Chelsea Annabel

Born September 23, 1995

at 9:59 a.m.

Weight - 8 lb. 0 oz.
Length - 20 in.

Riverview Hospital
Heron Point, Oregon

Mommy & Baby doing fine!

Dear Reader,

I can't imagine anything that generates more excitement in a family than the anticipation of the arrival of a new baby. It was certainly true at our house. Only, our "babies" arrived aged ten, eight and four, courtesy of the state of Oregon, with two bicycles and a guinea pig named Gertie.

But they were beautiful, healthy and bright, and we felt every bit as though a doctor had run out of the delivery room, shouting, "It's a boy! And another boy! And a girl!"

Since that day, thanks to our sons, new baby excitement has been generated by grandchildren, and as I write this, our daughter expects her first baby.

When the idea was "born" for romances involving the mothers of three babies born in the same hospital on the same day, I was nervous. Could I do this? Book research can take one only so far.

But fate intervened. My new editor was just back to work after *maternity leave*, and every book is a joint effort between author and editor. She promised to keep a sharp eye out for inconsistencies.

So we offer you, *Make Way for Mommy*, the second in my three-book series, Mommy and Me, a celebration of babies born without a father in the picture, and the mothers determined to change that.

Love ya,

Muriel

Muriel Jensen
P.O. Box 1168
Astoria, OR 97103

Muriel Jensen

MAKE WAY FOR MOMMY

Harlequin Books

TORONTO • NEW YORK • LONDON
AMSTERDAM • PARIS • SYDNEY • HAMBURG
STOCKHOLM • ATHENS • TOKYO • MILAN
MADRID • WARSAW • BUDAPEST • AUCKLAND

To Kathy, Gary and Baby Baker

ISBN 0-373-16606-0

MAKE WAY FOR MOMMY

Copyright © 1995 by Muriel Jensen.

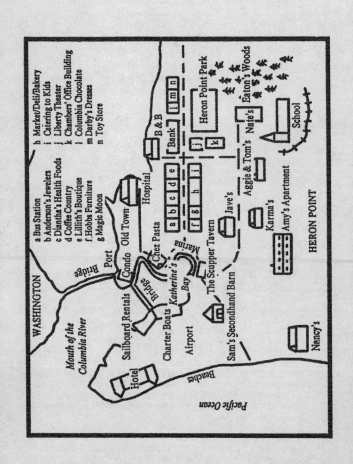

WASHINGTON

*Mouth of the
Columbia River*

Port

Bridge

Old Town

Condo

Chez Pasta

Hospital

Sailboard Rentals

Charter Boats

Bridge

*Katherine's
Bay*

Airport

Marina

The Scupper Tavern

Sam's Secondhand Barn

Hotel

Beaches

Pacific Ocean

a Bus Station
b Anderson's Jewelers
c Diantha's Health Foods
d Coffee Country
e Lillith's Boutique
f Hobbs Furniture
g Magic Moon

h Market/Deli/Bakery
i Catering to Kids
j Liberty Theater
k Chambers' Office Building
l Columbia Chocolate
m Darby's Dresses
n Toy Store

B & B

Bank

a b c d e

f g h i

Jave's

Aggie & Tom's

Karma's

Amy's Apartment

j

k

Nate's

Heron Point Park

l m n

Eaton's Woods

School

HERON POINT

Nancy's

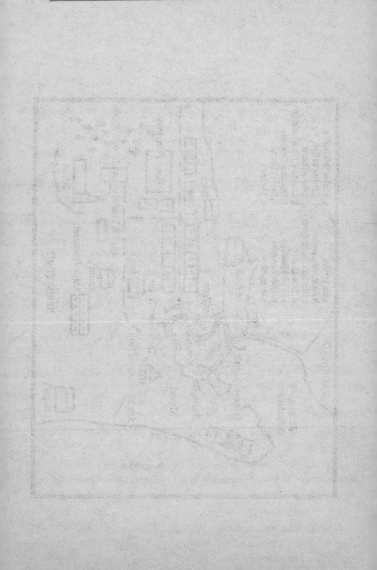

Prologue

This is what I know so far.

When I am born, I'm going to be called Chelsea Anna-bel, and I'm going to be special. That's because I have one father and two mothers. Other kids only get one.

We went to a hospital in Portland where they took stuff from my mother Cassie and Daddy to make me, then put it inside Aunt Jo.

Everyone was so excited when I began to grow that Aunt Jo started calling Cassie "Mama Cass," after a singer from the sixties in a group called the Mamas and the Papas. She plays their music all the time.

Mama Cass started calling her "Mama Jo," because it was taking the two of them to get me born.

Then there was an accident, and Mama Cass went to heaven. It's not bad for me, because I talk to her all the time, but Daddy and Mama Jo miss her a lot.

Mama Jo says when I'm born I won't belong to her anymore, I'll just be Daddy's. Sometimes she cries about it. I'm confused. I guess one mother can't just take the place of another.

It feels like we're going to work now. Mama Jo owns a coffee bar, but she can't have any coffee, 'cause it isn't good for me.

We live upstairs over the bar, so it doesn't take us long to get there. Daddy lives in a condo.

It's starting to get hard to get comfortable in here. My feet are up around my neck. But Mama Jo says in another month, I'll have all the room I want, so in the meantime, will I please stay off her bladder?

Whoops! Are we falling? I think we're falling. Yup. There's the stair against my bottom.

And there's a word I haven't heard before.

Chapter One

Josanne Arceneau struck every one of the last eight steps with her bottom and landed in a sitting position in the tiny, dark hallway. Her heart pounded in fear as she remained still, waiting to feel evidence that she'd seriously hurt her unborn baby—or herself.

She heard the faint sound of laughter coming from her coffee shop on the other side of the wall, traffic passing on the street just beyond the door, the honk of a horn, the bark of a dog—the sound of her own panicked breathing.

But she felt no pain. She'd half expected it to rip across her abdomen as the baby protested this rough treatment and demanded immediate freedom. But it didn't happen. Except for a gash on her right forearm where she must have snagged a carpet nail, she didn't seem to be hurt.

She ran a hand soothingly over the large mound of her pregnancy. The baby had been active day and night lately, and she waited for a kick to reassure her that the child was unharmed. Silence pulsed around her, disturbed only by the subtle, faraway sounds. She felt no response against her hand.

Her heartbeat accelerated, and she fought back a brand-new panic. Did lack of pain mean that the fall had caused a damage *deeper* than pain?

"Come on, Chelsea," she said, rubbing a little harder, more urgently. "Talk to Mama Jo. Are you okay?"

Nothing.

"Oh, Cassie..." Jo closed her eyes and called upon her sister as fear and grief tumbled together inside her. "You always fixed everything. Please let Chelsea be all right."

As Jo leaned a hand on the bottom stair to push herself to her knees, the door to the street flew open with a sudden jolt.

A tall shape was outlined against the late-August early-morning sunlight. It had broad shoulders, long arms braced in the doorway, and a tension about it she recognized easily. The scent of Polo blew into the hallway.

Jo looked up from her kneeling position, paradoxically relieved and distressed to see the father of her baby. He must have been next door in the shop for his morning double cappuccino and heard the thud.

"Ryan," she said, her voice strained with concern and lingering shock from the fall. "Hi."

He was on his knees beside her in an instant, one hand on her upper arm, the other on her swollen belly. Out of the backlit shadows, his angular face was taut with fear. "Did you fall?" he demanded.

She nodded, trying to drag in a breath. "Just the last few steps. I don't feel pain, but... I don't feel movement, either."

He held her gaze for one grim moment, then turned to look over his shoulder. Jo noticed for the first time all her regular customers gathered several deep in the open doorway.

"Call 911," he ordered calmly.

Devon, her white-aproned assistant, turned to comply.

"It's going to be all right, Jo." Diantha pushed her way to the front of the little crowd. She was a plump woman in her sixties, wearing a denim skirt and blouse adorned with silver-and-turquoise jewelry. Long gray hair was caught at the nape of her neck in a silver clip. "I charted your day. Aquarius is in your sign today—that's good for making love, and for making little children listen to you. Tell the baby she's fine, and she will be."

Ryan braced a forearm on his bent knee and turned to Diantha with impatience. Jo prudently forestalled whatever he would have said with a polite thank-you.

If only things were as simple as her neighbor in the health food store thought them to be. Diantha firmly believed that order in the universe meant order in one's daily life—if one simply complied with the astrological flow.

Jo concentrated on breathing regularly and remaining calm, hoping that would bring calm and comfortable conditions to the baby.

Ryan, his long-fingered hand splayed across her abdomen, probed for a kick, a roll, a movement of any kind. Jo willed the baby to move. But it didn't.

RYAN JEFFRIES felt Jo's slenderness in one hand and her almost-ripe pregnancy in the other. He refused to let himself panic when he felt no movement.

"The baby's all right," Jo said, her voice raspy and trembling faintly. "I know she is. Cassie wouldn't let it be otherwise."

He resisted an impatient response. He wasn't in the mood for his sister-in-law's cosmically spiritual approach to things. He'd lost his wife, and he didn't believe she still existed, on the fringes of their lives somewhere, assisting with their destinies. She was gone. He felt the yawning blackness of her absence every moment of his life.

"She's not an angel, Jo," he said quietly, as he wrapped an arm around her back and eased her into a sitting position on the second stair from the bottom. "She's just gone. How do you feel?"

He caught a glimpse of hurt and disappointment in her eyes. Then she gave a small shiver. He pulled off his suit jacket and placed it around her.

She wore a long, thin dress in some floaty fabric that fell almost to her ankles, and light brown hiking boots over baggy socks. The soles of her boots were as thick as snow tires.

He'd always thought Jo had atrocious fashion sense, but that was all part and parcel of her generally off-the-wall personality. With her passion for nature and her relaxed approach to life and living, she was like some sixties hippie caught in a time warp. He despaired of ever being able to relate to her—which was not a healthy situation, when she carried his baby.

And she knew it, too. He saw it in the pale blue eyes that watched him from under a riot of curly blond hair. It was always outrageously styled. This morning it was caught up high on her head, the long curly ends left to fall to her eyelashes and just above her ears, like a fringe.

"You believe what you want," she said finally, with a sigh. "I'll believe what I want."

The little crowd parted, and Devon appeared, his lean young face pale with worry. "Ambulance is on its way."

"Thank you." With a dark look, Ryan stopped the young man from coming any closer.

Devon wiped his hands nervously on his apron. "Can I do anything?"

Ryan shook his head. "Just give her room to breathe."

Heron Point Medics was located three blocks from downtown, and the whine of its siren could already be heard as it raced toward Coffee Country. Devon ran out to flag down the ambulance, and the little crowd peeled back from the door to make room for the emergency medical technicians.

"TAKE A DEEP BREATH, Jo, and don't move." J. V. Nicholas, Riverview Hospital's radiologist, turned knobs and controls on the ultrasound machine, and it made a whirring noise as he took an impression.

HI, Mama Jo! Wow! Am I going to have hair like that?
  Hi, Daddy!
  I can't wait to get out of here and into somebody's arms. Things are getting pretty tight.
  I'm okay. I can't kick anymore, because there isn't enough room in here, so I'll have to just wiggle.
  What? Oh, sure. Mama Cass says "Hi."

"GOOD. Got it," Jave said. "Okay, Jo. That should do it."

He turned off the machine and flipped on the light. He smiled at Jo, and at Ryan, who sat in a chair on the other side of the gurney. "Everything looks fine to me, but Dr. McNamara will want to check my pictures, of course. The baby was wriggling all over the place while we were photographing her."

Jo felt enormous relief. She even saw the set of Ryan's shoulders relax. Test after test had proven that Chelsea was unharmed by the fall.

"She might just have been surprised into stillness by the jolt," Jave said. "Or she might have dozed off. She's worked with you for eight months now behind the counter of Coffee Country. She probably thinks she can report to work on automatic pilot." Jave folded back the light blanket that covered her and helped her to a sitting position on the edge of the gurney. "I can't believe you showed up here without my caramel latte, though."

She grinned at him. "Thoughtless of me, I know. Come by when you get off, and you can have a double on the house."

"Thanks, but I've got a date with my brother, Tom, at the handball court. I don't want anything to slow me down."

He looked away as he spoke, an edge of tension in him. Jo wondered about it. He'd been at her first Lamaze class the previous week, as the coach of Nancy Malone, whom someone else in the class told her was the wife of a coast-guardsman. She'd thought that curious, considering the intimacy required between a mother-to-be and her coach. She knew it was common for single women to bring women friends as coaches, or men friends with whom they shared a special bond. But she doubted that it was customary for married women whose husbands were away to bring single men.

"How's everything at the bank, Ryan?" Jave asked, disturbing her speculations. "I keep watching for an Overstocked on Fifty-Dollar Bills sale, but it never happens."

Ryan stood, relief that the baby was safe making him feel energized. He was even able to expel the tension with a light laugh. "Money's a precious commodity. No one ever has too much, not even banks. How's the boat coming?"

"Greatly improved. We no longer have a hole in the deck of the *Mud Hen.*"

"Sounds like a definite plus."

"I thought so. But my brother thought we should have left it and seen if the fish could find their way in without so much effort on our part. Excuse me." The phone rang, and Jave reached across his equipment to answer it.

Ryan helped Jo to her feet and across the room to the dressing cubicle. "I'll wait for you in the hallway," he said. "Then we're supposed to go back to McNamara's office."

"I can take it from here," she offered, "if you have to get back to work. I feel fine."

He studied her consideringly for a moment, then shook his head. She wasn't sure whether it meant that he didn't consider her sufficiently competent to "take it from here," or that he *wanted* to stay with her.

"I'll be in the hallway."

Jo closed the curtains of the cubicle behind her and rolled her eyes to heaven. Ryan was an enigma. But she was giddy with relief at the moment, and she decided it didn't matter. The baby was fine. That was the important thing.

A little thrill of excitement ran along her spine. One more month, and Chelsea would be a living, breathing, squalling presence in her arms.

Relief was eclipsed for an instant by the realization that she wouldn't be in her arms for very long; she would then belong to Ryan. But she pushed that thought aside, knowing she'd find a way to deal with it. She would.

And for now, she had another month as Chelsea's mother. She rubbed the round protrusion affectionately and felt the baby squirm inside her. She smiled broadly. A month with Chelsea was a lot.

IT WAS MIDAFTERNOON when Jo and Ryan finally left the hospital with a clean bill of health for mother and baby.

They rode back to town in a taxi, because Ryan had ridden with Jo in the ambulance.

"Coffee Country, please," Jo said to the driver, a pretty young woman in a blue baseball cap with a picture of Elvis pinned to the front.

"Right." The woman turned on the meter and pulled away from the hospital's entrance.

"Scratch that," Ryan told her. "Take us to the Heron Point Condominiums, please."

Jo turned to him in surprise. "Your place? Why?"

"Because from now on," he replied, in a matter-of-fact tone that he hoped would discourage argument, "it's going to be your place, too."

Jo didn't stop to analyze why he felt the need to suggest that. She only knew she wouldn't let him. "The hell it will," she replied coolly. "Coffee Country, driver. Ignore this man. He's insane."

Ryan figured he should have known better. The tone had sometimes worked on Cassie, but only when she knew she could get her own way by subterfuge, rather than open argument. Jo knew nothing of such subtleties. With Jo, all-out war was the only option.

"The condo, driver," he said. "Ignore this woman. She hates Elvis."

The driver braked to a sudden stop at the road. Jo, in the process of putting on her seat belt, jerked forward. Ryan put a hand out to stop her.

The driver found Jo's gaze in the rearview mirror. "You don't like the King?"

Jo gave Ryan a lethal side-glance and smiled at the driver's reflection. "No, I don't. I'm sorry. I know it's un-American." Then, knowing she needed the woman's cooperation, she added placatingly, "But I liked his stamp. I even bought a firstday issue. Would you take us to Coffee—?"

Ryan put a hand on Jo's arm to silence her. "There are twenty steps up to your apartment," he said reasonably. "Today, you fell down eight of them. What if you'd fallen from the top? What if you'd fallen headfirst, or sideways, or..."

"You," she pointed out, "live on the second floor."

"My building," he said, "has an elevator."

"Your condo is a long way from my business, and I don't have a car."

"The bank is a block away from your coffee bar. I'll drive you in every morning and pick you up at night."

She folded her arms stubbornly. Resting atop the bulk of her baby, they were almost under her chin. "I open at six. You start at nine."

His scolding glance chided her for trying to put one over on him. "*Devon* opens at six. You show up at eight or eight-thirty, and I often start early."

"Ryan," she said urgently, knowing she had to get through to him, "it won't work. We can't live together. It *won't work.*"

"You're repeating yourself," he said, then added ove. the front seat, "The condo, driver."

"It *bears* repeating," she said forcefully, feeling more than a little desperate. "Ryan, we don't like each other. You think I'm an airhead, and I think you're a stuffed shirt."

He acknowledged that with a nod. "But we're having a baby together. Certainly that becomes the priority."

Jo was aware of the driver's wide eyes reflected in the rearview mirror as she turned onto the Coast Road.

"But we—"

"Look," he said, the hand on her arm tightening, "Can we save this for a more private moment?"

"No," Jo began, pulling away from him. "Public or private, my feelings on the matter are—"

The taxi driver screeched to a halt, pitching both of them forward, despite their belts. Then she made a wide turn around a UPS truck that had stopped in front of an auto-parts shop.

She smiled meekly in the mirror. "Sorry. Lost my focus, there."

Jo leaned back in the seat and decided the driver was too interested in their conversation to ensure the safety of a trip to *any* destination.

"Fine," she said curtly, turning away from Ryan to watch the very familiar passing scenery. "We'll go to your place, but don't think I'm moving in with you. Because I'm not."

Jo was no stranger to the condo. In the five years Ryan and her sister were married, she had attended many a holiday and family dinner there, and had often visited on a whim with a pound of the hazelnut blend Cassie loved, or a few ounces of the Spanish saffron whose price was exorbitantly high on the retail market.

In all that time, Jo and Ryan had simply tolerated each other. She'd known he considered her quirky and weird, and she'd always thought him stuffy. But they'd coexisted, because Cassie was the common denominator—petite, witty, optimistically determined Cassie, who'd been convinced there was a solution to every problem if one simply looked hard enough.

Ryan led Jo into the blue-and-gray clapboard building, punctuated by gables and cupolas, that rambled comfortably across Heron Point. He was silent in the elevator, then unlocked the door of number 27 and ushered her inside.

She hesitated, then drew in a deep breath and stepped into the large living room. She hadn't been here since she'd helped Ryan and her father sort through Cassie's things, right after the funeral, six months ago.

It was decorated in the shades of the river view beyond the windows—a cloudy, stormy blue, the gray of the herons that nested nearby, giving the point its name, the pristine white of the sea gulls that cavorted and called around the passing fishing boats.

Ryan pulled at his tie as he headed for the French doors and the small patio that hung out over the river. He pulled a caned chair away from the small glass table and gestured for her to sit. "Tea?" he asked. "Juice? Evian?"

"Evian, please," she replied, watching him a little nervously as he pulled off his jacket and tossed it at a chair. He'd always been very formal with her, and all their meetings since Cassie's death had been on neutral ground and conducted with civility and simple good manners—more like discussions of a business deal than an exchange of information regarding the pregnancy they had in common. He'd insisted on weekly reports on how she and the baby were doing.

But now that he'd removed the jacket, she could see the lean waist under his European-cut white shirt, the neat, taut hips in gray-and-white pinstripe, the shoulders that were formidable even without the jacket.

No. She looked away and simply listened while he opened the refrigerator door, reached into a cupboard, poured the imported water into a glass. She'd put this out of her mind for more than five years, and this was not the time to even let the thought form. God. She had to get out of here.

She pretended interest in the sailboarders taking advantage of the remnants of summer on the bay when Ryan brought her a tall glass. He put his own in the place opposite her and sat down.

He looked earnest and determined. She sought desperately to divert his attention.

"I've often wondered," she said, peering over the slatted railing, "if the right current could take you all the way to Hawaii on one of those sailboards."

She wasn't looking at him, but she could feel his gaze. She knew he saw through the ploy. "Well, maybe to Washington," he said.

"I guess I'd really rather go north, anyway. Sunny climes just aren't my thing." She chattered without turning away from the sailboarders. "I'd like to be where there are craggy mountains, lots of snow, cozy fires and moonless nights."

She heard the crackle of the cane chair as he leaned back in it. "Remember that you once broke a leg skiing," he said.

"Oh, I wouldn't ski. I'd sit by the fire, sipping Spanish coffee and writing moody poetry."

"You get drunk on one brandy. You'd have to write pretty fast."

He knew entirely too much about her. Jo turned back to him with obvious reluctance and met his quiet gaze. He studied her that way often, as though she interested but annoyed him. Which annoyed *her*. And it was time to confront the issue.

"Well, I can't go anywhere for another month, anyway," she said. "But that doesn't mean I'll be moving in here."

Ryan took her resistance calmly. He didn't intend to argue about it, because she thrived on that. She loved any opportunity to oppose him on anything. She'd always been that way. Cassie had insisted that her sister had never had a combative personality, that he alone inspired that reaction in her. And judging by how calmly and agreeably she dealt with friends, co-workers and customers, he could only believe it was true. He alone brought out this side of her.

But that was all right. She'd always made *him* edgy. They had bad chemistry.

But, for the next month, they had to find a way around their animosity. This baby was going to be born safely if it killed him. Cassie had been convinced there was a solution to every problem. He hoped she was right.

"A woman who is eight months along," he said, "should not be climbing all those stairs several times a day. It isn't safe. And I think at this stage of the pregnancy, you shouldn't be alone."

"At this stage of my pregnancy," Jo pointed out, "I shouldn't be upset, and you know that's what would happen if you and I cohabited. And it wouldn't be good for you, either. The best-run branch the bank has would suddenly be out of balance on a regular basis, or you'd be giving loans that had no chance of ever being repaid, and you'd end up unemployed."

He shook his head over her simplified view of banking. "I never let my domestic situation affect my work."

She snickered. "Because your domestic situation was always perfect."

He raised an eyebrow. "It was?"

She frowned. "Wasn't it?"

He shrugged a shoulder. "Depends on your definition of *perfect*. My life with Cassie was often wonderful, sometimes volatile, but always exciting. And, like many precious things, its value was in its *im*perfection. We were great together, but not because we never disagreed."

Jo blinked in surprise. In five years, all Cassie had ever said about Ryan was that he was the most delicious husband any woman ever had. Then she would close her eyes and lift her shoulders in an ecstatic little gesture that isolated her with her thoughts and made Jo embarrassed to even wonder what was on her sister's mind.

Ryan stared at the glass he was toying with and smiled to himself. Then he refocused on Jo. "So. We're two adults," he said finally. "Certainly we can get along for a month, until Chelsea's born. I promise to do my part, if you'll do yours."

Jo racked her brain for an excuse. She could not move in here. Her feelings would be too hard to hide, and then he'd *know*. It was hard enough to act nonchalant when he walked into the bar, or during their meetings about the baby.

"I think it's a bad idea," she said coolly, pushing her chair back and rising to her feet. But she didn't accomplish the maneuver with the grace and style she'd hoped would accompany it. She bumped the edge of the table with her stomach and dumped her water glass onto the floor, then backed away and knocked her chair into the rack of plants behind her.

She groaned as Ryan reached behind him on a small buffet table for napkins and dropped them onto the puddle. Then he came around to right the chair that had blocked her in the corner of the patio.

"Sorry," she said. "Thank you."

"You need a helping hand, Jo." His look said, *I told you so,* though those weren't precisely his words. "Before you kill yourself or destroy your surroundings."

The situation was getting desperate, she told herself. She had to get tough. When he took her hand to help her into the house, she pulled it away. He studied her in surprise for a moment, then stepped aside when she moved past him and went into the living room. The furniture was all plump and cushy, and she chose the only chair she felt reasonably sure she could still get out of—a Boston rocker.

"You don't like me," she said honestly. "That makes it impossible for us to live together, even for a month, even if we try to get along."

Ryan wandered into the house after her, but went to the window that looked out on the pilings below left over from a long-abandoned cannery. "*You* don't like *me,* but you agreed to carry the baby for Cassie and me anyway. My feelings wouldn't prevent me from seeing that you have all you need to be comfortable."

"Comfort," she said stubbornly, "isn't everything."

He turned away from the window to pace toward her. She sat in the rocker, looking a little like a flowered dumpling wearing snow tires. But there was something urgent in her eyes. He sat on the ottoman that belonged to the big chair opposite her.

"What do you mean?" he asked.

"I mean," she said, her voice a little high, as she rubbed her stomach, "that I have just four more weeks with Chelsea, and I want them to be...you know..." She groped for the right word and finally settled for "Intimate."

He spread his hands, confused by her reaction. "You're carrying the baby within your body. How much more intimacy do you require?"

Jo knew he would never understand. She'd sat in this very living room last Thanksgiving Day and listened to the plan Cassie had concocted that would allow her and Ryan to have a baby that was their very own creation, despite Cassie's inability to carry that life herself.

And Jo had agreed, because her sister was as precious to her as her own life—and because she'd loved her sister's husband from the moment Cassie brought him home to meet the family.

It had always been her secret, though her father had guessed it. And it would remain their secret into eternity.

She'd agreed to carry their baby as her gift of love to their life together. And had Cassie lived, she imagined, the prospect of handing this baby over to her would not have made the future look so bleak.

But Cassie was gone, and the configuration of their complex little family had changed considerably.

She saw Ryan's shoulders square and his eyes sharpen. "You aren't thinking about—?"

She forestalled him with a quelling look before emotion could overtake her. "Backing out?" she asked. "Of course not. We made a deal, and I'll fulfill my part. I just don't think I should have to give her up until it's time."

"Then you wouldn't want to do anything," he said quietly, "that would make you deliver early, like climbing too many stairs, and falling down them. If you stay here, you won't have that problem."

Jo opened her mouth to deny that was necessary, then remembered how close she'd come to just such a situation that morning. Certainly the baby was a more important consideration than her unrequited affection for the baby's father. Jo felt like some beleaguered character in an adventure movie, trapped in a room in which the walls were closing in, threatening to squash her.

She didn't want to live here, where *he* would be every spare moment. She didn't want to live with constant reminders of Cassie that would bring back that last day in vivid detail. But she didn't want to endanger the baby, either.

"So why don't you rest here this afternoon?" Ryan said. "I'll pack up your closet, and whatever else you think you'll need, and bring it back tonight. I checked with Devon while we were still at the hospital, and he said things were going fine. He's not taking this summer class for credit, so he just cut classes today." He glanced up at the oak-trimmed clock above the bar. "It's already almost three."

He was right, of course. She knew he didn't care about her, but he was genuinely concerned for the baby's safety. They did, at least, have that in common.

"Okay," she agreed. She would do this for Chelsea. But she had the most unsettling feeling that she was making a serious mistake.

GREAT! Mama Cass says she has wonderful memories of this place. I like it, too. Won't it be nice to have Daddy around all the time? Mama Jo?

Chapter Two

"The doctor's sure she's all right?" Devon, spooning a dollop of foamed milk into a demitasse of espresso, looked up at Ryan in concern. The mellow sounds of "California Dreamin'" came from the CD player on the shelf behind him.

Ryan nodded. "Positive." He suspected Devon was infatuated with Jo, despite the ten-year difference in their ages.

"That's great news. There you go, ma'am. Espresso macchiato." Devon handed the cup across the counter to a young woman in an elegant gray suit. "Tell her her regulars chipped in for this." He pointed to a tall green plant at the far end of the counter. "People have been stopping in all day to ask about her."

"Assure them that she's fine."

"Jeffries."

Ryan turned in the act of walking away. Devon met his gaze evenly, a mild challenge in his eyes. "Tell her I send my love," he said.

Ryan held his gaze an extra moment. "I will," he said finally. Then he turned to leave and found himself face-to-fingernail with Diantha.

"Didn't I tell you it would be all right?" she asked, shaking her index finger at him. Silver bracelets jangled. "You didn't believe me. But I knew. I knew. Aquarius came onto the scene today."

He'd always thought Diantha Pennyman was a little shy of plumb, but she was a good businesswoman, and he knew for a fact that she had as hefty an IRA as could be found in Heron Point. Still, he doubted the stars could be credited for her business acumen. And though there'd been a time when they guided ships, he didn't think they could guide lives.

"I'm glad you were right, Diantha," he said, and tried to slip past her.

She sidestepped him into a corner, as all the other patrons went about their business.

"You know, you shouldn't smirk at the heavens," she said, her unsettlingly clear gray eyes boring into his. "Particularly since you're a man who'd do something as unorthodox as plant his seed in a test tube."

Ryan drew a breath for forbearance. "It was a petri dish."

"That's beside the point. You stepped out in faith and took a wild chance that a life would be created, then successfully nurtured to birth in a surrogate womb. That's a lot like believing in the stars."

Ryan shifted his weight. "We rather thought we were believing in God."

She raised both eyebrows. "Who do you think made and moves the stars?" She pinned him with her gaze an extra moment, then stepped aside and let him pass.

Ryan took the steps to Jo's apartment two at a time. The coffee bar always made him feel a little as though he'd dropped into that alien bar in *Star Wars*. The people there were not only unfamiliar, but downright weird.

Jo's apartment was a small one-bedroom with colorful, mismatched furniture, and the artwork of friends on the walls. He supposed it was charming, if one could be comfortable in such a small space.

In her bedroom was a brass bedstead he and Cassie had helped her carry up the stairs after a church rummage sale, and a circa-1950s dresser with rounded edges and large round pulls.

She'd told him that all her "pregnant" clothes were in the top drawer of the dresser and the right end of the closet. Her purple velour bathrobe was the dividing line. She had a suitcase under the bed.

Everything fit in the case, with room to spare. He'd noticed over the past months that she didn't have that many changes of clothes. He bought coffee at the bar every morning and midafternoon, as a way of checking on her and the progress of their baby. When he suggested lending her his credit card to buy clothes, she'd given him a look that might have withered a man less accustomed to the ire of people turned down for loans, or whose boats or cars he'd helped repossess.

He hadn't broached the subject again. But maybe he'd have to brave it now.

He took her contour pillow from the bed, and remembered to get her shoes. He frowned over them as he put them in a grocery bag. There was a pair of absolutely flat black slippers, some Birkenstock sandals, and another very worn pair of boots, similar to the ones she'd worn today.

He thought it was no wonder she'd fallen in those boots. The tread was enough to steady an elephant on ice. Once they hit the carpeting on the stairs, they'd probably stopped her cold.

Shaking his head, he took a last look around the apartment, added water to a philodendron on a bookcase, then locked the door and headed for home.

JO PUTTERED in the kitchen. And putter was all she could do with the meager contents of the refrigerator and cupboards. In the refrigerator, she found Evian water, milk, beer, a large bag of apples, and a pound of coffee, from her shop, that she mixed personally and called Eye-opener. It was a blend of French roast and Continental, and even the decaf was like a surge of adrenaline.

In the freezer was a bag of ice, a box of Häagen-Dazs bars, a loaf of bread, and a pound of almond-chocolate coffee she'd put in Cassie's Christmas stocking. Her sister had been wimpy about her brew.

In the cupboard was a half-empty jar of mixed nuts, a revolving spice rack, a box of herbal tea, a jar of peanut butter and a box of crackers. She guessed Ryan ate out most of the time.

She made a cup of herbal tea and looked for something to do to avoid thinking. The condo was spotless. She knew Ryan had a housekeeper, because he came to the shop half an hour early the two mornings a week that she cleaned.

Soap operas could be entertaining, but she had no idea what was happening on any one of them, and she hated talk shows.

The bedroom Ryan had told her to use was large and airy and also spotless, and decorated in mallard green, white and burgundy. She'd used it for one night just last year, when a pipe in her bathroom sprang a leak and flooded her apartment and part of her shop. She examined the room's view of the bridge that connected Heron Point to Washington, then stood uncertainly in the middle of the green-carpeted hallway, wondering whether to try to take a nap she didn't need, or to explore further.

The master bedroom was across the hall. She wondered idly if it was tidy behind the closed door, then dismissed the thought. It was none of her business.

Then she turned to the last door at the end of the hallway. Cassie had intended to make it the nursery. Certainly that *was* her business.

But she hesitated before turning the knob. Since Cassie had been gone, she and Ryan had somehow managed to keep the baby out of their relationship, even though it was the only reason for it. They met to talk about it, he accompanied her to her doctor's appointments, and they'd agreed that when the time came, he'd be her Lamaze coach, just as Cassie had intended to be.

And even though she carried the baby, she'd felt oddly removed from all that would happen to it after it was born and Ryan took over.

But walking into this room, seeing all he and Cassie had planned for it, would be like a glimpse into its future. It would put her on a different footing with Ryan, and she wasn't sure that was a good idea.

I THINK IT'S A GOOD IDEA. Let's look.

THEN SHE DECIDED that she didn't care if it was or not, she wanted to see it. And she was trading her final month of solitude with Chelsea for Ryan's peace of mind, so she was entitled.

She pushed the door open boldly, then stopped just inside the door with an "Ah..." of approval.

WHAT, Mama Jo? What do you see?

THE ROOM was painted white, and a deep border of animal characters in primary colors paraded just below the ceiling, along with musical instruments, balloons and stars on a string.

A bright red carpet covered the floor, and the furniture was coordinated with the paper and a ruffly valance above a bay window with miniblinds pulled up to reveal the river view. A window seat was covered in the same fabric, and Jo sat on it to take in the rest of the room.

Bookshelves already held books, and a colorful shelf of sturdy plastic squares held a pale brown musical bear she'd bought when they learned the pregnancy had taken, a package of diapers, a little fern in a lamb-shaped planter that her father had sent, and several other odds and ends already collected from friends and relatives.

There was a rocking horse in one corner, and a child-size blue upholstered chair in the other. Jo picked up the bear and turned its key. Brahms's "Lullaby" filled the silence.

MUSIC. Mama Cass says it's a bear, and that you gave it to me. I can't wait to see it.

ABOVE THE BOOKSHELF was a framed photograph of the three of them—Cassie, Ryan and her—on her sister's wedding day. Ryan, in a morning coat, had an arm around each of them. Cassie was laughing happily, veil flying out behind her, the cleft in her chin that Jo had always envied very prominent.

She, Jo, was smiling under a coronet of rosebuds. Had anyone else, she wondered, noticed the wistful look in her eyes?

She unconsciously rubbed Chelsea. "There we are, baby," she said aloud. "Your parents."

Jo smiled at that thought, but at the same moment, a sob rose out of her that came from very deep inside and hurt abominably. Delight mingled with profound sadness.

She rubbed gently at the protuberance of Chelsea and accepted, not for the first time, how difficult it was going to be to give her up. Even knowing the baby was coming to this place of privilege and adoration.

Cassie would have smothered her with love, and she knew Ryan would, too, because she was part of Cassie.

"All Mama Jo is," she said, with a final pat for the baby and a toss of her head meant to dismiss any self-pity, "is the somewhat sophisticated paper bag that's holding you."

MAMA CASS says without you, I wouldn't be here. She thinks you should talk to Daddy.

JO STOOD, pushing against the seat to manage her bulk, and felt the seat flip up slightly as she let it go. Storage? she wondered. She peered inside and found it lined with cedar.

At the bottom of the fragrant space was a cloth bag with a drawstring. Jo recognized it as Cassie's sewing bag. Her sister had been an avid needleworker in her spare time, and had always carried projects back and forth to work at the bank or on Sunday drives.

Curious, Jo pulled out the bag. It was filled with finely spun yarn in soft baby colors—yellow, green, pink and blue. Only a dozen rows or so had been worked, in crochet, to produce about three inches of a baby blanket. A wooden hook dangled from the last stitch made in the middle of a row.

Jo pulled the work out to look at it more closely, and suddenly the perfect stitches in the barely begun project and the dangling hook seemed to exemplify for her Cassie's life and death, and she buried her face in the wool and wept.

RYAN HEARD THE SOUND the moment he opened the front door. It was soft and at the other end of the condo, but it struck at his heart like a blow.

He dropped the suitcase and the bag of shoes just inside the door, and the take-out food on the coffee table, and hurried down the hallway.

Jo was in the nursery. He should have guessed. It shouldn't annoy him that she'd looked in, but it did. This room was something he and Cassie had planned and begun together, and he'd finished it himself, with an almost ritualistic adherence to what his wife had wanted. It was absurd to consider Jo an intruder, and he wasn't sure that was the problem. But it seemed the more he missed Cassie, the more he resented her sister.

He was almost surprised to find Jo crying. She'd been so stoic at the funeral—as stoic as he was. They'd stood arm in arm—it was almost the only time in five years that they'd ever touched—and he'd felt her anger, as deep and roiling as his, and a grief that went deeper than any utterance could ever express.

He wished he could find that release somewhere. But feeling had clotted inside him, blocking any emotion from entering or leaving. He had to find a way to solve that, he knew, before the baby came.

He stepped into the room without a clue as to how to handle the situation. When Cassie cried, he'd simply wrapped her in a bear hug and held fast until she poured out what troubled her. But she'd loved him. She'd welcomed his caring bullying.

Jo simply tolerated him. But she was carrying his baby, and this sobbing couldn't be good for either of them.

HI, Daddy. Mama Cass says do *something!*

"Jo?" He put a hand on her shoulder. It startled her into turning. Her cheeks were flushed and blotchy from crying, and her eyes, usually clear blue and skeptical when they focused on him, were naked with grief. For an instant, he felt the same curious kinship with her that he'd felt at Cassie's graveside. It was grim, he thought, that the only bridge between them was pain.

She sniffed and squared her shoulders the moment her eyes focused on him. "I'm sorry," she said, her voice raspy and low. "I shouldn't have come in. I shouldn't have snooped. But I found this, and..."

Ryan's eyes went to the strip of soft-colored wool in her hands. It was unfamiliar.

"What is it?" he asked.

Jo shook her head, wiping the back of her hand across one eye, the heel of her hand across the other. "I found it in the window seat. I guess..." She drew a breath for composure. "I guess Cassie started a baby blanket."

He remembered suddenly the day she'd bought the yarn, at a little shop across the river. They hadn't yet been sure the pregnancy would take, and she'd called the purchase an act of faith. He'd just accepted an office with the Downtown Merchants Association, and she'd said the project would keep her busy while he was at meetings. He hadn't known she'd started it.

He studied the small strip of fine stitches and fought an overwhelming sense of loss. Cassie's life had been like that—beautiful and barely begun, the ending of it like a dropped stitch in the fabric of time.

He took the yarn from Jo, stuffed it into the bag and dropped the whole into the window seat and let it close with a slam. It seemed to pull both of them together.

"I brought home Chinese," he said, leading the way out of the room, then closing the door firmly behind her.

She preceded him into the living room. "Good," she said, striving for emotional equilibrium. She found it, as usual with him, in half playful, half serious animosity. "I was afraid you'd be expecting me to cook. I did make coffee."

He gave her a wry glance as he picked up her things. "I've tasted your cooking. You can stick to making the coffee. I'll lay this on your bed, if you'll get plates and silverware."

"Right." Jo carried the bag of takeout to the table and went about her assigned task. Ryan was back in a moment, his suit and white shirt exchanged for khaki shorts and a short-sleeved white sweatshirt with First Coastal Bank emblazoned across the chest.

They passed cartons of pan-fried noodles, kung pao chicken, fried rice and fried shrimp in a continual circle as they talked and ate. She'd been afraid their first meal together would be uncomfortable, but he'd chosen to discuss the very practical subject of their schedules for the next month.

"So you'd like to be at work by eight-thirty Monday through Friday?" he asked.

"Tuesday through Saturday," she replied. "Devon does Mondays, because he has no classes, and I do Saturdays so he can have his weekends."

Ryan nodded, then remembered the boy's message. "He asked me to give you his love."

Jo was startled for just an instant. The thought of Ryan delivering her anyone's love was enough to stir unwanted feelings. She felt just the suggestion of a blush rising at her throat, and fought it down with determined force of will.

"Devon's a buddy," she said, making a production of dipping a shrimp in duck sauce. "At nineteen, he's more sensitive than most mature men I know."

"And your regulars chipped in for a plant and card," Ryan went on. "I left it at the shop, because you spend so much of your time there, and I thought they'd probably enjoy seeing it on the counter when they come in."

Jo pretended surprise. "Also very sensitive. Mr. Jeffries, you surprise me."

"Really." He gave her an even glance as he dipped his shrimp in hot mustard. "You think all I do is foreclose on widows and orphans?"

"Oh, hardly. I know you have a reputation around town as the only banker who'll stake first-time entrepreneurs, single women in business, adventurous schemes that sound shaky to everyone else but that you see as potentially profitable."

Now he looked surprised. "Praise, from judgmental Jo? I must be misreading the message."

Jo rolled her eyes. "I know you're a fine, community-minded businessman. I'm just surprised you care about *my* business. I thought you considered it . . . flaky."

He gave her a noncommittal lift of his eyebrows over the rim of his cup.

Jo knew what it meant. She knew she should back away because the issue was potentially problematic, but she was often incapable of doing the diplomatic thing.

"It's me you consider flaky," she went on accusingly. "Because of Cassie, and the restaurant thing."

He inclined his head in a gesture that conceded her point. "She wanted it badly. You didn't want to work that hard. But I never called you flaky."

Trouble loomed closer and closer. She ignored it. "How many restaurants do you think Heron Point can support?" she asked. "I've worked in restaurants. All Cassie'd ever done was cook for you and cater for a few friends. The reality of restaurant work is hours of preparation and hours of cleanup broken up by sixteen hours of backbreaking fetching, carrying and tension."

Ryan remembered how hard Cassie had tried to talk Jo into entering into a partnership with her, and how disappointed she'd been when her sister couldn't be persuaded to come around.

He waved a hand, as though to dismiss the issue, and reached for the carton of rice. "Like I said. You didn't want to work that hard."

"She didn't know what she'd be getting into."

He couldn't let that pass. He looked into her eyes. "Yes, she did. She'd researched well. The old warehouse on the waterfront was an ideal location, and her cooking and your management savvy would have brought every tourist in the Northwest."

"It would have taken a fortune to get started," she said thinly.

"Not true. She had the loan, and it wasn't even through me. The Bank of Heron Point believed it'd go, too."

Jo was out of arguments—except for the real one, the one she couldn't share. She hadn't wanted to go into partnership with her sister because the plan was that Ryan would host on evenings and weekends, and she'd doubted that what she felt for her brother-in-law would remain invisible in such close proximity.

It had hurt to hurt her sister, but she'd felt sure then that she'd done the right thing. Now, as Ryan sat across the table from her, intelligent, loyal to Cassie, concerned for his baby—all the things she loved in him—she was still sure.

"It's a moot point now, isn't it?" she asked finally.

"You brought it up," he reminded her. Then he sighed, more than willing to put the unresolvable issue aside. "But, yes, it is. What else is on your schedule that we have to think about? You're involved in that Heron Point Has It project I'm chairing."

"Yes." She made herself concentrate on the subject. The plan for a communitywide commercial fair had generated a lot of excitement at the last association meeting, and was intended to show that everything the big city offered could be found in little Heron Point. All the restaurants and gourmet shops would offer food, gift shops would show samples of their wares, craftsmen would exhibit their work and be available for questions and consultation, community-service groups would distribute pamphlets and offer raffles and giveaways. "I have a couple of meetings with the restaurant cooperative's committee over the next two weeks."

He nodded. "I'll get you there. And I'll find some help to get you set up the day of the event on the chance Devon's tied up with school. I'm sure I'll be up to my ears in blown fuses and power outages. You know how the old fairgrounds building is."

It was strange, she thought, to realize that Chelsea would be almost two months old by the time the event was held. She could only wonder what her own situation would be then. The thought made her quarrelsome.

She shrugged a shoulder. "That'll be after Chelsea's born," she said. "You'll no longer be responsible for my welfare."

He frowned at her. "That's a coldhearted approach to this."

It was. But she knew that approach was the only one that would get her through. She pushed rice back and forth on her plate with the tip of her fork. "It was the deal we made in the beginning, remember. I carry the baby, then she's yours. I was welcome to be a doting aunt, but it would confuse a child to have three parents."

Ryan put his fork down quietly and leaned back in his chair, his dark eyes assessing her. She wished she could seal her mouth closed. One moment she made harsh promises to herself about remaining on the fringes of his life without a fuss, and the next she came off sounding like a shrew with self-esteem problems.

"I want her aunt to be a part of her life," he said.

"I know." She tried to sound amenable. "I just meant that you won't feel the same... duty... to Chelsea's *aunt* as you do to me now, while I'm carrying her."

She spoke the words with the utmost reasonableness, but Ryan heard all the unresolved issues underneath. Cassie had insisted there would be none. She and Jo, though as different as night and day, had been as close as it was possible for two sisters to be. She had complete faith in Jo's generosity, she'd told him. In her integrity, and in her love.

And it might all have worked as Cassie projected it would—if she had lived. But her death had changed everything. Now Jo would be giving this child to him, and not to her sister. And she didn't like him. That was bound to compromise her generosity.

He resisted the pull of panic.

"Do you want to talk about this?" he asked calmly.

She looked at him blandly, pretending to misunderstand. "About what?"

He was almost afraid to say the words, afraid they'd make her run. But he had to. It was what their lives were all about for the next month. "About giving me Chelsea."

There was a hard lump in Jo's throat. "There's nothing to talk about. I promised Cassie. And I promised you." She forced herself to smile. "All I meant was, that our relationship—yours and mine—will change. When Chelsea's here, you'll no longer have to worry about how I get to meetings, because I'll be back in my own apartment, living my own life. Will you pass the chicken, please?"

Jo ignored his pensive gaze and chattered on about anything and everything on her schedule that she could remember, and a few things she invented, in the hope of making him forget that little exchange.

They finally tidied up together, and she excused herself to retire to her room.

"I'll be ready to drive you at eight-fifteen," he called after her.

She turned at the head of the hallway. "Do you work on Saturday?"

"A couple of hours. But I'll be back to pick you up at five." His eyes roved her bulbous silhouette. "You're sure it's a good idea to be on your feet that long at this stage?"

"I'm doing okay so far," she said. "And I have a chair in the back I can use when it's quiet."

"All right. Your bathroom should be well stocked, and the TV-VCR remote is in the bedside-table drawer. But if you need anything, I'm right across the hall."

"Right. Thanks."

Jo put the few things in her suitcase away, then put the case itself in a corner of the cavernous closet. She read a chapter in the book she'd bought months ago on pregnancy and birth, she watched evening television, she tossed and turned and had trouble getting comfortable.

She was finally dozing off when the phone rang. The ringer was turned off in her room, but she heard it across the hall in Ryan's bedroom. Anyone who had ever run a business, she thought, trying to settle down again, was attuned to the sound of a telephone.

A knock on her bedroom door brought her up on her elbows. "Yes?" she asked.

Ryan's head peered around the door. "Did I wake you?"

She shook her head. "Something wrong?"

"No. But your father's on the phone. He got worried when he couldn't reach you at home, so he called me."

"Oh." She pushed herself up awkwardly. Ryan came to push her contour pillow aside and stuff the plump pillow she'd discarded behind her. Then he reached under her arms and pulled her up.

The contact left her breathless for an instant. Then he handed her the phone and walked away, apparently without noticing that there'd been nothing between his hands and her body but thin white cotton.

"Hello?" she said into the phone, her voice a little unsteady.

"Jo. Baby, are you all right?" Matthew Arcenau's voice came loudly and urgently over the cross-country connection. He taught American history at a rural Connecticut high school. He claimed the beautiful surroundings made for a perfect semiretirement. "Ryan says you fell."

"I'm fine," she assured him quickly, clearing her throat and repeating the declaration in a firm tone. "I'm fine. I've had every test possible, and the baby and I are both doing beautifully."

"Well, that's a relief." His tone quieted. Then there was a moment's hesitation. "I'm glad you're staying with Ryan. I was worried about you being all alone at this stage of the pregnancy."

"Oh, he's kept close tabs on me all along."

"I know. I just feel better knowing there's someone with you at night." She heard a smile in his voice. "You're the one who always needed a night-light."

Jo laughed lightly. "I've gotten over that, Dad."

"In some ways, maybe. You're not as tough as you're always trying to make us believe."

"Am too."

"Are not."

"Can you drink Turkish coffee?"

There was a pause, then a rumble of laughter. "It tastes like tobacco."

"Point proven. I'm tougher than you are. So, don't hassle me. How's school?"

"Great. I've got a good bunch of kids this year." He said that every year. "But I have a sub lined up, so I can visit when the baby comes. Ryan says it's all right with him. What do you think?"

"Um . . . that'd be good." It would be wonderful to see him, and it would be good to have her father's support then. She'd promised herself she wouldn't become maudlin about giving up the baby. But she doubted that anything about it would be easy. She was sure her father knew that.

"You're still . . . okay about everything?" he asked. His voice was gentle, almost a whisper. "I mean, I'm sure if this is going to be too hard on you—"

"What?" she asked wryly, interrupting him. "I can decide not to have the baby?"

"Jo . . ."

"I have no choice, Dad." She sighed, remembering the colorful little strip of crochet. "I made a deal with Cassie. I have to follow through."

"Maybe...another solution will present itself," he said, with an innocence she had to applaud but ignore.

"Yeah." She laughed. "Maybe I'm carrying a hidden twin, and there'll be one for each of us."

NOPE. Nobody here but me.

THERE WAS a moment's silence, and then her father said briskly, "Well. I just wanted to be sure you were well. Keep me posted, and I'll keep in touch. I'll make reservations to be there around the twentieth. That all right?"

"Great." Her due date was September 23.

"Okay. Good night, baby. Let me talk to Ryan before I hang up."

"'Night, Dad." Jo shouted for Ryan to pick up the phone. The moment she heard him on the line, she hung up. She leaned back against the plump pillow, thinking that this deal with Cassie rated right up there with the time her sister had talked her into sneaking into the movie theater, when they were ten and eleven. They'd been chased by a vigilant usher, leapt from the ladies' room window, and ended up in the Dumpster of the pizzeria next door. They'd smelled like the Meaty Pizza Special for days.

Ten minutes later, Ryan peered around the door again. He stopped there, saw that she'd reclaimed her pillow and gotten back down under the covers on her own.

"Everything all right?"

"Fine. Thank you. See you in the morning."

That remark had been meant to dismiss him. But he remained, somehow invading her space from across the room.

"How do you feel?" he asked.

She sighed. "Like the Meaty Pizza Special," she replied.

He raised an eyebrow. "The what?"

"Never mind. Private joke. Good night." That was less subtle.

Ryan got the point. With a shake of his head, he pulled the door closed behind him.

Chapter Three

Jo saw it all happening again. She was dreaming. Somehow, she knew that. But it was all as clear as the day it had really happened. And she didn't want to go through it again. She didn't.

She could stop it, she knew. All she had to do was resist. But it was getting harder and harder. Every time the dream came back, it took her a little farther.

She saw Cassie and herself, walking along a busy Portland street. They were shopping. Handled bags hung from their fingers, and their near arms were laced in each other's.

Cassie was ecstatic. "It worked!" She was laughing. "Can you believe it worked? We fertilized an egg and put it inside you and you're pregnant with *my* baby!"

Jo felt her own warmth and happiness as though she still inhabited that image in her dream. She heard her own delighted laughter. "I can't believe I can do something you can't. You and your faulty womb. Imagine it taking *three* people to make a baby."

Cassie smiled up at her. "I hope the baby gets all your good qualities while she's inside you. Your generosity, your fearlessness." She sobered suddenly. "I know everything about this isn't easy for you."

"It's a labor of love," Jo replied, her voice emphasizing the significant word in the hackneyed phrase, which had been sincerely spoken. "And when I'm *in* labor—" she laughed "—remind me that I said that."

It was going to happen now. She felt the horror coming, the dark, awful moment. She saw herself with her back turned, looking in a shop window, seeing the reflection of Cassie stepping out into the street as a big, dark car sped toward her. A sudden paralysis of her entire body made it impossible to do anything but watch. She screwed her eyes closed.

Then she felt pain in her leg. And that was strange, because that wasn't the way it had happened. It hadn't been her. It had been Cassie.

Wrenching pain in her right leg woke Jo out of her fitful sleep. Leg cramp. She'd had them before, but this one was a doozy. She tried to struggle out of bed to stand on it, forgetting where she was, and collided with the bedside table. She gasped and fell back again, groaning as the cramp tightened and the bulk of her stomach made it impossible to reach.

The overhead light went on, and Ryan stood there, barechested, in a pair of gray fleece shorts. A corner of her mind considered it amazing that she could awake, in pain, out of an emotional dream, and still notice her brother-in-law's physical assets. He had straight, strong legs, and a chest just meant to inspire security in a woman.

"What?" he asked, his eyes dark, as he hurried to the side of the bed. "Tell me you're not in labor."

"No." She grimaced as the pain tightened even further. "Leg cramp. And I can't stand up." She stretched a hand out toward him, desperate for help.

He caught it and pulled, arching that arm around his neck as he got her on her feet. He wrapped his other arm around her back.

Jo felt the baby wriggle, adjusting to the change in position. Out of habit, she patted her with her free hand.

Ryan walked her back and forth at the foot of the bed as she worked the cramp out.

"Getting better?" he asked.

"Barely," she replied, still feeling the rocklike tension in her calf. "This one's a killer."

He paced her across the room. "You get them a lot?"

She slanted him a grin. "Part and parcel of the advanced stages of the third trimester."

She didn't realize she was perspiring until he stopped her when they reached the window and wiped his hand across her brow.

He looked solicitous, worried, and for the flash of an instant she felt the precious gift of a man's tender concern.

Ryan felt her warm, damp flesh under his hand and looked into her eyes, eyes made turbulent by distress. She hung from his neck, the bulk of her stomach bumping against him, and he was aware of having to make an effort to remain clinical. His instinct was to touch her in comfort, to soothe her. But this was Jo, who probably wouldn't welcome the gesture. Although she seemed grateful enough for his supporting strength.

As they paced back across the room, the baby moved inside her, and he felt it against him, a completely surprising and mystifying experience. It paralyzed him for an instant.

DADDY? Hi. What are we doing up?

JO SAW something change in his eyes, from serious concern to absorption, fascination. And she knew what it was. Over the months, despite their regular meetings and his presence at her appointments with her obstetrician, neither of them had been sufficiently comfortable with the other for him to touch her to feel the baby's movement.

That morning, when he did it instinctively, out of concern, the baby hadn't moved. Now it was wriggling steadily, apparently impatient with her pacing. And the way he supported her weight, her stomach was wedged against his waist.

She felt sudden sympathy for him. She knew how much he'd loved Cassie, and she was well aware of his grief. Still, she'd known Chelsea would be his the moment she was born, so it'd been hard to think of him as deprived.

It hadn't occurred to her that he was missing out on a large part of the expectant-father experience because he and she weren't intimate.

Without hesitating to think about it, she took the hand with which he held her arm around his neck and placed it high on her stomach, where a tiny fist or elbow waved impatiently. The gentle protrusion moved visibly across her stomach, under his fingertips.

Ryan's dark eyes reacted, then looked into hers with a brilliance that touched her. She smiled, sharing the moment.

"Diantha says that Librans are doers," she said, "and exert impressive physical energy. She predicts she'll like tennis, hiking and aerobics."

He laughed, It was a rich, deep sound in the brightly lit silence of the condo. "I suppose what we just felt was backhand practice."

I WAS JUST TRYING to find my thumb. Ah. There it is. 'Night.

"PROBABLY. I guess since I'm up, she thought she should be too."

They exchanged a smile, and then the atmosphere in the room shifted abruptly. Suddenly the baby wasn't the only element she was aware of in his touch. She felt every one of his fingertips through the cotton over her tender stomach, the warm but ironlike arm that still held her close, the strong, solid thigh that helped support her weight.

Old longing, suppressed in deference to his love for her sister, rose virulently out of the past. It came back, not as memory, but as reality. It pulsed with life, and beat like a little hammer at the base of her throat.

She saw Ryan's expression change, and quickly, guiltily, removed her hand from his.

Ryan felt the small jolt of sexual awareness with total surprise. Jo was his sister-in-law. She didn't like him. She annoyed him. She was reasonably pretty, though she dressed like an example of "What's Out." And she was eight months pregnant.

That was it, he thought, searching his mind for a reason for this niggle of feeling. It was some mistaken impulse from brain to body because of the lateness of the hour and the unique circumstances. He was confusing concern for her, as the host mother of his child, with interest.

And with that thought came a flood of memories of Cassie and everything she'd been to him, of her determination that they find a way to bear a child, of her absolute delirium when the doctor had confirmed that Jo was indeed carrying their baby.

Then guilt overrode everything else he felt. God. It had only been six months. What was wrong with him? He dropped his hand from Jo and stepped back so that he was supporting her only with a forearm clasping hers.

She looked away.

He cleared his throat. "Better?" he asked.

"Yes." The sudden distance he'd placed between them brought reality sharply into focus for Jo. She might feel lust, but Ryan still loved her sister, and probably always would.

She made her way back to the bed without hobbling. The cramp had relaxed somewhat, but an uncomfortable tightness remained. She wished she could reach it to rub it away.

But not every pain could be rubbed away. She'd learned that the hard way, a long time ago.

Ryan stood by to lend support if necessary, but she made it back into bed without help. He drew up the blankets, careful not to touch her, then crossed the room to turn off the light.

He left with a quiet "Good night."

JO CONFRONTED her reflection in the door of the microwave at seven-thirty the following morning. She pointed a butter knife at herself.

"You are not going to live with this theatrically tragic feeling of unrequited love throughout this child's life," she told herself. "He never even *noticed* you, except as an annoyance, and he's only sparing time for you now because you're carrying Chelsea. Your hormones are hysterical, and that instant of sexual awareness last night meant only that you're a jerk. The fat lady sang even before you met him, because he was already in love with Cassie. So *stop* it!"

RYAN PULLED a black-and-gray argyle sweater over his head, and looked out at the view of the river from his bedroom window. He still felt strangely shaken by what he'd felt the night before when helping Jo.

He'd analyzed the incident, if it could even be called that, and he understood what had happened. It was probably only natural that emotion over his first contact with Chelsea should sort of overlap onto the woman whose body sheltered her. That was all it was. No reason to panic. No reason to wallow in guilt. It meant nothing significant.

In fact, this unusual circumstance of having to share space with Jo was going to be a misery, unless both of them relaxed. He had to discuss that with her.

He was surprised to find her in the kitchen and the coffee brewing fragrantly when he walked in. She seemed to be muttering to the microwave, or to herself. She wore a long blue cotton skirt this morning, and a blue-and-black sweater that hung like a tarp to her knees. And those same fat-soled boots.

"Good morning," he said, noticing that she'd set two places at the table, with bowls and mugs.

She turned, her eyes wide and...guilty? "Hi," she said. "I was just...psyching myself up to face the day. You didn't hear me, did you?"

He reached into the drawer for spoons. "No. Why? Did I miss something enlightening?"

The toast popped, and Jo concocted a story as she put them on a plate and buttered them, glancing at him as she worked. "Not enlightening. Embarrassing. I always get myself going by telling myself that a dark, handsome stranger's going to walk into the shop to order a double cap and fall madly in love with me."

He smiled as he placed spoons on the table and reached to the counter for the napkin holder. "Anyone in particular?"

"No. A rock star, maybe, or a humanitarian."

He laughed. "A broad choice. But I thought you were a Heron Point flower, adapted to your environment. Would you be happy anywhere else?"

"Oh, I wouldn't leave. He'd abandon his past and stay here to help me with the shop."

"Ah." He took the plate of toast from her and placed it on the table. "You think a rock star or a humanitarian would want to stay here? I mean, would he want to stage a concert in the basement of the Methodist church? Or add on a wing to the one-room Heron Point Library?"

She met his gaze steadily. "For love of me, he'll do anything."

"Of course," Ryan said. "What was I thinking? What are the bowls for?"

She took a plate out of the refrigerator and handed it to him. It held a bright red-and-yellow Jonathan Delicious. Then she reached into the freezer for a paper-wrapped ice-cream bar. "Apple for you, Häagen-Dazs for me." She frowned. "I couldn't find cereal."

"Yes," he said, taking the plate from her with a skeptical frown. "We have to go grocery shopping. But how come I get the apple? You're the one we're supposed to keep healthy."

"My gums bleed easily." She smiled, obviously pleased with herself for having a legitimate reason to get the ice-cream bar. "Another bonus of the third trimester."

The day was overcast and cool, dark gray clouds hanging heavily over the purple gray hills on the Washington side of the river. They merged seamlessly with the dark gray water.

Downtown started quietly on Saturdays, and it was virtually deserted now, except for people coming and going from the bakery down the street.

Ryan pulled up in front of the coffee shop, then walked around the car to help Jo out. She took his hand, reminding herself that the gesture was nothing but a simple courtesy. When he held on to it, she realized he meant only to help her step from the street onto the sidewalk.

When he still didn't let her go, she felt her hand begin to tingle. She reminded herself firmly of this morning's speech into the microwave.

"Can I come in for a minute?" he asked.

She was now certain he had something on his mind, but she couldn't imagine what. Some alteration to their deal, perhaps? But why? He already had every advantage on his side.

"Of course," she said. She unlocked the shop, then locked the door again as the little bell above it tingled cheerfully. Out of habit, she went behind the counter. She noticed the tall ficus at the other end that must be the gift from the regulars, but she didn't move toward it. She had to know what Ryan had on his mind. He sat on one of four stools pulled up to the counter. Six tables-for-two took up the rest of the small space, and beyond the swinging doors in the back was a small meeting room.

Ryan wondered how to approach the subject of their situation for the next month. Then the antique coffee poster of an old Turkish proverb framed on the wall behind Jo's head caught his eye. He'd always liked it. And part of it related significantly to what he wanted to say.

He pointed to it, and Jo turned to look.

"'Coffee should be black as hell,'" he read, "'strong as death, and sweet as love.'"

Jo turned to him, her eyes perplexed, as she waited for him to explain.

"Strong as death, and sweet as love," he said again. He crossed his arms on the counter and focused on her, his expression grave. "You and I have to come to terms with spending the next month together."

She nodded faintly, certain that was true, but wondering precisely what he meant. She couldn't help the little sprig of hope that pushed through the acceptance inside her.

"Death is strong," he said. "We've both lost Cassie, and though you like to think she still exists on the fringes of our lives, affecting them somehow, she's physically gone. And we're left to finish what the three of us started together."

'Scuse me. Make that four *of us. I'm the star here, you know.*

Jo nodded again, her heartbeat picking up, her breath stalling somewhere in her throat.

"Love is sweet," he said.

Her heart kicked at her ribs. Or was it the baby? She waited.

"I think we've both put our love for Cassie into Chelsea. And we both want, more than anything, for her to be born healthy and happy."

"Yes."

"This month is critical for the baby, and for us."

Afraid to think or analyze, she simply listened.

"So we have to learn to be friends."

Friends.

"I think we should put aside all our preconceived notions of each other, and try to come to a new understanding. We need to cultivate harmony."

Harmony. The little shoot of hope inside her shriveled and died. She accepted that she'd been foolish to ever think it might flower into... Well.

So here they were again. He wanted to be friends, and she wanted to kill him.

But she, too, wanted harmony for Chelsea. She folded her arms. "Well, I made breakfast. The next move is yours."

His level gaze chided her for being flippant. "I'm not suggesting you do anything for me. But I'd like us to be able to relax around each other, to create a healthy atmosphere. Aren't babies supposed to be able to see and hear by the eighth month?"

I CAN SEE what's going on in here, but all I'm getting from out there is light. I can hear everything, though.

JO REGRETTED teasing about what was obviously an earnest proposal. She nodded. "Librans, particularly, according to Diantha. They love music, flowers and perfume. They like aesthetically pleasing surroundings."

Something softened in his eyes. "Then that should be our mission. A happy home for Chelsea's last four weeks of warm-up. Think we can do it?"

"Of course," she insisted brightly. But she added to herself that it wouldn't be easy.

"All right." He slid off the stool and offered his hand. "Peace."

She took it. "Friends," she agreed. She felt warmth and solidity in his grip, and that calmed her, despite the futility of her hopes and dreams.

She could do this. It would be good for Chelsea.

Ryan was convinced this was a good idea. Her hand felt small and fragile in his, reaffirming his decision to watch over her. Her blue eyes were curiously sad, despite her smile. He didn't understand that, but he was sure there was a lot about his sister-in-law he'd never understand.

"Pick you up at five," he said.

She nodded. "I'll be ready."

He left with a smile and a wave, and Jo turned on the CD player and went about the business of opening up shop, telling herself it was going to work. For a month, she could be his friend. His harmonious friend.

Then she took the change from the safe in the back, put it in the cash register, and found herself looking at the poster above it that Ryan had quoted.

He hadn't related the "black as hell" part of it to anything, she thought. But she did. That was what her future was going to look like, if she had to restrict all the love she felt for Ryan and Chelsea to that of a sister-in-law and an aunt.

Chapter Four

There was no other alternative, Jo decided. She had to ask Ryan for help. He probably wouldn't appreciate being awakened at seven-thirty on a Sunday morning, but her living here was his idea. He had to deal with the consequences.

She took her fleece jacket off the foot of the bed and went to his bedroom door. It was slightly ajar, and she peered around it, expecting to find him fast asleep in the opulent dark blue bedding.

Instead, she was completely surprised to see him seated at the foot of the neatly made bed, in shorts and a T-shirt, tying the laces of a running shoe. He looked up. His rich, dark hair was combed, his eyes were bright, his angular chin was shaved. She felt a pang of guilt over the bed she'd left rumpled, and the hair she'd simply brushed quickly and stuffed under a wool beret.

"Good morning," he said, coming to pull the door open farther. His eyes ran over her in assessment. "Everything all right?"

"Um . . . yes." She took a step backward, experiencing an unsettling sense of awareness as he pushed aside the door that separated them. He stood braced on long, strong legs. Muscular arms flexed as he studied her, hands on his hips.

"Get over it," she told herself firmly. "He wants you only to be harmonious and friendly." She smiled casually.

"You going for a jog?"

He shook his head. "I could never get into that. I'm going to the gym." His eyes roved her fleece jacket and her hat, then met her eyes with a frown. "Where are you going at this hour?"

"For a walk," she said. Then, bracing a hand against the molding, she held up one foot, on which a walking shoe rested, still untied. "But a curious thing happened during the night. Either the baby's doubled up and doing yoga, or she's grown suddenly. But I can no longer tie my shoes. Would you mind?"

I THINK WE GAINED A POUND. Must have been the ice-cream bar.

RYAN KNELT BEFORE HER without reply and braced her left foot on his bent knee. He tugged on the tongue of her shoe and straightened it before pulling the laces tight and making a neat bow. He pulled the ribbed hem of her gray sweatpants over the tops of her socks. He repeated the process with her right shoe, then rose smoothly to his feet to frown down at her.

"Walk?" he asked. "Outside?"

She looked at him a moment, wondering if this was a trick question. "Right," she replied finally. "Outside. Along the river and around the point. Why? Where do you usually walk?"

"I don't," he replied, going to the bedroom window to look out.

He snapped a cord and pulled the partially opened drapes all the way back. Fabric that matched the bedspread swirled fluidly and settled into neat columns on both sides of the window. Even from across the room, Jo could see the broad expanse of fog that obscured the river and the town that occupied its banks and the hills around it.

"It's cold and damp," he said, reaching to a bedside chair for a gray sweatshirt, which he pulled on. When his head emerged from the neck, he said briskly, "I'll drive you wherever you need to go. No point in your getting chilled."

Jo resisted a surge of annoyance. "Where I need to go," she said patiently, "is for a walk. To get exercise and see what's going on in the world."

He leaned down to snag the handles of a light brown leather gym bag and came toward her. "Not much to see in that fog. What did you want to do? Stop in at church? Get something from the bakery?"

He flipped off the light and turned her toward the hallway with a hand on her shoulder.

She held her smile firmly in place. "I want exercise. But if you want something from the bakery, I'll gladly pick it up on my walk." She preceded him through the living room to the condo's front door.

"Jo," he said, his tone suggesting that he would be reasonable only to a point. And that they were about to reach it. "You'll get chilled. You'll chill the baby. I don't want that."

Jo turned to him, no longer pretending to smile. She gave him the full impact of her most determined glare. "Let's get something straight, Jeffries," she said. "I've moved in here so that you can rest easy about the baby's well-being, because you are the baby's father. But you're not my husband, and you're not going to make me turn this child into some kind of hothouse flower to suit your antiseptic ideas about life.''

One hand on the doorknob, he raised an eyebrow. "Anti—"

"Antiseptic!" she repeated, enunciating carefully. "You are welcome to go exercise indoors, breathing recycled, carbon-sanitized air while you pit your muscles against machinery." Aware suddenly that she'd raised her voice in her vehemence, she took pains to quiet it before going on. "Chelsea and I, on the other hand, will breathe in fresh air, the perfume of flowers and grass and the river, while we get a cardiovascular workout by strolling under the trees, by the ducks, and over the bridge, with a view of the marina.''

Wow! I wish I could see all that stuff.

EXASPERATED, Ryan pointed toward the window, and the all-encompassing fog. "You won't *see* anything."

She shook her head against his claim. "Of course I will. You can already see the sun behind it. The fog will be gone by the time I get to town. Now, will you please open the door and let me go?''

He considered her a moment. She was wearing sweat bottoms, one of her many tentlike sweaters, and a gray fleece jacket several inches shorter that didn't come close to closing over her stomach. Her hair was stuffed into a magenta wool beret that deepened the color of her cheeks and contributed to her waiflike appearance.

"No," he said, putting his bag down.

She focused on him pugnaciously, her hands on her hips. "Look, Ryan..."

He couldn't help but grin. She looked like an A-frame on which someone had strung laundry.

"I'll come with you," he said. He pulled a pair of weight-training pants out of the bag and slipped them on.

She rolled her eyes. "Aw, come on, Ryan. We'll just spoil it for each other. You probably stop at every red light, even when there's no traffic, and I stop at every heron and just stare until I've had my fill. You'll just want to raise your heart rate, and I just want to feel the wind in my face." She grew suddenly grave. "You'll probably hyperventilate. You're not used to real air, you know. You might poison your system. You'd better stay with your plan and go to the gym."

He wouldn't give her the satisfaction of seeing him grin. He merely pushed her gently through the door into the carpeted hallway and locked the condo's door behind him.

"If I let you go out alone at this hour," he said, leading the way to the elevator, then turning to look at her, "in that getup, you'll get arrested for vagrancy."

"If I were sensitive to a yuppie's opinion of my appearance," she said, angling her chin, "that might hurt my feelings, because I've outgrown all my cool-weather clothes. But the truth is, it's hard to put your fashion trust in people who wear their labels on the *outside*." She pointed a short-nailed index finger at the label on the back of the neck of his sweatshirt, and then at the one on the waistband of his pants.

A melodic bell rang, and the elevator doors parted. He gestured her inside. "Funny. I offered you my credit card to go shopping, but you glared at me."

The car started down with a little jerk, and she caught hold of the bar to steady herself. Instinctively braced against the movement, he took hold of her other arm.

She gave him a quick glance that he didn't understand, though he did note that it held mild accusation and vague disdain. Then the doors parted and she stepped off, pulling away from him and starting across the condo's lawn to the trail that led around the point.

The fog was thick and damp against his face, the air cool and pungent. He picked up his pace as she disappeared into the swirling stuff ahead.

He caught up with her and matched her smaller steps on the narrow, sandy trail, which was bordered by seagrass.

"What did that mean?" he asked.

She glanced up at him again, her expression bland. "The label thing? You have to admit it's a faddish—"

He shook his head. "I mean the look. Why were you offended by my offer to pay for your shopping? I know you're a self-sufficient businesswoman, I just thought you might appreciate a little help with the extras."

She jammed her hands into the pockets of her jacket. "You thought," she said quietly, "that you could make me look the way you'd like me to look—at least while I'm carrying your baby."

He kept pace beside her, with no outward appearance of temper, even as he thought that he'd never known a woman who could bring him as quickly to anger as she could.

"And how do I want you to look?" he asked challengingly.

She shrugged a shoulder as she walked on with a sure and steady stride. "I suppose like Cassie always looked. Like a Donna Karan model with a Victoria's Secret alter ego—the perfect combination of efficiency and simmering sex. Well, that isn't me."

He would have agreed that was certainly true, but the subject seemed to make her strangely vulnerable, despite her honestly clinical discussion of it.

She heaved a sigh and said candidly, "I was never the pretty one. I was the quirky one, so you'll just have to take me as I am."

"You're very pretty," he told her. "But since Cassie was pretty, too, you probably learned that being quirky got you more attention."

She stopped in her tracks for a moment, her eyes wide, accusing—and faintly stricken. Then she started walking again, her gaze focused on the horizon, her pace picking up.

"We're straying from the subject," she said. "I don't want you to buy me clothes."

"That's fine. But I had no ulterior motive in offering you my credit card. Since we're not emotionally involved, it doesn't matter to me whether you look like a Donna Karan model, a Victoria's Secret alter ego, or a very large bag lady. I just thought you might be getting uncomfortable in your nonmaternity clothes, the closer you get to term."

"That's thoughtful of you," she said, in a tone that betrayed her true sentiments, "but I'm fine."

"Good," he said coolly.

"Good," she replied. He was sure it was just to get the last word.

They followed the trail through the marina. Jave and Tom were at work on the *Mud Hen*. The boat, Jo saw, was an old cabin cruiser built in the early part of the century. It had a lapstrake hull and mahogany trim. Ryan detoured to say hello. Jo wandered after him.

"Hey!" Jave waved a paintbrush at them from the bow as they approached. He wore a torn sweatshirt that bore splotches of the white deck paint on his brush. "Want to come aboard?"

Ryan turned to Jo, who shook her head and smiled. "Thanks," she said to Jave, "but I don't fit on anything smaller than the *Queen Mary*. How's it going?"

At the same moment she asked, Tom surfaced from below decks, his clothes covered in the same paint Jave sported, wearing a painter's cap backward. Loud rock music came from below, and Tom gyrated outrageously to the sound as he brought Jave a canned soft drink.

Jo and Ryan exchanged amused glances. Tom had been a regular customer of Coffee Country since Jo had opened the shop, and he was still a fireman. Since the fire a year ago that had killed his friend and put him in the hospital, she'd empathized with his struggle to put the past behind him and start over as a carpenter and general craftsman.

Jave rolled his eyes. "I'd have had this boat seaworthy a week ago," he said, "if I'd been working by myself."

"Hi!" Tom's dance stopped abruptly when he noticed them, and he waved over the side. "Come on up. We've got mineral water and iced tea, too."

Ryan shook his head. "Thanks. We're just out for a walk. Saw Jave working and thought we'd say hi."

"We'll take you on a harbor tour when we get her going," Jave said. "Pretty soon." He inclined his head toward Tom. "Depends on how much help I get from Little Brother."

"Make your jokes," Tom said, with an air of superiority. "When it comes time to find the fish, you'll be begging for my help."

Jave frowned ruefully at Ryan. "Unfortunately, that's true."

Ryan shook his head. "Should have left the hole in the deck, so they could jump in on their own. Take care."

"Don't you think that's strange?" Jo asked under her breath as they walked back along the dock to the road. A water hose had been stretched across the planks, and Ryan took Jo's elbow to help her over it. "About Nancy Malone and Jave, I mean."

The trail now took a subtle but definite incline, and Jo, distracted by her thoughts, looped an arm through Ryan's for support. He noticed, but pretended not to.

"Strange in what way?" he asked.

"Well, Nancy's married," Jo said. "When we were at the hospital, the staff in OB was talking about how she's going to be the model mother for the opening festivities for the new birthing rooms."

Riverview Hospital's redesigned OB facility was a source of excitement in Heron Point. It included birthing rooms in which the expectant father, and whatever other family members and friends the mother approved, could remain with her during labor and birth. They were decorated like bedrooms out of *Better Homes and Gardens*.

The austere and lonely hospital room was a thing of the past—at least in OB.

He didn't understand the problem. "And?"

"And," she said, as though it ought to be obvious to him, "Jave is her Lamaze coach. That doesn't seem strange to you?"

"No," he replied.

"Why not?" she asked, obviously perplexed. "She's married, and her husband's friend is her Lamaze coach? Come on. Women alone in their pregnancy usually choose another woman as their coach. Like Karma Endicott, the accountant, who comes with that girl from your bank."

"Ah." He did, at least, know the young woman who worked at his bank. "Roberta Dawson."

"Right. You don't see her there with another man. Yet Nancy Malone comes with Jave."

"If he's her husband's friend, chances are he's her friend, too."

"But..." She rubbed her swollen stomach. "Delivery is an intimate thing."

He nodded. "And a personal one. And no time for prudery. If she's comfortable with him, that's what counts. So it shouldn't matter to anyone else."

She angled him a rueful glance. "Are you telling me to mind my business?"

He put a theatrical hand to his heart. "Heaven forfend! I just don't think you should lose any sleep over it, if Nancy and Jave are comfortable with it."

They'd crested the hill that led to town and turned onto paved sidewalk. Jo was apparently unaware that she still held his arm. He continued to pretend not to notice, thinking that it was curiously pleasant. He missed a lot of big, important intimacies since Cassie's death, but he missed many of the small things, too. Like the easy trust of her hand in his arm.

He wasn't mistaking Jo for Cassie, he knew, but he liked the feeling anyway. He recognized it as another small step toward healing. He knew he would never heal completely; he and Cassie had loved each other too much. But it was important for their baby that he make life's demanding adjustments.

He heaved a sigh as they walked on.

Jo looked up at him in mock concern. "I heard that," she said teasingly. "Getting winded? Doesn't your treadmill at the gym incline this steeply? Want to find a bench, so you can sit down and catch your breath?"

"Who," he asked, with a pointed glance at her hand, clutching his arm, "is holding on to whom?"

She studied it a moment in surprise, then withdrew it and put it in her pocket. "I was climbing for two," she said briskly. "But it's downhill from here. Didn't I tell you the sun would be out before we got to town?"

She pointed to the horizon formed by the hilltops of Washington, across the river, meeting a bright blue sky. The fog was now simply a gauzy ribbon clinging to the foothills. "You'd have missed this view at the gym."

"True." He had to concede that. In the six years he'd lived in Heron Point, he'd never seen it from this particular angle. He'd driven this way in the car, but then his attention had been focused on the road, watching for all the children and pets that lived in this old neighborhood and ran across without checking the traffic.

It was beautiful. Two lines of turn-of-the-century homes meandered down the hill toward the river in colorful splendor. Some were newly repainted, others charmingly faded, but all were fronted by the rich green grass always in evidence in rainy Oregon, even in early fall.

As they passed a yellow-and-white house, a Golden Retriever ran from the porch steps to the chain-link fence, tail wagging as she barked excitedly at Jo.

"Hi, Buttercup," Jo said, reaching over the fence so that she could scratch between the dog's ears. The bulk of the baby made the movement difficult, but Buttercup stood on her hind legs accommodatingly and whined in ecstasy at the attention. "This is Ryan. Ryan, meet Buttercup, former contender for field trials champion in Oregon, but now just a happy house dog."

MAMA CASS says she was going to get me a puppy when I was born. Can we have one? Huh?

RYAN REACHED OVER the fence to stroke the dog, who butted her nose trustingly against his hand, and greeted his ministrations with the same whining delirium.

"Buttercup told you all this?" he asked Jo with a grin.

Jo laughed lightly. "Her master is a police officer who comes in for coffee every morning before his shift."

Ryan gave the dog a final pat, and they moved on. Buttercup followed them to the very edge of the fence, barking a protest at their departure.

"So, you're kind of like a bartender," he suggested, stopping at the curb as a late-model station wagon passed, filled with children wearing their Sunday best. "Listening to personal stories, probably giving advice?"

The curb was high, and he offered her his hand for balance as she stepped down.

"I'm a good listener," she said, "but I leave the advice to Diantha. At least she has astrology to back it up. Bill! Hi!"

They'd reached the other side of the street, and Ryan looked for the man or boy responsible for her greeting, but saw no one. Then he noticed a black tuxedo cat, sporting white markings that resembled a mustache and a bow tie. He was young, and approached Jo with a playful, stiff-legged prance.

"Hi, baby!" she said, trying to bend. Remembering suddenly that she couldn't, she turned to Ryan with a smile of appeal. "Would you pet him for me? But don't touch his tail—he doesn't like that."

With a long-suffering groan, Ryan squatted down to stroke the cat, who studied him suspiciously for a moment, then rubbed obligingly against his knee.

A calico kitten scampered over from across the street and bumped her way in between the tuxedo and Ryan's hand.

A KITTEN WOULD BE OKAY. Could we have a kitten?

"CAMOUFLAGE!" Jo exclaimed. "How're you doing?" To Ryan, she added, "You can rub her anywhere. She loves attention. But watch yourself. She plays like a predator."

She'd just spoken the words when the purring kitten rolled onto her back, grabbed Ryan's hand in her front paws and ripped at it with her back feet.

Ryan tried to withdraw his hand with a spirited oath, and lifted it waist-high, only to find the kitten still attached, still attacking. Jo gently extricated Camouflage, who purred, then whopped her on the nose with a paw. Jo laughed and placed the kitten on the nearby gatepost.

Ryan studied the angry red scratches on his hand. "You didn't tell me we'd be walking through Wildlife Safari," he said, taking her elbow to pull her along. "How many more species will we be encountering before we get to town?"

She took his hand in hers and examined it. He experienced an instant's disassociation from the world around him. Her touch filled the moment—the softness of her fingertip, the light rasp of her index fingernail as she traced a scratch, the bump of her shoulder against his upper arm as she leaned close to him in her inspection.

"You'll live," she said finally, dropping his hand.

The magnified moment dissolved, and he put it out of his mind, striving for normalcy. She seemed completely unaffected. "Sure, but I'll be scarred," he said. "I suppose their masters are also customers of yours?"

"No, I just met them on my walk. Aren't they great?"

"And they told you their names?"

She gave him the scolding look the question deserved. "They wear tags. Anyway, I can't have pets in my apartment, and I wouldn't have one downtown, anyway. It's too dangerous. So I have to get my pet fix around here.'' She asked curiously, ''Have you ever had a pet?''

He shook his head. ''My parents both worked and didn't think it was fair to leave one alone. Then Cassie and I were in the same situation. And, frankly, I don't like the idea of having to set my schedule around a pet that has to be fed and let out, requiring me to be home at definite intervals, or preventing me from taking trips.''

Jo stopped in her tracks and blinked up at him. ''Ryan,'' she said. ''That's precisely what the baby will do to your life.''

They'd reached the edge of the downtown area, where the blocks of houses were replaced by small shops and other places of business. Bright sunlight bounced off store windows and the windshields of cars.

''Really,'' he said, with a dry glance at her, as they stopped at the traffic light at Heron Point's main intersection. ''I thought I could just put her in my briefcase and take her to work with me. Or maybe drop her off at Coffee Country, and you could put her on a shelf till I get off.''

''She can hear everything, you know,'' she said in a scolding tone as the light changed to green. ''Sarcasm is not a nice thing to teach her.''

Ryan stepped off the curb. ''Neither is the notion that her father's a thoughtless jerk who hasn't made any plans for her care.''

''Have you?'' she asked in surprise.

He'd taken several steps across the street, and when he looked back and saw that she wasn't following, he went back to catch her hand and pull her after him. ''Of course I have. I told you I was going to call Mrs. Bennett about moving in when you go back to work.''

*MRS. WHO? I don't think I'll like that. I want to go to
work with Mama Jo. Mama, tell him.*

JO TRAILED after him moodily, remembering that he had
mentioned talking to Helen Bennett. She'd built an impressive reputation around town as an infant nanny. At
sixty-two, she preferred small babies to toddlers that had
to be chased and corralled.

It shouldn't surprise her that he'd actually done it. He
was very responsible and reliable, especially where the
baby was concerned. She simply found it unsettling that
he'd arranged circumstances so that she would eventually
be unnecessary—at least where Chelsea's daily care was
concerned.

On the opposite side of the street, he stopped and looked
down into her forlorn expression. "You're the one," he
reminded her in mild concern, "who suggested Mrs. Bennett."

"I know." She drew a deep breath and shook off the pall
of depression. She forced a smile. "That'll be perfect. Can
you buy me a cup of tea and a brioche?"

Ryan studied the melancholy look in her eyes an extra
moment, and then, since she'd initiated an abrupt change
of subject, let the matter drop. "Ah...sure." He looked
up the deserted street where the bakery was, and saw that
it, like most of the shops downtown, was closed. "But
where?"

"The bakery at the supermarket has them, and a table
where we can sit."

They talked about nothing significant while they ate in
the market, which was also deserted at this hour of a Sunday morning. Warm, sweet smells surrounded them, en-
closing them in a cozy atmosphere directly at odds with
how they felt in each other's company.

Ryan watched as Jo talked. She'd pulled off her beret, and a riot of curly blond hair fell to her shoulders and down her back, frizzy and rumpled and somehow completely captivating.

He'd never noticed before that the millions of tiny corkscrew curls appeared gilded where they caught the light, and made her look like something from a Botticelli painting. His eyes wandered over it, but he still caught every subtle little nuance in her voice.

She was telling him about a fundamentalist customer who'd gotten into an argument with Diantha, and though she spoke animatedly, he could hear that her enthusiasm was forced and fraudulent. There was an underlying sigh in her tone.

Jo knew she was babbling, but he was watching her with that casual attention that always made her feel he saw and understood more than he let on. And that he would eventually know more about her than she knew herself.

And there was so much she had to keep from him.

Even as that thought formed, a flush filled her cheeks and rose to her hairline. She cursed the honest nature that made it so difficult to hide what she felt.

She pulled at the neckline of her sweater and fanned herself with a napkin. "What was that you said about getting chilled?" she asked, deciding that if he was wondering what had brought on that rush of color the better part of valor would be to distract him by putting him on the defensive. "We'd both be more comfortable now in bathing suits." Then, glancing down at her rotund form, she added with a laugh, "Well, not necessarily glamorous, but more comfortable."

Ryan wondered about the blush. He couldn't imagine a reason for it, unless she truly was overheated. But then, he'd never understood her anyway, and he doubted that he ever would.

He was also confused by his feelings for her. At the moment, he was looking at her with new interest. In the somewhat normal sweater she wore, and with her hair tumbled but simply flowing free, and not in one of the bizarre styles she usually preferred, she was attractive. The very notion robbed him of logic.

He'd always considered her everything he stood against—disorderly, irreverent, liberal. But he seemed strangely unaware of those facts at the moment. He saw only that her cheeks were pink, her eyes were bright, her hair was wildly beautiful—and she was carrying his baby.

For an instant, the convoluted method of the baby's conception was forgotten, and he felt a very elemental attachment to the woman who was pregnant with his child.

That mellow mood lasted until Ryan realized he and Jo were staring at each other—and that her blush had deepened. He downed his coffee.

"Ready?" he asked, slapping their empty paper cups together and tossing them at the wastebasket.

"Ah...yes." She studied him for one uncertain moment, then stood awkwardly, draping her fleece jacket over her arm. The air was charged, she noted, and she didn't know why. So she found stability in the antagonism that was their conversational currency.

"The next leg of our journey is uphill, you know," she warned him, gathering up their napkins and dropping them in the basket. "It's even harder on a full stomach. You want to hop a cab, and I'll meet you at the condo?"

Ryan felt himself relax. It was strange, he thought, that fighting with her was comfortable.

"Get real," he said. "I could carry you back and not even raise my heart rate."

"Ha!" She snorted. "I'd like to see *that* happen." Then she stopped his progress toward the door with a tug on the sleeve of his sweatshirt. "Can you buy a bag of day-old bread?"

He frowned. "Why?"

"So we can feed the sea gulls near the cannery."

He withdrew a fistful of change and held it open to her. "God. You mean there's more to Jo's Wild Kingdom?"

She shook her head at him as she took three quarters. "You're supposed to be in harmony with your surroundings, Jeffries."

"Yeah, well, usually my surroundings involve receipting machines and bank vaults. They don't require petting and feeding."

She asked the clerk for a bag of dried bread, then turned back to him while she waited. "You've got to remember that machinery isn't life, Ryan. Life is people, nature." She sighed deeply and pretended that she bore the weight of a great burden. "I have *so* much to teach you, in such a short time."

Chapter Five

"Miss Arceneau! Josanne!"

Jo stopped in the middle of the hospital corridor and turned to find a tall young woman chasing her down. She carried a clipboard and was waving excitedly. Jo had seen her around the hospital on her regular visits, and assumed from her nonuniform garb that she was some sort of administrative personnel. She waited with a combination of interest and perplexity for the woman to reach her.

"Whew!" the woman exclaimed as she came to an awkward stop in front of Jo. She was tall and angularly built, dressed in a green cotton dress with too much lace. Her long hair was lank and silver-blond, though apparently some attempt had been made to curl it, and she wore little makeup. Clear-framed, frumpy glasses rested on a small, well-shaped nose. But she had a smile that lit her eyes and warmed Jo with its sincerity. "I'm Amy Brown, public relations director for the hospital. Thanks for waiting for me." She made a production of drawing a deep breath. "Jogging just isn't my thing, and as you can see, I'm not built for speed. May I have a few minutes of your time?"

"Of course." Jo allowed herself to be led to a small office off the reception area at the back of the hospital. Ryan hadn't been able to accompany her to her appointment this morning, but had sent his assistant to drive her. She'd been headed for the pay phone to call for her ride back when Amy Brown intercepted her.

"Would you like some tea?" Amy asked. "Cocoa?"

Jo shook her head. "No, thank you."

Amy nodded, pointed Jo to a chair and took the one behind a small, orderly desk. "Then I'll get right to it. I'm sure you're aware of the hospital's new birthing rooms. We had something about it in the *Herald* just the other day."

Jo nodded. "Yes. I'm looking forward to using one."

Amy sat a little straighter, her eyes beaming. "That's precisely what I want to talk to you about. In order to 'launch' our birthing rooms, so to speak, we've planned to shower with gifts the first mother to use one of our rooms. We've gotten the merchants involved, and they've donated the most remarkable prizes for the first baby born there."

Jo nodded. "That was in the article. And Nancy Malone's your model mother, isn't she? She's in my Lamaze class."

Amy shook her head, her expression indulgently accepting. "She isn't anymore—our model mother, I mean. She's...abdicated."

Jo tried not to look too interested. She'd known there was something strange going on there. "Why," she asked, "would she do that?"

Amy thought about her reply for a moment, obviously picking and choosing her words carefully. "Well...it seems we sort of...were confused by her records, and presumed she was married."

Jo couldn't hide the interest now. "Isn't she?"

Amy shook her head. "She's divorced. That was no problem for us, of course. We'd have still been delighted to use her, but she... Well, it's all very complicated. But the upshot is, we need a new model mother." She smiled at Jo. "Would you consider taking on the role? You're due just about the same time Nancy is."

Jo couldn't decide which issue caught her interest more strongly—that Nancy Malone wasn't married and was therefore entitled to be seen all over town with Jave Nicholas, or that Amy Brown wanted *her* to assume the position of model mother.

She obviously had to explain a few things—and then she wanted a few things explained to her.

"I'm flattered, of course," Jo said, "but you're probably not aware that my circumstances are rather unique."

"I know you run Coffee Country, and that you're single," Amy said. "A completely outfitted nursery would be a real boost to your budget, wouldn't it?"

"It would," Jo answered, "if the baby were mine."

Amy's eyes widened. Then she leaned back in her chair, looking very much as though she required an explanation but, considering her quest for someone to take Nancy's place, didn't particularly want to hear it. She seemed to suspect it would rob her of her candidate.

Jo explained about Chelsea's unorthodox conception, then Cassie's accident. "My sister and brother-in-law had made all their plans for the nursery when we learned the pregnancy had taken," she said. "Then, when Cassie died, Ryan finished and furnished it down to the last detail." She smiled apologetically at Amy. "I'm sorry, I thought everyone in town knew the situation. And there isn't a thing we need."

Amy nodded ruefully. "I just moved to Heron Point a couple of months ago. I guess I should have talked to Dr. Mac before approaching you, but I noticed you when you came into Emergency last week, and when Nancy with-

drew, I thought you'd be perfect." She sighed, raising her
hands in a gesture of defeat. "I'm sorry I wasted your
time. I hope I didn't . . . upset you, or anything."

Jo pushed herself laboriously to her feet. "Of course
not. I'm sure you'll find another candidate. In fact," she
added with sudden enthusiasm, "my Lamaze class has
several other couples, and a single woman who—"

Amy shook her head. "I checked. The other couples are
going to Portland for their deliveries, and Karma Endicott, the single woman, isn't due until the end of Octo-
ber."

Jo smiled sympathetically. "If you can't find another
model mother, maybe you'll just have to delay the opening a month."

Amy walked Jo to the door. "Thanks. I was so sure this
was a great idea, and that mothers would be pushing each
other out of the way to get all the gifts for their babies."
She shook her head, obviously mystified. "But everyone's turning me down instead. Go figure the American
consumer. Where are you parked? I'll walk you—"

They'd just stepped out into the hall when their conversation was interrupted by a man's impatient bellow.

"Josanne! God! You scared me to death. What are you
doing in the PR office? Don't you ever take a direct route
anywhere? You were supposed to call the bank when you
were finished, so someone could pick you up. You don't
call. So we call Dr. McNamara and he says you left the
office an hour ago."

Ryan, the sides of his conservative gray suit jacket
thrown back and braced there by the hands on his hips,
frowned down at Jo, obviously displeased.

She resisted an annoyed reply, deciding he was making
more than enough noise for a hospital corridor all by
himself. Instead, she said politely, "Amy, I'd like you to

meet my brother-in-law, Ryan Jeffries. Ryan, this is Amy Brown, the hospital's PR director.''

Ryan dropped his annoyed-lordship posture and shook Amy's hand.

"I apologize," he said, with a glance at Jo that made it clear the apology did not extend to her. "When I couldn't find Jo, I got a little nervous. Particularly after her fall the other day. I thought—"

Amy smiled at him and shook her head. "I should apologize to you. I'm the one who stopped Jo on her way out and delayed her. So please don't shout at her. It was all my fault."

Ryan replied politely, but did not appear entirely appeased.

A short, square nurse with the air of a drill sergeant marched past. "Call Tom Nicholas," she said, without pausing in her steps. "And next time you leave your office unattended, take your beeper, and other people won't have to take your messages." She gave a curt nod in Ryan's direction. "Mr. Jeffries."

Ryan nodded back. "Nurse Beacham."

"Tom Nich—" Amy repeated, a shamelessly thrilled note in her voice. Color filled her cheeks, and she looked suddenly befuddled. She turned one way, and then the other, took a step, collided with her office door, then seemed to remember her guests and turned back again.

"Thank you for giving me your time, Miss Arceneau," she said to Jo, then added to Ryan, "And forgive me for frightening you." Her expression of professional concern was replaced suddenly by a glowing smile as she turned and stepped into her office and closed the door firmly behind her.

Jo looked up at Ryan, forgetting his irritation for a moment. "Tom Nicholas? Are they—?" She held up two crossed fingers, the gesture suggesting a relationship.

Ryan interrupted her. "I don't want to talk about Tom Nicholas," he said, taking hold of her arm and drawing her with him down the corridor. "I want to talk about why it never occurred to you to call, if you knew you were going to be late."

"Ryan," she said patiently, "I was heading for the phone when Amy stopped me." She explained briefly about the model mother-birthing room situation and Amy's offer of the position to her. "Of course, I had to refuse."

"And that took an hour?"

"No, it took about ten minutes. But I—"

"Then where the hell were you?"

She stopped at the glass doors to the outside to growl at him exasperatedly. "I spent a little time at the nursery window, all right? When the birthing rooms are in use, babies will stay with their mothers, and we oglers will have nothing more to look at. Anyway, I got to looking at all those pretty babies and thinking that in just under three weeks, ours will be—" She hesitated, then corrected herself. "I mean, *yours* will be here. It was a startling notion, so I kept staring and thinking about it. I guess I was longer than I realized."

MAMA CASS *says I'm cuter than any of them. And, Daddy? She says stop shouting.*

RYAN'S TAUT FEATURES softened. He shifted his weight, then assumed that displeased-lordship stance again, though far less convincingly.

"Okay," he said quietly. "But I wish you'd remember that we're in this together, and that while you're carrying the baby and feeling great and taking walks in the fog and dawdling at your doctor's appointment, I'm watching everything from a worrisome distance. All I know is that you seem awfully small to be carrying this burden, that I'm worried every moment that something could go wrong with you or with the baby, and when you take off in your independent way I go mildly crazy."

That admission was a major concession to her, Jo knew. Far more vulnerability than she'd ever thought he'd admit. It put them on somewhat equal footing—a status she'd never imagined he'd accord her, given that the baby was half Cassie's, and she, Jo, was only there because of the unusual circumstances.

She smiled fractionally. "Mildly?" she asked, her tone challenging.

He let a smile slip. "Okay, wildly. So, have a heart, would you? Come on. I'll take you to lunch before I take you back to work."

"I'd love that. Can we go to Chez Pasta?"

"Wherever you like."

"Can we stop at Dairy Queen after for fat-free yogurt?"

"If you'd like that."

"Will you buy me the Jeep Cherokee I've been admiring at Lum's Auto Center?"

He had helped her into his red Volvo, and walked around to slip in behind the wheel. He cast her a cautionary glance. "You're pushing it, Jo."

She buckled her seat belt and laughed wickedly. "Your guilt reflex was working so well, I thought I'd go for it. You'll never guess what I learned from Amy."

He turned the key in the ignition and headed for the exit to the road. "What?"

"Nancy Malone isn't married, she's divorced. So that's why Jave Nicholas is her Lamaze coach."

He considered that a moment, then shook his head. "That doesn't necessarily follow."

"Sure it does. They must have a relationship. I bet that's why she gave up the model mother position. Because she wanted him more than she wanted the gifts."

Ryan turned onto the road, heading in the direction of Chez Pasta. "I think you're employing creative reasoning."

She shook her head pityingly. "It's all so obvious. But you're so left-brained. You don't believe anything that isn't substantiated by columns of figures or an audit. Want to make a small wager?"

He pulled up at a red light, and turned to look at her. She saw laughter in his eyes, and was pleased by it. "On what terms?" he asked.

"I'll bet you Nancy and Jave are married by the time she has her baby. If I win, you can buy me a new winter jacket. If *you* win . . . what do you want?"

He rested the inside of his wrist against the top of the steering wheel and thought.

"Remember my budget," she put in.

He nodded. "I'd rather go for some kind of service, anyway, so that you'd have to remember every time you did it that I was right and you were wrong."

"You're a pillar of nobility."

"I try." The light turned green, and he accelerated. "How about," he asked, giving her a quick, smug glance, "latte delivered to me at the bank every afternoon for a month?"

"But . . . you'd have to wait awhile for it," she pointed out seriously. "I mean, we won't know until her baby's born, and by then Chelsea will be, too, and I'll be home."

Ryan glanced at her again as they sped along the road that paralleled the river. "No problem," he said. "I can wait until you go back to work. As long as I collect."

When she went back to work, she thought, Mrs. Bennett would take over Chelsea's care, and she'd be relegated to aunt status.

"Yeah," she said quickly. "Right." She fidgeted and looked out the window.

"What is it?" he asked, with another worried look in her direction. "Don't tell me you're concerned that *I'm* getting the good end of the deal?"

She warned herself sternly to get it together. She laughed and backhanded his upper arm. "Of course not. Your end of the deal is already forfeit, anyway. I'm sure of it. They're in love. They'll be married by the time that baby comes. If I have dessert," she asked, "do I have to give up yogurt at the Dairy Queen?"

"BREATHE IN . . ." Serena Borders, the Lamaze-certified trainer, directed as she walked among the couples seated among pillows on the carpeted floor. "Then breathe out, concentrating on expelling every negative thought, every concern, every idea clamoring for your attention. Breathe out and relax. Empty your mind. Clear even your dreams away."

Jo lay in the spoon position, a pillow between her knees, trying to concentrate on the instructions. But Ryan, spooned behind her, was fidgeting.

She propped herself up on an elbow and turned to whisper to him while Serena paused to give Karma Endicott instruction. "What's the matter?"

"They're faulty directions," Ryan complained, though he held his position. "How can you listen to instructions and clear your mind? Your mind has to be busy to concentrate on what she's saying. And you have to think about breathing."

"No, you don't. It's instinctive."

He propped himself up on his elbow, too, to dispute that. "Well, normally it is, but when someone tells you how you should be doing it, then you have to think about it to do it right. So, you can't."

"Jeez, Jeffries," Jo whispered. "You make everything so hard. Just breathe and go with it. I can't believe emptying *your* mind would be such a big deal. And this is our third class. You should be into this by now." She turned and resumed her position.

He stared moodily at the back of her head. Her mass of curls was caught loosely at the nape of her neck, then seemed to explode from the tie like a spurt of gold rain.

He closed his eyes. He was tired of noticing her hair. But then he felt tired of everything today. He was tired of people with no money and no means of acquiring any wanting to borrow from the bank. He was tired of employees needing time off and forgetting to schedule it ahead of time. He was tired of careless errors and of slipshod double checks that missed them.

He pushed himself to a sitting position at the teacher's instruction and positioned himself behind Jo. He drew a breath, wishing the class was over and they could go home. He would retire to his room with a brandy and the *Wall Street Journal* and try to forget for a moment that he had no idea what the hell was happening to his life.

Eight months ago, it had stretched before him like a ribbon of promise—good position with the bank, beautiful, loving wife, baby on the way, however unconventionally.

Even after Cassie's death, he'd known precisely what he had to do—protect the baby they'd made together, by watching over Jo until Chelsea was born. Then he would love Chelsea and see that she had everything she wanted.

It had been so clear.

But he seemed to be losing that comfort level lately. The closer the time came to his baby's delivery, the less secure he felt about what had once seemed so simple.

He was going to be a father. A single father. And his child was a girl. He'd have Mrs. Bennett for a while, and Jo would be around to help, but ninety-nine percent of the responsibility for her happiness, her health, her sense of security, eventually even her image of herself as a woman—would be his. That was a daunting thought.

And then there was Jo. Their relationship was undergoing a subtle change. He couldn't quite define it, or even understand it in the most basic sense. He just knew it was making him nervous.

He'd never noticed her much before, except as an annoyance. Now he found himself aware of her most of the time. He guessed it was because she'd moved in with him. Proximity was bound to make them more conscious of each other.

But he had an unsettling feeling it was more than that. He didn't know what, and he wasn't sure why, and all he wanted to do was put it out of his mind. But they were in a Lamaze class, with its touchy-feely approach to delivery.

He understood its value. He'd even been the one to insist they take the class when Jo was reluctant—probably for the same reasons he was now. But today, particularly, it was making his life difficult.

"All right," Serena said. "Let's work on our full body massage."

Jo assumed the gently stretched position in a brisk and clinical manner, and prayed for the strength to hold herself aloof throughout the exercise. She could do it. All she had to do was concentrate.

Ryan was right, she thought as he placed a hand on her head according to Serena's directions. It was difficult to clear one's mind and concentrate at the same time.

Although, in an unexpected sense, it seemed to be working. As his hands moved from her head to her shoulders, she wasn't thinking, she was simply feeling.

His hands were long-fingered, and broad from little finger to thumb, and left a wide swath of sensation from the tip of her shoulder to the middle of her back. A tingle rippled along under her skin in the path of his fingertips, and she had to concentrate to prevent herself from fidgeting. Concentration prevented relaxation, but she stopped herself from moving by pretending she was stone. The trick served her purpose, but not Serena's.

"Jo Arceneau!" the trainer exclaimed, for all to hear. "You're like concrete!" But instead of being displeased, the woman turned to Ryan with a satisfied smile. "Coach," she said, "this is excellent training for you. Tensing up will be the mother's instinctive reaction to pain and fear and doubt. It's *your* job to remind her to relax, and to apply your hands to her body in a way that'll make her notice your touch over her own pain. Now, what have I taught you?"

Jo's body turned from stone to putty as Ryan dutifully proved that he'd paid attention. "I apply sufficient pressure," he said, his thumbs on her spinal column, his fingertips rayed out toward her sides as he rubbed in a slow downward motion, "to help her relax, always listening for her reaction. If she's distracted, I ask where she wants to be massaged, and let her dictate how lightly or how firmly."

He reached the back of her waist, then his thumbs dipped down to the small of her back. "I'm careful here, because this might relieve her pain, or cause it. So I listen for feedback."

OH, right there, Daddy. Down. Over. A little to the right. Ahh . . .

SERENA LAUGHED. "And sometimes you'll get that very explosively, if you've touched an area that causes more pain. But just remember that every cell in her being is at a heightened pitch, and she's just reacting at that level. So what must you do?"

Ryan stroked his way up her back again with firm but gentle confidence. "I remain calm, keep my voice down, and try to fulfill her needs, whatever they are."

"Excellent!" Serena patted his shoulder. "You're so good, I might lend you out to other mothers with less competent coaches."

She walked away, and Ryan dropped his hands from Jo, surprised to find them less than steady. His heartbeat was erratic, too, and his breathing shallow. His brain, far from relaxed, was thinking how soft Jo felt for a woman who was generally angular and athletic. It was probably the pregnancy.

The moment Ryan's hands fell away from her, Jo felt the absence of his touch, as though a lack could be a tangible thing. Tension began to build in her again, and with it came the old guilt and confusion.

He didn't want to be doing this, she knew that. Oh, he wanted to study the Lamaze method for the sake of his baby's safety and ease of delivery, but he didn't want to have to coach her. He was doing it because he had to.

She had to remember that. No matter how comforting his touch, how exciting and promising, any further effects of it were entirely in her imagination.

Jo glanced around the room as Serena moved among her students, and saw Nancy Malone and Jave Nicholas laughing together and gazing into each other's eyes with a look of love that was unmistakable. She remembered her wager with Ryan. She was going to win that jacket.

Karma Endicott, the attractive accountant who stopped in regularly for house-blend tea but was always too busy to chat, was practicing breathing exercises with stern-faced concentration.

Easy for *her* to concentrate, Jo thought dryly. She had another woman as a coach, not a man with strong, distracting hands.

Groaning at her own foolishness, Jo struggled to her knees as Serena declared the class over. Ryan offered her his hands to help her to her feet, but she couldn't help staring at them for a moment, thinking how ironic it was. Those hands represented everything she wanted—except permanence. She had to keep reminding herself that she had only until the time Chelsea was born, and she had to be satisfied with that.

She placed her hands in his and glanced up at him as he smoothly pulled her upright. His dark eyes were unfocused, and his thoughts clearly miles away. Automatically he helped Jo with the old fleece jacket, and picked up their pillows and stacked them in the corner with the others.

"Hi, Mr. Jeffries," Roberta Dawson said. She was Karma Endicott's coach, and worked at the bank. "You were quite a star tonight. Can we line you up to help Karma if I lose my nerve?"

Ryan smiled politely. "No, thanks. I think I'll be good for one time only. And the closer it gets, the less sure I am about it."

Roberta agreed. "Me too. It seemed so easy—and so far away—at first. Now I'm tempted to be out of town when Karma's due."

Ryan nodded. "I know the feeling."

Jave tossed his and Nancy's pillows onto the pile. "You're both experiencing prenatal jitters. They have a sound medical basis. Relax, and everything will be fine."

"Ha!" Roberta said, with a teasingly scornful look at Jave. "Doctors! They think they know everything about medicine. This is terror, pure and simple." Then she winked. "See you next week. See you tomorrow, Mr. Jeffries."

"Ryan," Jave said, "I'd like to see you tomorrow, too. Do you have a small block of time in the afternoon?"

Ryan noted that Jave looked beyond him as he spoke, to Nancy, who was in earnest conversation with Serena. He was smiling unconsciously, his usually steady expression disgustingly besotted. Ryan saw his chances of winning the bet slip considerably.

"Sure," he replied. "I'm back from lunch at two o'clock. Would that work for you?"

"Great. My whole afternoon's clear."

Ryan was quiet on the drive home, but Jo thought little about it. In the two weeks she'd lived with him, she'd learned he wasn't one to make small talk comfortably.

But by the time they stepped off the elevator in the condo's hallway, she knew he was experiencing more than a simple unwillingness to chatter. He seemed angry.

He reached into his pants pockets for his keys. Jo saw his frown deepen as he reached into his other pants pocket, then patted the pockets of his jacket.

"Would you open the door, please?" he asked, with stiff courtesy. "I don't seem to have my keys."

Jo sensed trouble. "I'm sorry," she said. "I don't have my keys with me. Maybe you—"

"What do you mean, you don't have them with you?" he demanded, still furiously patting pockets.

She wasn't in the mood for this. She didn't know what his problem was, but her back hurt, her head hurt, and her libido was in a confused and sorry state. All she wanted was to go to bed and watch "Murphy Brown" reruns.

"I mean," she said, her patience strained, "that I do not have my key with me. I don't know how to clarify that any further."

"I had two made for you," he reminded crossly.

She shifted her weight. So did the baby. "I know. But one's at the shop, and the other's in my tote bag. Maybe you—"

"Why," he asked, interrupting her, "would you not carry one with you?"

"Because," she said, in the same annoyed tone he used, "I was going to be with *you*. I thought, foolishly, it seems, that you would know where *yours* was!"

They glared at one another for a moment, he leaning a forearm against the doorway molding in complete exasperation, she with her feet squarely planted to relieve her sore back.

"Interesting," he said finally, his voice now quietly angry, "that the same woman who can be so independent in some ways refuses to take responsibility for herself in others."

Anger rose in her like heat up a chimney. "We're no longer talking keys, are we?" She forced herself to speak quietly, knowing Mrs. Drummond across the hall probably had her ear to her door. "I'm getting a little tired of

arguing the restaurant deal. I...didn't...want...to do it!"
She enunciated emphatically. "This is a free country, you
know. I know Cassie wanted it, and I'm sorry I disappointed her, but I came through in the end, didn't I?!"
Despite her resolve, she forgot Mrs. Drummond across the
hall and spoke in an increasingly louder tone.

"Jo..." he began quietly, cautioningly.

She pointed to her protruding belly. "I made it possible
for you and Cassie to have your baby!" she shouted. "I
know you wish I'd been hit instead of Cassie, but unfortunately I—"

He put one hand to the back of her head and one over
her mouth. He leaned over her until they were nose-to-nose
and then he said sternly, "Stop it now."

Two tears slid down her cheeks and onto his hand. She
nodded quickly, horrified that she'd spoken the thought
aloud.

He dropped the hand over her mouth, but the one in her
hair clamped at the nape of her neck, and he said in a low
growl, "Don't you *ever* say that." He drew a breath that
sounded as though it hurt, then added, "I'd give anything
to have her back—anything but someone else's life. Except, maybe, my own."

Jo felt as though her world had exploded at that admission. She'd certainly entertained the thought for months,
but she couldn't believe she'd spoken it aloud. She felt naked and exposed, yet vaguely comforted by his vehement
and unmistakably honest denial of her claim.

"I'm sorry," she whispered.

"I hope so," he said. Then in a curiously tender gesture, given the circumstances, he pulled her head to his
chest for a moment and held her there while he heaved a
ragged sigh.

She finally drew away, a light warming in her breast. She sniffed and cleared her throat. "Maybe your... ah, your keys fell out in the car," she said. "I remember in class you took them out of your pants pocket and put them in your jacket. Maybe...maybe they fell out when you tossed your coat in the back."

He considered that a moment, then turned back to the elevator. "Wait right here."

The moment he stepped onto the car, Jo sagged against the wall, exhausted, spent. She stood without thinking, feeling strangely composed of pain and promise throbbing in every little corner of her being.

MAMA JO? Mama Cass says stop being a twit. Can we go to bed? All that breathing made me sleepy.

RYAN WAS BACK in a matter of minutes, his expression still moody and tense. But he held up his house keys as he stepped off the elevator. "You were right," he said.

"Why don't you keep them on the same ring?" she asked.

"Too bulky, with all my bank keys," he replied. "This way I can put them in separate pockets."

He unlocked the door and stepped aside to let her in. The condo was quiet and cool, the dusk over the river visible from the living room window.

"All that relaxation is exhausting," Jo said, turning immediately in the direction of the bedrooms. She felt as though she were standing on the high end of a teeter-totter. "I'm going to go to bed early, maybe watch TV for a little while."

He seemed relieved. "Me too. Want me to bring you a cup of tea before I turn in?"

She shook her head. "Thanks, but I don't need a thing. See you at breakfast."

"Good night," he said.

She smiled and disappeared into the hallway.

Ryan made himself a cup of cocoa and poured a generous measure of brandy in it. He stepped out onto the patio with it, and scanned the familiar view without seeing it.

He knew why he'd accused her of refusing to accept responsibility. He'd been angry at her, and he'd wanted to hurt her in some way. That was uncharacteristic of him, but then, so was confusion—and that was all he felt at the moment.

The Lamaze class had been even harder than usual tonight. He'd absorbed the instructions, but he'd been conscious every moment of Jo's full, round body under his hand.

Her bone structure felt very fragile, yet every curve of her was full and ripe with the impending delivery.

If it was simple lust he'd felt, it might be more understandable. He'd been celibate since Cassie's death.

But his awareness of Jo's body was more complex than sexual deprivation. It was as though she were becoming for him the personification of woman. She seemed delicate but strong, swollen with the baby, yet curiously graceful, high-strung sometimes, then serenely competent at others.

She was all the enigmas, all the mysteries, all the ambivalence, that was female. And he found himself inextricably drawn toward her, like every sane man in the world attracted by what he knew to be illogical.

It didn't make sense. He hated things that didn't add up. But there it was. He'd tried to reason those feelings away for several days now, but tonight, when he lost his temper, had been proof.

He examined his alternatives as he sipped the doctored cocoa. He decided he had only one. He would ignore the whole thing and hope it went away.

Even as the thought formed, he knew it to be cowardly, but he was in no shape for heroics tonight. He was lonely, confused, depressed and exhausted. And any other course of action would probably horrify Jo, hammer him with guilt, and ruin the friendly relationship they were trying so hard to build. He couldn't risk that.

His mind replayed her distraught declaration, and he winced against it. He was horrified that she could think the thing, horrified that he might have done anything to nurture such a thought.

He put his cup in the sink, then went to rap on her bedroom door with a new resolve.

There was an instant's silence. Then she called, "Yes? Come in."

He pushed the door open, but stood firmly on the threshold. "You all right?" he asked.

She was reading, and looked at him over the book balanced on the hill of her stomach. She seemed subdued, vaguely wary. "I'm fine," she said. Her foot moved under the bedcovers. "I'm sorry I shouted at you."

He leaned a hand on the doorknob and put his other in his pants pocket. "I verbally attacked you. You had every right to shout. Jo..."

He considered his words carefully. There was a lot between them—divergent interests and personalities, the awkwardness of their situation, their shared grief, and a weird confusion that seemed to be taking on a life of its own. But there was one point on which he wanted her to be clear.

"I swear to you," he said gravely, "that it has never crossed my mind that you should have died instead of Cassie."

She smiled gently. "Poor Ryan," she said, leaning her head back against her propped up pillows. "Cassie and I put you in quite a fix, didn't we? We thought we'd set up the perfect situation, and then, when fate stepped in, you were destined to lose. If the poor old man having a heart attack behind the wheel of that car had hit me, you'd have lost your baby." She shook her head with the fatal acceptance of someone faced with God's supremacy. "Some choice. Your wife or your child."

He hadn't intended to step into the room. But he was determined to make his point, and he couldn't do it from the doorway. He went to sit on the edge of her bed.

"First of all," he said, "since Cassie died, I've felt as though my life's been broken in two. But I don't feel like a victim of fate. I had Cassie. She loved me. It was far too short, but it was mine and it will always be mine."

Tears brimmed in her eyes. He took her hand, his throat tight with emotion, as he went on.

"I don't think I can count myself a loser. I feel very, very lucky that you and the baby are fine."

Jo squeezed his hand. She'd loved Cassie, too, and valued every moment they shared as sisters and friends. Her memories were warm, and many were filled with laughter. It was difficult to feel abandoned when she still carried her love and her baby.

But, God, how she wished she were more to Ryan than simply the surrogate pregnant with his child. Before Cassie and Ryan were married, when he used to join them for holiday dinners, she would taunt and verbally tease him to cover what she truly felt. Then conversation would swell around the table and she would remain quiet and simply watch him—pretending that Cassie was out of the picture, that he'd come to dinner with her family because he loved *her,* Jo.

She would imagine living a suburban life, buying a station wagon, going to school functions and chauffeuring children who were blond like her, but with Ryan's defined features and dark eyes.

Then Cassie would laugh about something with that hearty abandon that had always made everyone turn in her direction, and she, Jo, would look up to see Ryan smiling at Cassie with that look in his eyes that made Jo know for certain his love could never belong to anyone else.

She sighed and pulled her hand away. "I forgot to be *harmonious* tonight," she said, giving special emphasis to the word. "I guess Lamaze class wore me out. I'll do better tomorrow."

Ryan stood. He'd said what he wanted to say, but he wasn't sure he'd gotten through. That worried him, but she looked tired. He suddenly felt very old.

"Sleep well. Did you have your banana today to ward off the leg cramps?"

Jo smiled, that small policing gesture making her feel that things were approaching normalcy. "Yes, I did. You sleep well, too. I'm making pancakes in the morning."

"Oh, no!" he said, without pausing to monitor his reaction. Then he saw her raised eyebrow and added quickly, "I mean...really? Are you sure? Wouldn't you rather sleep in, and I'll..."

"Diantha gave me a foolproof recipe," she insisted, knowing now that things *were* back to normal. She felt herself relax. "Using rice flour, Egg Beaters, and fruit juice concentrate."

I'LL SLEEP IN, thanks.

"OH..." he said feebly. "Good. Well. I'd better let you rest up, if you're going to tackle cooking."

"You might be pleasantly surprised," she told him challengingly as he walked to the door.

He smiled blandly. "Hey. I'm an optimist. Good night."

Jo watched him walk through the door and close it behind him. She smiled with the bittersweet thought that he was a far more interesting man than even she'd imagined.

SHE HAD the Cassie dream again. She saw everything repeated in slow motion, saw the sweater that had claimed her attention in the shop window, the reflected image of Cassie stepping off the curb and the big car on a collision course with her. She felt the terror again, the paralysis.

She awoke panting and perspiring. She listened for some indication that she'd disturbed Ryan, but the house was quiet.

She lay back, rubbing the baby. She felt her move under her hand. She patted her, telling her everything would be all right—and prayed that she was right.

I DON'T LIKE THAT DREAM, Mama Jo. And Mama Cass says put that memory away and everything will be all right.

Chapter Six

"What do you think?" Jo asked.

Ryan chewed the rubber disk which had little flavor other than extreme sweetness, and wished he had an alternative to swallowing. He hated the thought of the latex-like mixture in his mouth moving into his digestive system and becoming a part of his body.

But Jo was standing over him with a raised spatula and an expectant expression—he pardoned himself for the involuntary pun—and he gave serious thought to his personal safety if he was to tell the truth.

Her hair was piled high on her head, curly golden ends dangling from a green ribbon. She wore a long white sweater over a green skirt, and an apron hung from her neck, the ties, too short to meet around her considerable girth, dangling uselessly at her sides.

He had no choice. He swallowed. He guessed it must be what swallowing a balloon felt like.

"It's very filling," he said diplomatically, trying desperately not to taste.

Her soft blue eyes widened with distress. "Diantha said it was foolproof!"

He glanced at the plate of pancakes that lay before him, looking very much like small, round carpet samples. The texture of the rice flour even gave some of them a sixties-shag look.

"Well..." He took a quick sip of coffee. The woman did make the world's best coffee. "It's overcast and rainy today. Isn't the barometer supposed to affect cooking?"

"I think that's baking," she said. She took the fork from the side of his plate, speared three layers of pancake covered with butter and syrup, and put it in her mouth. She chewed contemplatively, but then her expression changed abruptly to one of distaste.

He handed her his napkin. She put it to her mouth, then turned away to the trash can concealed under the sink and tossed the bite away.

She brought a carton of milk and a box of granola to the table. "You should have told me they tasted like leather," she said scoldingly, going back to the cupboard for bowls and spoons.

"I was thinking filleted bungee cords," he said.

She giggled and sat opposite him, pulling a cup of tea toward her. "I don't know what made me think I should try to cook, anyway. Must be some kind of nesting frenzy, or something."

He laughed lightly. "It helps to know one's limitations. The baby's afghan is coming along well."

It was. She brought the project back and forth to work, and it had grown to about half its final size. The intricate pattern in pastel rainbow colors was familiar now, after dozens of repetitions, and she was confident she would have it finished by the time the baby arrived.

"And you do make great coffee," he added, pouring granola into her bowl, then into his.

She dabbed desultorily at the granules with her spoon. "I don't want to have limitations."

He passed her the milk. "Limitations are a fact of life."

She poured a small amount, then passed it back.

She hated to accept it, but she knew that to be true—particularly in her case and in her present circumstances. The thought depressed her. "Well," she said with a sigh, "as long as I'm not required to like it."

"I don't think so."

"Good." She pushed her bowl away with sudden ill temper and prepared to stand. "I think I'll pass on breakfast and have a bagel at work."

He leveled a dark, even gaze on her. "Uh-uh. You need the milk, and the food value in the grains. A bagel won't do the same thing for you."

He was right, but she didn't have to like that, either. She pulled the bowl back toward her and gave him a rebellious glance. "I'm doing it because you're right, not because you said so."

Ryan, spoon poised over his bowl, tried to make sense of that remark and failed. He decided he didn't have to understand it, as long as she ate the cereal.

"YOU'RE KIDDING." Ryan studied Jave Nicholas, who was sitting in one of the upholstered chairs in the small conversation area in his office, and wondered why he was surprised. He'd guessed as much last night at the Lamaze class. "*When* did you get married?" Jave looked smugly self-satisfied. "Last weekend. And let me tell you, it was no small feat."

Ryan nodded. He had shed his suit coat and Jave had a jeans-clad leg hooked over the side of the chair. "We all thought she was married to a—"

"I know. A coastguardsman." Jave shook his head, as though that falsehood had caused him considerable trouble. "She'd just moved from New York after an unpleas-

ant divorce, when Amy Brown at the hospital got this idea
about the birthing room extravaganza."

Ryan nodded, remembering the afternoon she'd tried to
talk Jo into taking Nancy's place.

"She saw Nancy's records from New York, and they
indicated a husband. She presumed Nancy still had him,
and that she'd be the perfect all-American mom for the
project. When Nancy saw all the gifts she'd be getting for
the baby, she knew that it was far more than she could ever
provide the baby alone, so she agreed to do it, and let Amy
go on thinking she did have a husband. She explained his
absence by saying he was away on a Coast Guard cutter on
a security cruise."

Ryan grinned. "When'd you figure it out?"

"Almost right away," Jave replied. "But she insisted I
was mistaken. When I had her dead to rights—when the
cutter put into Long Beach, California, for repairs and she
didn't know it—she finally came clean. But her first marriage had been so bad, it took me a long time to convince
her that marriage to me would be different."

"And how do your boys feel about a new mother and a
new baby?"

Jave shrugged a shoulder. "I'm sure we won't always be
like an episode of the 'Brady Bunch,' but the boys love
Nancy, and they're excited about the prospect of a new
baby. At least until she starts keeping them up nights and
breaking their toys."

"So, you know it's a girl?"

"Yep. Yours, too. We're going to have a lot to learn. Me
with my boys, and you being a complete novice."

Ryan rolled his eyes. "I've got a nanny lined up until the
baby starts walking. I'm sure I'm in for a lot of character-
building experiences."

"Kids are great. You'll love it." Then he drew a deep breath, and his eyes filled with empathy. Ryan had come to know that those gestures usually preceded an expression of sympathy. "I'm sorry Cassie isn't here to hold her baby."

Ryan fought the old knot in his throat, the anger that surged without warning. "Well. Jo insists she's watching over us—like some kind of guardian angel, or something."

Jave smiled. "Jo's a gift to mankind. You're lucky to have her for a sister-in-law. I imagine it isn't every woman who'd be willing to carry her sister's baby." He sobered suddenly. "And it'll be doubly hard for her to give the baby up with Cassie gone."

Ryan handed Jave a folder that contained trust-account paperwork. "She doesn't have to give her up completely," he said, resisting an instinctively defensive feeling. "I mean, she's still the child's aunt."

"I know." Jave tapped the folder against his other hand. "But she's carried the baby all this time. I've seen it before. It'll be more difficult for her to hand the baby over to someone else than she ever imagined, and I'm sure far more difficult than *you* ever imagined it could be for her. And with Cassie gone, she's lost that unique tie. You might remarry one day."

"No," Ryan said.

"You think that now."

"No," Ryan said again. "And Jo's okay with this. We've talked about it."

Jave stood and offered his hand. "Good. Well, I'm just warning you that women become pretty irrational about their offspring. So you'll take care of Malia's trust fund for me?"

Ryan shook his hand and walked him to the door. "With her new trust account, your little daughter will be as well set up as your boys. Take care. Don't forget that promise of a harbor tour when the *Mud Hen*'s operational."

"Right."

Ryan watched Jave stride through the bank and out the door toward his GMC, parked across the side street. His mind, already cluttered with memories of his argument with Jo and the unsettling acceptance in her eyes that had resulted, was now overburdened by Jave's remarks.

It'll be more difficult for her to hand the baby over to someone else than she ever imagined—and I'm sure far more difficult than you ever imagined it could be for her.

When Jo became pregnant, the gifts of modern medical science had seemed like such a boon to their lives. Now that fate had interceded and the dynamics had changed, it appeared to be turning into another situation that was bound to produce a loser—Josanne. Maybe the message was, he thought, that it wasn't safe to manipulate the hand life dealt you.

A headache forming between his eyes, Ryan looked over the quiet bank, then went back into his office and checked his calendar. He had no appointments after Jave. He called his assistant manager to tell her he was taking a few hours off, then grabbed his jacket off the oak rack near the window and left the bank.

"IF SHE'S BORN on your due date," Diantha said, sitting at the far end of the counter in Coffee Country, "she's going to be a finicky eater, and probably develop food allergies."

Her index finger in the handle of a short glass mug, she sipped at a mocha and leafed through ten or twelve notebook-size pages stapled together. "But she'll be nurturing. Hospitable, compassionate, even philanthropic. She'll treat everyone as part of her family."

Jo sat on a stool behind the counter, her chin in her hand as she watched her friend read the chart she'd produced.

Diantha turned a page. "She'll have a keen intellect, and a—"

"She gets that from me," Jo interjected.

Diantha looked at her over the rim of her glasses. "She gets it," she replied, "from natal Mercury in Scorpio."

"Of course."

"Her mental powers will not be bogged down by sentiment."

"That," Jo said with a grin, "she gets from her father."

Diantha put the sheets down and brought her cup to her lips. Silver bangles moved musically at her wrists. "How're things with you and Ryan?"

Jo raised an eyebrow, pretending surprise that Diantha would ask, when everyone knew they were simply in-laws—though in-laws in a curious position. But she knew she wasn't fooling anyone. She wasn't sure where Diantha got her intuitive powers—from the stars or from some innate ability to read minds—but she saw far more clearly into people than anyone Jo knew.

"We're coexisting," Jo replied, taking a sip from the long-neglected cup of raspberry-and-rosehip tea at her elbow. "That's all we're required to do."

"Mmm . . ." Diantha put her cup down. She met Jo's gaze evenly. "When are you going to ask him to marry you?"

"*What?*" Jo shrieked. Color flooded her face, and Tom Nicholas, reading the newspaper at a small table at the front of the room, looked up.

"If the gossip is that good," he said, with a grin at the women, "I want in on it."

Jo laughed lightly. "Di's telling shocking stories. Go back to your stock quotes."

He looked offended. "I'm reading the comics," he said. "So if you're not going to share, could you at least keep it down?"

Jo turned back to Diantha and whispered indignantly, "*What* are you talking about?"

"As if you didn't know," Diantha whispered back. "You love him. You're carrying his baby—not in the traditional meaning of the term, granted, but the fact remains. He's frustrated by his attraction to you. Seems to—"

"He is?" Jo asked, stiffening suddenly on the stool.

Diantha nodded. "Seems to me you're holding all the cards."

Jo looked doubtful. "How do you know?"

Diantha sipped her coffee. "I read the stars."

"I mean *really* how do you know?"

Diantha frowned at her. "You mean I spent all morning preparing a chart for you, and you're a nonbeliever?"

Jo bobbed her head from side to side uncertainly. "Let's just say I'm intrigued but skeptical." Then she looked her in the eye. "What makes you think he's attracted to me?"

"He takes care of you," Diantha replied. "Do you really think that before you moved in with him he came in here every morning and every afternoon just for coffee?"

"He didn't?"

"Of course not. He was checking on you."

"He was checking," Jo told her, "on his baby."

Diantha narrowed her eyes and focused on the coffee menu behind Jo's head. "I don't think so. I think he's drawn to you—and he's not sure why, or even if it's a good thing."

Jo listened to her friend in complete surprise and consternation. "I... You... I don't *think* so."

Diantha folded her arms on the counter and leaned earnestly toward Jo. "I *do*. Cassie will always be with the two of you, but in subtle, possibly even unconscious ways, you're both beginning to realize that having a baby is about *life*—and that can't help but put death in the background, even the death of someone you both loved so much. And that clears the way for..." She shrugged and smiled. "For whatever the two of you will allow to happen."

MAMA CASS SAYS give Diantha a free mocha.

"I THOUGHT the stars dictated what happened," Jo said challengingly.

Diantha nodded with confidence. "I believe they affect events. But how events affect us is our own decision."

Jo leaned toward her and said quietly, "You're getting batty in your middle years, Pennyman."

Diantha laughed throatily and patted her cheek. "Who else would keep company with you? So here." She pushed her cup aside and thrust the sheaf of papers at her. "Get acquainted with this profile of your child, and—"

"She's not *my* child." Jo said, bracing her hands at her back as she shifted her weight carefully off the stool. "She's Ryan's."

Diantha repeated her earlier words significantly. "How events affect us is up to us."

"Heavy," Ryan said. "Is this a private philosophical discussion, or can anyone join in?"

Jo and Diantha turned in surprise as Ryan took the stool next to the one Diantha occupied.

"Now what would a mercenary banker," Diantha said dryly as she picked up her wallet and keys, "know about philosophy?"

He pulled at his tie. "We lend money. You don't think that requires a philosophical outlook?"

"Good point." She laughed and slapped his shoulder.

"Don't let them fool you," Tom called from his corner. "They've been telling dirty stories and shrieking."

Ryan turned to Jo with feigned shock. "Miss Arceneau. I'm horrified."

She waved a careless hand. "We were just gossiping." Then she turned quickly away before he could see in her eyes precisely who they'd discussed—and what. "Ready for your afternoon latte?"

" 'Bye, all," Diantha called as she headed for the door. "Tom, I've got that Vitamin E cream you asked about."

"Great." He folded the newspaper and replaced it on a shelf covered with other newspapers and magazines, then followed Diantha out the door, with a parting wave for Jo and Ryan.

The door closed behind them, and silence settled over the coffee bar.

"No latte," Ryan said to Jo.

She turned from the refrigerator, an eyebrow raised. "Juice? Mineral water?"

He shrugged off his suit coat and placed it on the stool beside him, then pulled off his tie. "No. I was wondering if you could get away this afternoon."

She blinked, startled by the suggestion. She glanced up at the clock. "Devon's due in about fifteen minutes," she said. "But why?"

He raised his hand in a gesture of helpless resignation. "Because you won the bet."

"What bet?" she asked, then remembered. "You're kidding!" She squealed, suddenly all smiles, and came to stand just opposite him at the counter. "Nancy and Jave are getting married?"

"Already did it. Last weekend. Just the family." He considered her thrilled expression. "I didn't realize you were such a proponent of matrimony. In fact, you've turned down two proposals since I've known you."

She rolled her eyes. "A redneck and a Republican. Please."

"Ah, yes." He grinned and folded his arms on the counter. "You're looking for a rock star or a philanthropist. I keep forgetting."

"Chelsea's going to be a philanthropist, according to Diantha." Jo ran her thumb along the edge of the small stack of pages and handed it to him. "She ran her chart with this new software she just bought. She claims the baby will also be a finicky eater and very intelligent."

Ryan gave her a skeptical smile, but lifted the top page of the chart. "Aren't all babies finicky eaters?"

"I wasn't. I loved spinach and asparagus when I was a child."

Ryan concentrated on the page, then marked a line with his index finger and read aloud. "Once she forms an opinion, she will stick to it stubbornly." He glanced up with a wince of concern that Jo found charmingly disarming. "That doesn't sound good for me."

Jo laughed, instinctively covering his hand with hers. "If it's any comfort, I was glancing through the chart and saw something about great charm and personal attractiveness. It's in one of those First House paragraphs."

The instant Jo felt Ryan's knuckles against the soft pads of her fingertips, the warmth of his skin against her sensitive palm, she saw his eyes fly up to hers, startlingly dark and deep.

But they contained no annoyance at the intimacy, she noticed, no suggestion that she'd intruded where she didn't belong. Mesmerized by that acceptance, she stared into his eyes.

The bell over the door tinkled merrily as it opened, admitting three women juggling bags and bundles and laughing loudly.

Jo drew her hand away quickly, and was surprised when Ryan smiled at the guilty action.

"You...ah, you look that over," she stammered, wiping her hands on her apron as she backed away from him, toward her customers. "Devon should be here any minute."

Jo's hands were shaking as she pulled out cups for three Borgias. Everything inside her was trembling, too. She had the strangest feeling that, for reasons she couldn't imagine, some barrier had been removed from between them.

She didn't know what it meant, and couldn't guess what it portended—she simply liked the way it felt. She hummed softly to herself as she reached for the orange syrup.

Chapter Seven

"Actually, this isn't a very practical idea," Jo said, hanging back as Ryan led the way toward a small cluster of stores two blocks away from Coffee Country. "I'm only going to be pregnant for two more weeks. It'd be silly to buy a jacket now."

She knew he was headed for Darby's, an exclusive women's clothing store she'd avoided since wandering in to look it over one day and discovering that a scarf she admired was over a hundred dollars.

"I mean, you were only going to get free lattes for a month," she said. "And everything in here is astronomically priced."

"Free lattes *delivered*." He grinned over the distinction. "That doubles the value to a busy man."

She remained rooted in place when he opened the shop's elegant stained-glass doors. "A busy man," she said, "doesn't take a woman shopping in the middle of the afternoon."

He remembered suddenly the impulse of guilt and confusion that had led him from the bank.

"There are moments in life," he said, "that defy order and duty."

Her eyes widened. "Wow. You *do* have a philosophical bent."

"I have my moments." He opened the door wider. "Let's go."

She remained where she was, peering uncertainly into the fragrant, moodily lit rose-and-green interior. "We should be at a wilderness outfitter's, shopping for a tent or a tarp."

He rolled his eyes and caught her hand. "How you do go on. I thought we could get you one of those fling-coat things." He made an awkward sweeping gesture with one hand, while pulling the door closed with the other.

Jo narrowed her eyes in confusion. "Fling things?" she repeated.

"You remember," he said, taking her elbow and pulling her toward a clerk. "It's narrow at the top and kind of floats out widely at the bottom. Cassie had a gray one she wore all the time. If you got one of those, it'd fit you now, and *after* Chelsea's born."

Jo remembered Cassie's coat, but she had no idea what the style was called.

"A swing coat!" Lauren, the clerk, proclaimed after Ryan's unself-conscious description. The young woman was so perfectly made up, groomed and dressed that Jo fought an impulse to poke her, to see if she reacted.

Lauren cast an assessing glance over Jo's impossible proportions and nodded. "A good idea. We have a fine selection. Follow me."

Ryan and Jo fell into step behind her as she led the way through the elegant shop, like Napoleon leading the French army over the Alps.

Ryan, an arm hooked around Jo's shoulders as though he were afraid she might try to escape, smiled smugly. "I told you I knew what I was talking about," he said under his breath.

"Oh, right," she answered in a teasing whisper. "You called it a 'fling' coat."

"Fling, swing," he said, dismissing his misnomer. "I knew it related to some sexual indiscretion."

She laughed aloud. She couldn't help it. She'd never seen him in quite this kind of a mood. He was always polite, and often kind, but he'd never been so deliberately amenable before. He seemed to have set out this afternoon not only to buy her a coat, but to be charming.

She should resist him, she thought. This kind of coziness between them wasn't safe.

But Lauren claimed her attention when they reached the coat department, and for the next half hour she was completely distracted as Lauren helped her in and out of every pattern of swing coat on the racks.

Ryan waited patiently in a pink brocade chair, her tote bag, her beret and her old fleece jacket at his feet.

She looked wonderful in neon colors, Ryan decided, and wondered if that was why she usually chose them. He was sure if that was true, her choice was unconscious, because nothing about her style of dress was intended to flatter her person in any way.

It was probably more likely that she loved brightness in color, as she did in everything else about her life. Everything she did seemed to be just a step beyond what everyone else preferred. It was as though, he thought with sudden insight, she pushed everything to its limit to make a statement of recklessness or courage.

"That one," he said, when Lauren helped her into an electric blue coat with a mandarin collar, softly molded shoulders, crown-shaped gold buttons and yards of wool that floated softly down at the sides and back to just around her knees.

I LIKE THIS ONE, too. It's very soft. And it makes it even warmer in here. Now, if only there was more room!

HER PROTRUDING STOMACH hiked the front up several inches, but she looked stunning in it all the same.

He went to stand beside the clerk, eyeing Jo critically.

"He's right," Lauren said. "That's the one. Look at what it does to your eyes."

Jo looked at herself in the mirror. "All it's supposed to do is keep me warm."

Lauren looked horrified at the notion that a woman's clothing should be simply functional. She came to stand behind Jo, to fuss with the collar and smooth the shoulders.

"That's a barbaric idea," she said with a sudden smile. To that point, her manner had been as glossy as her appearance. "Clothes reflect the woman inside." She reached down to the thick forest green carpet to pick up Jo's magenta beret and twirl it on her finger. "I thought a woman who wears a beret would know that. I believe everything you put on your body, consciously or unconsciously, says, 'This is me.' We think we're holding all our little secrets so closely, but our bodies and our instincts betray us. Deep down, we want to share who and what we *really* are. I think we do that with what we wear."

Jo looked at her in openmouthed surprise. This beautiful Barbie-woman was the last person from whom she'd have expected such deep thought.

The woman apparently read her thoughts, because she gave her a so-there tilt of her chin.

Jo looked back at her reflection, a little unsettled. The coat was beautiful, and hung in elegant lines, despite the intrusion of her pregnancy. And the color did seem to darken her eyes and brighten the color in her cheeks.

She'd brushed her hair and tied it up in a knot before leaving the shop, and it looked unusually tidy—almost stylish. The idea alarmed her. She'd always gone out of her way to flout conventional style, in favor of her own personal expression of it.

Was this what Lauren meant? she wondered. Did she like this coat because somewhere inside her was a woman who wanted to look chic and elegant, rather than free and comfortable?

She dismissed that thought as the product of weariness and the continual confusion Ryan caused in her, and brought the issue back to what a coat should be all about.

Was it warm?

It was.

Did it reach across her stomach?

It did.

Would she be able to wear it after she delivered Chelsea?

She would.

She lifted the right sleeve in search of the price tag. Her eyes widened at the three digits, and she started to unbutton it.

"We'll take it," Ryan said, then raised a hand to silence Jo's attempt to protest.

Lauren, still holding the beret, held it up and studied it critically. "Maybe we should find you a hat to coordinate with the coat?"

Jo took the hat from her with a firm shake of her head. "Thanks, but I like this one."

"Come on," Ryan coaxed. "Just have a look. Those colors don't go together, do they?"

Jo placed the hat on her head at a rakish angle. "Cassie gave it to me. It goes with everything."

Ryan looked to Lauren questioningly.

She studied Jo closely, smiled, then raised her arms in a gesture of helplessness. "When a woman's comfortable with the way she looks, *everything* works—even electric blue and magenta."

Jo made a face at Ryan as Lauren walked to the gazebolike area in the middle of the shop where the counter was located.

"I could be warm," she whispered, "for a third the price of this coat."

"But you couldn't look as beautiful," he said with smiling gallantry. "Lauren?" He turned his attention to the clerk, who looked up from lining a box with tissue. "Perfume?"

"Perfume?" Jo repeated. "Ryan, perfume is not going to keep me warm on a..."

Her protest trailed off as Ryan followed Lauren across the shop.

Jo remained at the counter. She watched Lauren and Ryan engage in a brief conversation. Then Lauren uncapped a bottle, spritzed it on her wrist, and held up the slender, graceful line of it to Ryan's nose.

He dipped his head to sniff. Jo felt deep, hot emotion, and recognized it immediately for what it was—jealousy. Fortunately, that also allowed her to chide herself for being stupid, and to come to her senses.

That wrist-to-the-nose process was repeated several more times, with other fragrances, and the two finally came back to the counter with two bottles.

"Floral or musky?" Ryan asked.

"I never wear perfume," she said frankly, with an apologetic glance at Lauren.

"Diantha said," he reminded her, "that the baby would be sensitive to smells. She'll be closest to yours."

Jo took a blue-and-silver bottle from him. "And I smell like French roast coffee." Because she was wearing long sleeves, she spritzed the contents on the inside of her left hand. Then she held her fingertips to her nose. The scent was floral, a little stronger on the side of gardenias.

Ryan took that bottle from her and gave her the other. She sprayed it on her right hand. That fragrance was deeply, sumptuously heavy.

"The floral," Jo said, handing the bottle back.

Lauren took them. "Are you sure? Rendezvous—" she held up the musky fragrance "—is heavy-duty stuff."

Ryan took both of Jo's hands in his and lifted them toward his face as he leaned down to intercept first one fragrance, then the other. The backs of her hands were cradled in his much larger palms, and his strong fingertips closed around her hands to keep them still.

Jo felt the air catch in her throat, her heartbeat stutter. She stood quietly under his touch, her entire being absorbing the sensation of being the subject of his complete attention.

He turned to Lauren and gently shook Jo's left hand. "This one."

Lauren went back to the display for a boxed perfume. "The floral it is," she said.

They left the shop, Ryan carrying the green-and-rose box that contained Jo's coat, Jo carrying her perfume in a decorated gift bag. The shopping had tired her, and she took Ryan's arm as they walked slowly back toward the bank parking lot.

"Worn-out?" he asked.

She nodded and rotated her shoulders. "A little. My back hurts all the time now."

They stopped at the light, and he put a hand to the small of her back and gently rubbed while they waited.

She couldn't help a little moan of relief when her tense muscles loosened a little. "What could I pay you," she asked with a little laugh, "to do that continually for the next two weeks?"

He grinned. "The service comes free with Lamaze coaching. Serena is always reminding us that coaching starts long before labor. Do you like cabbage?"

"Ah..." Jo required a moment to switch her thoughts from his comforting reassurance to his completely unrelated question. "Yes. I love cabbage," she finally replied, with a puzzled glance up at him. The light changed, and they walked across the street. "Why?"

"Would you like stuffed cabbage for dinner? You can wait in the car while I pick up what we need."

MAMA CASS says say no—*fast!*

SHE STOPPED in her tracks in the middle of the sidewalk in pleased anticipation. Stuffed cabbage was one of her favorite meals.

"I'd love it!" she said. "My mother used to make it, but Cassie didn't like it, so we didn't have it that often. Isn't it an awful lot of trouble?"

He shook his head and pulled her along toward the car. "It'll be worth it. Cassie obviously never fixed them, but my Polish grandmother made the best *golabki* in the whole world. You're in for a treat, Josanne."

He helped her into the car, and she waited in a little cocoon of mellow warmth for him to slip in beside her and drive her home.

WHITE SHIRTSLEEVES rolled up to his elbows, and wearing a blue-and-white-striped "Cordon Bleu" apron, Ryan expertly blanched and separated cabbage leaves, mixed a filling of hamburger, rice, egg and seasonings, and sat beside Jo at the table, sharing the duty of neatly rolling the cabbage leaves around the filling.

"How long will they have to bake?" Jo asked, placing a roll next to a row of others in the long pan between them.

"Almost an hour," he replied. "Why? Will you need an hors d'oeuvre?"

She looked hopeful. "Like what?"

He cast her a knowing glance. "Mini bagel pizzas. Pepperoni."

She stared at him. Another of her favorite things. "I *love* those!"

"I know," he said dryly. "When Cassie bought a package to see if she could improve upon them with her own recipe, you ate them all before she was able to analyze them. Remember?"

She did. She concentrated on making precise corners on her cabbage roll. "I'd just spent all day at the children's fair at the park. You spend twelve hours with a pack of five-to-eight-year-olds wanting you to read to them and paint their faces and see if *you* don't crave carbohydrates."

He folded the sides of a cabbage leaf around the filling placed at the top, gave it one tuck to keep the filling in place, then completed the roll with one long sweep of his hand. "I imagine I'll have the opportunity one day in the not-too-distant future." He placed that roll in the pan, then went to the kitchen to pull a flat box out of the freezer.

I, Jo thought, will probably not. I'll be running a coffeehouse somewhere in Alaska, because I will no longer be able to stand being near both of you and not loving you as I want to. I'll wind down toward spinsterhood with an old dog, a passel of cats, and clothes even more bizarre than I wear now. Except for my blue swing coat. I'll always feel different when I wear it.

"Speaking of community events," Ryan said, closing the door on the microwave and setting the timer, "does the county carry its own insurance on the fairgrounds, or does the host of the event have to provide it?"

She came out of her cheerless thoughts to concentrate on the moment.

"For Heron Point Has It, you mean?" She placed a dollop of filling at the top of the last cabbage leaf. "The downtown association carries its own. You don't have to worry about it."

"That's a relief. Something to drink with this?"

"Tea, please."

"What's Coffee Country going to be serving?" he asked conversationally as he took plates and cups down from the cupboard.

Jo watched him move skillfully around the kitchen, his long-muscled biceps flexing as he pulled the oven door open. "Um...you know. All the things we serve. Biscotti, shortbread, scones..."

"Mmm... Sounds good." He came back to the table to take the pan of cabbage rolls from her, and saw that one roll remained unfinished—the one she'd been working on while watching him. He raised a questioning eyebrow. "You waiting for that one to roll itself?"

"Ha, ha," she said, and quickly finished it and placed it in the pan.

"Good work," he said, taking it to the oven. "Why don't you sit in the recliner, and I'll bring you your hors d'oeuvres as soon as they're done."

Jo couldn't stand it another moment. "Are you softening me up to tell me something unpleasant?" she asked.

He closed the oven door on the baking pan and set the timer. Then he turned to her, hands resting loosely on his hips. "You needed a coat that closed, the perfume was really for the baby, and we have to eat. There's nothing here to make you suspicious."

Jo shook her head, denying his denial. "Not so. You took off in the middle of the afternoon, spent far too much money, bought a fragrance that was even more than I'd have paid for the *coat,* and now—" she waved a hand in the direction of the kitchen surrounding him "—all of this."

She saw just a trace of discomfort pass over his expression. It was barely visible, but she was finely attuned to every nuance in their curious relationship.

"All right," he said finally. He leaned a hip against the counter and folded his arms. "I…was thinking about you today…"

He paused, obviously thinking over what he intended to say.

Jo felt every life-sustaining function in her body slow dangerously. Every nerve ending trembled, waiting. *I was thinking about you today.*

"What…" she asked softly, "did you think about?"

"How generous it was for you to do this for me and Cassie," he replied. His voice was quiet and sincere. The kitchen was harshly lit, but beyond, the living room lay in the long shadows of early evening. He sighed and met her eyes. "How hard it's been for you with Cassie gone."

She couldn't deny that, but her entire being was focused on what she hoped he was about to say. *Maybe there's a solution here we haven't considered, Jo. When we try, we get on fairly well together. Why don't we—?*

"I love this baby," she said, her voice husky with feeling, "as much as you do."

He came back to the table to take the chair he'd vacated earlier. "I know. That's why I wanted to . . ."

Every thought in her head fled. Her heart pounded, her blood raced, her breath threatened to strangle her.

"To what?" she breathed.

He placed his hand over hers on the table. She turned hers to catch his fingers, a charge of power running up her arm, straight to her heart.

"To try to let you know that I appreciate you. That I want to keep you warm and comfortable. To try to pay you back for all you've—"

Despite the bulk of the baby, Jo shot up out of the chair as though she were her old size-eight self once again.

"Pay me back?" she asked, in a dangerously quiet voice. Then she repeated again, in utter disbelief, "Pay me *back?*"

Somewhere deep inside, she knew this was simply a matter of semantics. But her emotions weren't deep inside at all. They were right on the surface, throbbing for release, bursting through, powered by longing and pain and profound disappointment.

She had not wanted to hear that these wonderful few hours had been intended to pay her back for anything. She'd wanted to know that they were the beginning of something new, and for no reason at all.

Ryan understood he was in trouble the instant he saw her light blue eyes turn to the color of lead.

"I've told you over and over," she said, in a voice he didn't even recognize as hers, "that I agreed to have this baby because Cassie wanted it more than anything in the world. And that's the spirit in which I'm seeing it through. Her love for you started this baby, and my love for *her*, and now for Chelsea, is bringing it to life." She was fairly trembling with fury.

"Do you think for one moment," she demanded, "that *anything*—particularly a coat and a bottle of perfume— could ever repay me for the feelings invested in this baby?"

Ryan was totally surprised by her reaction. What he'd intended to express was diametrically opposed to what she'd apparently heard. He felt himself slip back into the familiar morass of their inability to communicate—only this time, even after their wonderful afternoon, there was nothing comfortable about it.

"Jo..." he began, reaching for her wrist. "I meant—"

"I know what you meant," she said, snatching her wrist away. "You just don't want to be beholden to me for anything when she's born, so that when you don't need *me* anymore, she'll be all yours!"

She turned on her heel and waddled from the room. She stormed into her bedroom and flung the door closed behind her. Instead of slamming, it made a hollow thunking sound. She turned to see that it had struck Ryan's hand. He'd followed her.

He slammed it behind him, and they stood together in the dark room, which was lit only by the glow of a halogen light from the condo's parking area.

He jabbed a finger at her shoulder. "You're wrong, Josanne," he said, in a breathless tone that betrayed temper barely controlled. "I had no ulterior motives, except to let you know that I care. But you have to throw it off by pretending it isn't good enough, or that it isn't offered with the degree of perfection you deem necessary. Well, I don't pretend to know what motivates you, but over the years I've begun to see a pattern. Is it that you don't know what to do with admiration when you get it, or that you don't think you deserve it?"

"Get out of my room," she ordered in a deadly whisper.

He ignored her. "Something's responsible for the bizarre getups and your acidic manner. You're trying to keep men away from you, aren't you? In fact, I could conclude that you're trying to push me farther and farther away from you, so that when I'm not looking you can run off with the baby."

This time she physically pushed him. He didn't even budge. "You say one more word—" she choked on a sob "—and I *will* run!"

"Don't try it, Jo," he warned. "You'll never get past me."

He reached behind him and yanked the door open, then slammed it again and was gone.

COME ON, Mama Jo. You can't run. You can barely walk. And that kind of talk upsets me. And when I get upset, I get restless, and you don't want that to happen in this tight spot.

Chapter Eight

Heron Point—possibly even the entire world, as far as Jo could see—was shrouded in fog. The annual fall pattern of low fog that burned off by midmorning had firmly established itself.

Jo turned away from her bedroom window and pulled her coat on over stirrup pants and a sweater. The weather seemed to parallel her life—except that for the past three days, she'd known no sunny afternoons.

Since her fight with Ryan, they'd barely spoken. He'd driven her to work and picked her up, and she'd made breakfast and cleaned up after he prepared dinner—but they'd done everything in silence.

And she never had eaten the cabbage rolls. She hadn't come out of her room for dinner that night, but she'd tried to sneak one in the early hours of the morning and been unable to find them. They hadn't been in the refrigerator or the freezer, or the trash. She'd settled for peanut butter on a celery stick instead, in bitter disappointment.

She knew she'd been horrible, but so had he. Of course, she'd been worse. And she'd started it.

She'd never been one who found it impossible to apologize for being wrong. It had always seemed as important a function of pride as accepting praise for being right.

But she kept remembering him cradling her hands in his as he leaned over them to sniff the perfume. She remembered him telling her she looked beautiful in the coat. She remembered his laborious preparations for the cabbage rolls that had virtually disappeared without ever being tasted—by her, anyway.

And he'd done all that to "pay her back." In retrospect she could admit that he'd meant nothing dishonorable. She'd become so upset because what she'd *wanted* to hear him say was "I'm falling in love with you."

She'd tried a dozen times since then to tell him she was sorry, but every time she approached, he turned away. She was sure it was more than coincidence.

She wrote a note that said she was going for a walk before breakfast and taped it to his bedroom door. Then she pulled on her beret and headed out.

She stood in the hallway and pressed the button for the elevator. After a moment, the up signal flashed, the bell rang, and the doors parted—revealing Ryan in jeans and a distressed-leather jacket, holding a small bag of groceries. He hadn't shaved, she noticed, and he looked sexily dangerous. A tingling vibration communicated itself from him to her.

His grim expression changed to one of surprise, then angry suspicion. He stepped off the elevator and blocked her path onto it. "Where are you going?" he asked.

Her only intention had been to take a walk, but confronted with his open suspicion, she felt her face flush and knew she must look as though she'd just cleared out his bank account and intended to take his car and his baby as far away as possible.

"I...ah, I..."

He caught her arm and pulled her back toward the condo. "I told you you wouldn't get past me," he said, maintaining a grip on her arm as he put the grocery bag on the floor and reached into his jacket pocket for his key.

"This is ridiculous!" Jo said, anger curiously absent from her reactions to his faulty conclusion. She was very tired of being at odds with him. "I was going for a walk," she said reasonably. "I do this all the time, remember? That is, I used to, until Hulk Jeffries became my bodyguard. I even left a note on your bedroom door. Go check, if you don't believe me. Go..."

Mrs. Drummond's apartment door opened suddenly, and she appeared in blue velour robe and slipper socks to reach for *The Oregonian* on her floor mat. Her jet black curls were standing upright, like rows of question marks. She looked embarrassed, and reached up to smooth them.

Then she said, with sudden enthusiasm, "Mr. Jeffries, I've never enjoyed a meal as much as I enjoyed those cabbage rolls. Thank you so much! I even had my sister over for dinner last night, and I still have another two or three meals in the freezer."

He smiled and nodded. "Glad you enjoyed them." Then he turned the key in the lock, pushed the door open, reached for the grocery bag and hauled Jo inside.

She rolled her eyes and leaned wearily against the closed door. She pointed toward the bedroom. "Go look. I left a note."

"The note wouldn't prove anything," he said. "Just that you could say you were doing one thing when you were really doing another."

Exasperated, she held her arms out at her sides. "Where could I go in this condition—on foot? Do you want to check my pockets for your car keys?"

He dismissed that notion as impossible. "I had the car with me."

"And where did *you* go?" she asked, beginning to un-button her coat, figuring the walk was out after all. "You didn't even leave me a note, and you don't see me accus-ing you of... of abandonment."

"I went to the bakery," he said, passing her the grocery bag. The suspicion had left his expression, and he now simply looked tired.

She peered inside the bag. It contained brioches from the supermarket's bakery. She looked up at him, wondering if what she held in her hands was an olive branch.

MAMA JO? Mama Cass says you got lucky with the cab-bage rolls. Take the bakery buns and make peace. You were wrong, anyway.

HIS NEXT WORDS answered the question. "I'm sorry about the other night," he said, hands in his pockets. "I had no right to... make those judgments."

She shrugged a shoulder. "I'm sorry, too. It was my fault for attacking you. I know that isn't what you meant."

They looked at each other, each almost afraid to go on and risk the sudden truce. Jo finally pulled her coat off and turned toward the kitchen. "I'll put on the coffee and make some tea."

He rubbed his stubbly jaw. "I have to shave," he said.

"Oh, don't" was on the tip of her tongue, but she bit it back. Instead, she said, "Go ahead." Then she couldn't resist taunting him. "Unless you're afraid I'll make my escape while you're gone, and you'd be more comfortable if I came into the bathroom with you?"

He gave her a look that acknowledged the taunt, then slid down to take in her generous proportions. "Thanks, but you wouldn't fit in the bathroom. I figure the bri-oches will keep you here until I get back."

She turned away to the kitchen. "Only if I eat yours, too."

IT HAD BEGUN. Ryan wrapped an arm around Jo's shoulders as they left Dr. McNamara's office after her weekly visit, and walked out to the car. He felt both exultant and terrified.

According to the obstetrician, Jo had experienced lightening and engagement—medical terms that meant the baby had "dropped" and that her head was in position and about to begin the gradual trip down, though actual birth could still be a week or more away.

MAMA JO? Are you using gravity boots?

SHE WAS REMARKABLY CALM at the moment—even serene. But he knew that situation could change in an instant. They'd lived in relative peace in the four days since their brioche breakfast, but her wild and abrupt changes of mood kept him alert. He never knew from one moment to the next whether he would have to comfort a sobbing woman, or laugh with one who was delivering one-liners about her size.

To his surprise, she wrapped an arm around his waist and looked up at him with a smile that was empathetic. "Scared?" she asked.

"Profoundly," he replied with a brief laugh. "You?"

She nodded. "Yes. But I'm excited, too. I can't believe we're on the brink of finally seeing what Chelsea looks like."

"Jo! Hi!" Jo and Ryan turned to see Amy Brown hurrying across the parking lot toward the hospital. She was flushed with excitement. "Guess what?"

Jo did. "You got your model mother?"

PLAY
ONE MILLION
BIG BUCK$
ONE MILLION
AND YOU COULD WIN THE
$1,000,000.00
PLUS JACKPOT!
YOUR *PERSONAL* GAME CARD INSIDE...
HARLEQUIN

◄ **DETACH AND MAIL CARD TODAY!** ▼

BIG BUCKS

TWO WAYS TO WIN BIG BUCKS!

HURRY! This jack pot must be claimed!

YES! I have played my BIG BUCKS game card as instructed. Enter me in the MILLION DOLLAR Sweepstakes III and also enter me for the Extra Bonus Prize. When winners are selected, tell me if I've won. If the Lucky Charm is scratched off, I will also receive everything revealed, as explained on the back and on the opposite page.

LUCKY CHARM GAME!

Claim 4 FREE books AND a FREE Mystery Gift!
Scratch Here ▷

154 CIH AWMV
(U-H-AR-11/95)

NAME _____

ADDRESS _____ APT ____

CITY _____ STATE _____ ZIP ____

NO PURCHASE OR OBLIGATION NECESSARY TO ENTER SWEEPSTAKES.

© 1993 HARLEQUIN ENTERPRISES LTD.   PRINTED IN U.S.A.

1. Uncover 5 $ signs in a row . . . BINGO! You're eligible to win the $1,000,000.00 SWEEPSTAKES!

2. Uncover 5 $ signs in a row AND uncover $ signs in all 4 corners . . . BINGO! You're also eligible for the $50,000.00 EXTRA BONUS PRIZE!

THE HARLEQUIN READER SERVICE®: HERE'S HOW IT WORKS

Accepting free books places you under no obligation to buy anything. You may keep the books and gift and return the shipping statement marked "cancel". If you do not cancel, about a month later we will send you 4 additional novels and bill you just $2.89 each plus 25¢ delivery and applicable sales tax, if any.* That's the complete price, and – compared to cover prices of $3.50 each – quite a bargain! You may cancel at any time, but if you choose to continue, every month we'll send you 4 more books, which you may either purchase at the discount price...or return at our expense and cancel your subscription.

*Terms and prices subject to change without notice. Sales tax applicable in N.Y.

"Yes!" Amy shrieked. "Coast Guard family. Just moved here a month ago. She's very excited, and I'm thrilled to death! She's just been admitted, so I want to be around for the grand finale."

"Wonderful!" Jo patted her hand. "Well done."

Amy's beeper went off, and she rolled her eyes, switched her purse to her other arm so that she could reach it, then frowned as she read the digital display.

"Yeah?" she mumbled to herself. "Well, you can just wait until I'm good and ready."

"What?" Jo asked.

Amy looked up at her, as though surprised she was still there. "What? Oh, nothing. Just mumbling to myself. So, you're about to do your thing, too, aren't you?"

Jo nodded. "All the right things are happening. My due date's a week from today." Then she shooed Amy toward the building. "Don't let us keep you. I know you don't want to miss anything. Good luck."

"Right." Amy waved as she started off. "See you next week. You take care of her, Mr. Jeffries."

"That I will," he promised.

"I wonder who that call was from," Jo asked as Ryan unlocked the passenger side door of the Volvo. "She didn't seem particularly thrilled by it."

"Tom Nicholas, maybe?" Ryan suggested, lifting her feet for her and putting them into the car. This had become a ritual over the past few days.

Jo turned to him with a frown. "Why do you say that?"

"Just a guess. She had a message from him the last time we saw her, remember?"

"That's right. Do you think they've had a falling-out? The last time he called her, she was so excited, she was barely coherent."

He nodded, slipping in behind the wheel. "I remember. Well, you know how love is," he said.

"No," she replied candidly. "I don't. How is it?"

He met her eyes. "Wonderful, difficult, happy, sad, tragic, funny, enervating, debilitating—everything that exists in this world, and its direct opposite."

She frowned at that explanation, seriously interested. "And how do the two of you ever get anywhere?"

"Ah...well..." He stared through the windshield. "You don't really have to *get* anywhere. You just have to *be,* and love sort of generates its own propulsion. And you really have very little control over where it takes you. All you have to do is sustain each other along the way."

She turned slightly toward him, fascinated by his description. "How did a practical, organized man like yourself even *want* to enter into a...a...situation so unstructured?"

He folded his hands at the top of the steering wheel. "Again, it's not like you have a choice. Had I been asked by anyone, I'd have declined. But Cassie came to work at the bank, and from the moment I saw her, I knew I had no personal future without her."

MAMA CASS says to hug Daddy.

CASSIE. Jo felt no resentment that her sister's name had come up. After all, she, Jo, had asked Ryan about love, and the love of his life had been Cassie. He had no other reference point.

And she was carrying Cassie's baby. It didn't matter that she had sheltered and nurtured its body for nine months, that she'd grown to love it with everything she was and more. When Chelsea finally made her appearance a week or so from now, she would be half Ryan and half Cassie. And Jo's job would be done.

The sudden, desperate loss she felt made a fist of emotion in the pit of her stomach.

"I'm exhausted," she said, in a carefully neutral voice. "Can we go home instead of going to lunch?"

Ryan put his key in the ignition, frowning in sudden concern. "Right away."

At home, he tried to put her to bed, but she insisted on lying on the recliner. "It's easier to get out of," she said as he placed a sunflower-patterned cotton throw over her. "And could you get my crochet bag before you go back to work?" As he headed down the corridor, she called after him, "I think I left it on the floor beside my bed."

Ryan found it immediately and took it to her. The bag was now stuffed, the project almost three feet long. She'd worked on it faithfully on breaks at work and in the evenings. He always felt an odd twinge when he saw it. Cassie had begun it, and Jo was finishing it. Just as they'd done with Chelsea. It amazed and touched him what women would do for one another.

He microwaved a cup of tea for her and placed it on the lamp table at her elbow.

"Anything else?" he asked cheerfully.

Something about the look in her eyes made him force a carefree mood. She smiled pleasantly, and she had that same air of serenity about her, but it had a quality of fatal acceptance in it that he didn't trust. It had come over her, he remembered, when he mentioned Cassie.

She shook her head. "Nope. Got everything. Thanks. You want me to put potatoes in the oven for dinner, or anything?" She smiled grimly. "I'll even remember to poke holes in them this time."

He laughed lightly. "Thanks, but I'll bring home take-out. Chinese? Italian? Mexican?"

"How about—" she thought with great concentration "—that bow-tie pasta salad from Chez Pasta, and the Macho Nacho appetizer from the bar?"

He leaned over the chair to make sure he'd understood her. "Bow-tie salad and nachos?"

"Yeah."

"And...you're going to have them together?"

She didn't seem to see a problem. "Yeah. And could you pick up cannolis for dessert?"

He felt his stomach roil. "Sure."

"Thanks," she said quietly.

Her hair was down in a wild mass around her shoulders, and her cheeks were pink with weariness. Her eyes were bright, her skin was flawless, her fingers were long and slender on the blanket. Under it, his baby mounded like a little Everest.

He felt drawn to her like the sea to the shore, as though God himself had ordained this movement at the moment of Creation.

Before he could second-guess the impulse, he closed the gap between them and kissed her mouth.

Jo's heartbeat rose into her throat as she read the intention in the dark eyes focused on her lips. She parted them, startled, at the same moment that he claimed them. But all she felt was the tender warmth of his mouth for what was but a brief instant—but one that played over in her mind for the hours he was gone, as though that kiss had taken an eternity.

She ate half of everything he brought home, including half of *his* cannoli. And each of them studiously avoided any mention of the kiss. When they'd finished eating, she asked brightly, "You want to go for a walk?"

He looked up from wiping off the table. She closed the door on the dishwasher and the few utensils they'd used.

"At night?" he asked.

She frowned. "This isn't Central Park, Ryan, it's Heron Point. I thought we'd just walk along the river a little way."

"You said you walked to see things," he reminded. "You can't see anything at night."

"At night you walk to *smell* things."

He tossed the sponge at the sink and looked doubtful. "What kind of things?"

"I'll show you." She took his arm and pushed him toward the coat closet. "Come on. I've got to work off some of this." She patted her watermelon stomach.

He grinned. "Good idea, but it won't work. You still have to give birth to it."

She rolled her eyes. "You know what I mean."

He laughed and handed her her coat and beret.

The fog that was in place every morning when they looked out the condo window was already lying over the water like a length of thick gauze. Foghorns blared from the channel where ships sailed upriver to Portland, and sometimes anchored, waiting for a berth at the port.

Jo and Ryan walked along the well-lit dock arm in arm, drawn together by a force neither understood or tried to explain. It was like the kiss neither understood nor regretted.

They stopped about a quarter mile from the condo and leaned their forearms on the railing.

"This is so stimulating," Ryan said in teasing tones of feigned boredom. Fog covered everything, and there truly was nothing to see.

Jo reached a hand up and covered his eyes. "What do you smell?"

"Why are you covering my eyes?" he asked. "I can't see anything."

"Because you're distracted," she said, "by the fact that there's nothing to see. Concentrate on the smells."

"Okay." He sighed, let himself concentrate for just a moment on the cool softness of her hand against his cheekbones and the bridge of his nose, then worked on answering her question. "Ah . . . salt water, diesel oil, creosote . . ."

Jo murmured, "God, you're stubborn," and turned his face in the direction of the mouth of the river. "Breathe deeply," she instructed.

He complied. And then he got it—lungfuls of some indescribable natural perfume that must have drifted on the air and rolled with the ocean into the river to come to this place and this point in time with this particular combination of fragrances.

"Oh," he said on a breath, trying to filter and separate the components. "I smell Bangkok," he said, "the Serengeti, some Alpine meadow, and a . . ." He sniffed, catching a whiff of something sweet. "Paris, I think," he said. "A bakery on the rue de Rivoli."

She dropped her hand from his eyes and giggled. The fog seemed to act as soundproofing, and kept the musical sound lingering at his ear.

"What a nose," she said admiringly. "That was pretty specific. Why the rue de Rivoli?"

"When I was in college," he said, "I did my junior year in Paris. A friend and I went there for croissants every morning." He smiled down at her. "You think the brioches at the market's bakery are delicious? You should have tasted those. Anyway . . . the aroma would wake us up, it was so wonderful. But so far, I've done all the work. What do you smell?"

They leaned shoulder to shoulder on the railing, enclosed in their misty world. Water lapped against the invisible pilings, and a foghorn warned against trespassing too close.

"Well, frankly, I've never broken it down that way," Jo admitted. "I've just always thought of it as...invitation. Promise. The fragrance of tomorrow."

"So, you want to travel?" he asked.

"No." Her denial was quick. "Not an invitation to visit the source of all those exotic fragrances, but the invitation to accept that they're out there, and the promise that the world is a wide and exciting place."

He looked down at the face at his shoulder. "A world that you don't want to see?"

She shrugged a shoulder. "Not at the moment, anyway. I guess it's weird to feel excited just *knowing* what's out there."

He put an arm around her shoulder. "It isn't weird. It's a sort of Joian philosophy."

She laughed and looped an arm around his waist. She looked up at the sky, but it was hidden by the fog.

He followed her gaze. "Looking for a star to wish on?"

"No." She leaned her head back in the hollow of his shoulder. "I was looking for Chelsea. Some people believe babies are stars before they're born."

IT ISN'T TRUE. We just like to be stars after *we're born. I can't wait.*

"NO KIDDING." He was a little surprised to find himself straining to peer through the fog. But the sky was virtually invisible. "Is she the North Star, do you think?"

She laughed lightly. "Probably. I imagine her as big and boisterous."

"Incidentally, your father called the bank today to ask if I still had my Volvo, and what the dimensions of the trunk were."

She blinked. "What's he bringing?"

"He wouldn't say. I can only conclude it's big." He squeezed her shoulder. "Are there any more smell tests, or can we go home now?"

They stood arm in arm, and she was leaning into him. He supported her weight easily, casually. Several hours ago, he had kissed her. Yet there was nothing different about him that she could see to indicate that they had blundered onto new ground. She felt it, though she didn't understand it, and she wanted him to feel it, too.

"No," she replied, "but there is a taste test."

He raised an eyebrow. "After pasta salad, nachos and cannolis?"

She ignored that. "It also involves closing your eyes."

"Jo..."

"Do it, Ryan, or I'll send you out for anchovies and orange juice at 2:00 a.m."

With a groan, he closed his eyes.

The obstruction of the baby prevented her from getting close enough to stand on tiptoe and reach his lips with hers. So she put a hand to the back of his neck and tipped his head down toward her.

His eyes opened, and she saw a quick surprise in them, then an admission that it had to be, an acceptance that it was inevitable. He didn't take the initiative from her, but he didn't resist, either.

Jo put her mouth to his, felt his interest and attention, and tried to put into the gesture all the emotion that was blossoming up inside her. *I love you,* she told him with the artful attention of her lips. *I've loved you for so long.*

There's something here, Ryan. Can't you see it? Can't you feel it?

She looped her arms around his neck, drawing him closer. *I know we're opposites, but we're finding ways to deal with that, aren't we? I think we could be happy.*

His response was tentative for just an instant, but then she felt her emotion ignite his, and he crushed her to him, Chelsea squirming between them.

HAVE I MENTIONED that it's already very tight in here?

HE KNEW there were a dozen reasons why this shouldn't happen—he'd been widowed only seven months, this was his sister-in-law, the woman who carried the baby he'd made with his dead wife, the woman who was 360 degrees different from himself. Well, maybe that wasn't true anymore. Living and giving had seemed to lessen the distance between them considerably.

And she was warm, generous, funny, and touchingly brave. Something in her called to him, and something in him was eager to respond.

It occurred to him to wonder if that was love. He'd experienced it once, but loss made it seem like an eternity ago. Jo put her lips to his ear at that moment, and he lost whatever fragile grip he'd had on thought. So he simply went with what he felt.

Desire erupted in him like steam from a geyser. He kissed her hair, her eyes, her cheeks, her jaw. He nipped at her earlobe, and when she uttered a little cry of pleasure, he raised her face in his hands and plundered her mouth.

Jo was giddy with ecstasy. He felt it. He knew! Then she became giddy from lack of air and pushed at his chest, wresting her lips from his with a little laugh that drifted around them in the fog. She leaned her forehead against his throat and laughed lightly. "The baby needs oxygen," she said breathlessly.

GASP!

THE BABY. Ryan felt it wriggling against his own abdomen—alive, and eager, probably, to escape the confined space of the womb and join the world. Cassie's baby.

He felt Jo in his arms, warm and laughing, her breath against his throat, and felt quite literally as though the past and the present were trying to tear him in two.

He'd been so careful all this time, resisting his attraction to Jo, sure it was all wrapped up in the pregnancy. But in the midst of this kiss, he'd almost forgotten the baby—until it moved against him. And even now, when memories of Cassie intruded, he found it difficult to open his arms and set Jo free.

But she took the responsibility from him. As she stepped backward, out of his embrace, he looked down into her eyes and saw the laughter wiped away. Pain had replaced it.

He took hold of her arms as she tried to move away. "Don't look like that," he pleaded. "I wanted that kiss as much as you did."

Her lips took on a wry twist as she looked deeply into his eyes. "Yes," she said quietly, mockingly. "I can see that. You look utterly miserable. Let's go home."

"No." He pulled her back when she tried to turn. The night was damp and cold, and he moved his hands from her arms to tie the top button of her coat. He couldn't analyze what he felt, but he didn't want her to think he felt nothing. "We're not in a simple relationship here," he said reasonably. "I've been . . . attracted to you since I moved you in with me, but I want to understand what's at the heart of it.''

"The heart," she pointed out quietly, "usually generates love."

He framed her face in his hands, his brow furrowed. "Jo, surrogate motherhood between sisters generates *confusion* for the widower of the one, who is also the father of the other's baby! No matter how I add it up, someone gets subtracted! I need time to think about this."

DADDY. *Mama Cass says she's already gone. She wants you to think of you and me. Please snuggle up against me again. That was nice.*

SHE SUBSIDED, knowing he was right. She wanted it to be simple, because what she felt was so clear. But it wasn't simple—particularly not for him.

"You're right," she said. "I'm sorry."

"Don't be sorry." He put an arm around her and started back slowly toward the condominium. "Just be patient."

Patient, Jo thought as the foghorn bleated its lonely call. She had a week left before Chelsea was born. And she'd come to love the baby and her father so much that she couldn't imagine living on the periphery of their lives after the birth. She was beginning to understand that she would have to be as important to them as they were to her, or she couldn't stay. She would be gone.

Patience—at least more than a week's worth—was not an option.

"WELL, my God, Jo!" Matthew Arceneau, tall and bony and professorial, with shaggy white hair and a beard, leaned down to try to wrap his daughter in his arms. "You look as though you're about to fly away."

Jo turned to one side to make it possible to get closer, and reached her arms around his neck. "This approach usually works best." She laughed as he kissed her cheek soundly. "I'm far too leaden to fly away, believe me. I'll probably hatch a T-Rex or something. It's so good to see you, Daddy."

HI, Grandpa! Mama Cass says to tell you she loves you. And she sends love from Grandma, too.

THEY STOOD in the tiny terminal at the Coast Guard air station at Heron Point, which rented an airstrip to the commercial short-hop carrier that had flown Matthew in from Portland.

Ryan excused himself to collect his father-in-law's bags, but Matthew caught his arm. "You'll need my help," he said, pushing Jo gently to the terminal's single bank of green vinyl chairs. "We'll be right back, Joey."

"How is she doing?" Matthew asked Ryan as they went to the small, warm office at the back of the terminal where luggage was placed in the middle of the floor to await collection.

"The doctor says she's healthy," he replied, avoiding the man's eyes, reading the implication in the question. Matt Arceneau had been his father-in-law for six years, and Ryan was well aware of his fierce love and loyalty for his daughters, and the deceptively charming mailed fist that was behind all his efforts to do what was best for them. "And the baby's great. He doesn't foresee any problems. Which bags?"

"All my stuff has a Continental flag sticker on it," Matthew replied, pointing to one blue tweed garment bag in a far corner, and another, smaller leather bag on the opposite side. He headed for an item that rose from the middle of the sea of luggage like the *Queen Mary*—except the queen was a lion.

Ryan stopped with his hand on the garment bag and watched in amazement as Matthew picked up the stuffed toy, which must have sat five feet tall, and gingerly made his way back out again.

Both bags in hand, Ryan met him near the door. "What *is* that?"

Matthew grinned, stroking the elaborate mane. "My granddaughter's first stuffed toy." Then he sobered again. "But, how *is* Jo?"

Ryan sighed and gave up trying to hedge. "She's serene, in charge, efficient and eager one moment, then tearful and worried the next."

Matthew nodded. "Well, that's pretty par, as I recall. Hormones in a flap, you know. All part and parcel of the process. The day before her mother delivered her, she hit me with a tent stake in the middle of the outdoor department at Sears. Thought I shouldn't be looking at sporting goods when she was shopping for a nightgown to take to the hospital where she was going to have *my* baby."

Ryan laughed. "I didn't realize being a father was so dangerous."

Matt looked him in the eye and shook his head. "Being a father is wonderful. It's being a husband that's dangerous. Don't you remember?"

Ryan tried to think back, but the details of being married to Cassie seemed as though they'd happened a lifetime ago, to someone else. He was surprised to discover that, when waiting for the baby kept the essence of his life with her so near.

Ryan shook his head. "I remember mostly that we laughed a lot, loved each other madly, and that she was always concocting schemes I was sure would never work out. But she was convinced there was a solution to every problem, if you wanted something badly enough. And, somehow, she always found one.''

Matthew smiled a little sadly, apparently also remembering that quality in his daughter. "So, how are *you* coping, Ryan?'' he asked. "Are you ready to be a single father?''

He didn't hesitate. "Of course. That's the hand I've been dealt.'' He turned back to the terminal, gesturing Matthew to follow. "Come on. Jo will be wondering what's happened to us.''

"Maybe,'' Matthew muttered quietly as he fell into step behind him, "you should pick up another card.''

Jo looked up from the magazine she was perusing as Ryan and her father approached. She took one look at the giant lion and shrieked, "Simba!''

Ryan raised an eyebrow. "You've met before?''

"He's the Lion King!'' she cried, reaching up for the toy. Her father placed it on the floor before her. It stood taller than she did. "Oh, Daddy...'' She smoothed the fuzzy orange mane with her hands, then ran a fingertip down the length of its nose. "Chelsea will love it!''

"Okay, let's go,'' Ryan said. "We've got reservations at Chez Pasta for seven o'clock.''

Matthew picked up the lion. Jo smiled from her chair. "I'd like to, but I can't.''

Ryan frowned. "Why not?''

She looked around surreptitiously, then admitted under her breath, "Because I'm stuck.''

Ryan rolled his eyes and put the bags down, exchanging a grin with Matthew, who stepped back with the lion.

"Well, don't be upset with me,'' she said, raising her arms as Ryan squatted down to assess her position.

"Daddy's the one who suggested I sit here. On my own, I'd have concluded that a wraparound waiting-area chair was not a good choice, but I was trying to be cooperative."

Matthew snickered. "Ha! For twenty-nine years of her life, she's a hellion. *Now* she chooses to cooperate."

Ryan gently forced his fingers in between her stomach and the kidney-shaped table arm attached to the chair. "Okay, slip sideways," he instructed.

DADDY, you're bending my foot.

SHE LOOKED AT HIM as though he were insane. "Ryan, I don't even move *forward* very well anymore."

"Jo..." His tone held amusement and mild impatience. Then he placed his other arm around the back of her waist to pull. "Put your arm around my neck. If I miss my ravioli with sausage, I won't let you forget it."

She inched sideways, tried to slip out, but the three chairs attached to the one in which she sat rose with it.

She sat back with a sigh, her arm still hooked around his neck. Their noses were an inch apart. "There isn't much I *want* to forget," she whispered for his ears alone.

His dark eyes held hers for an instant, and she thought she saw a smile there. Then, realizing they were beginning to collect an audience, Ryan inched her backward a little farther, pushed a little harder on her stomach and instructed a young boy observing with a Tootsie Pop in his mouth to sit in the next chair.

"Okay, now," he said. The boy sat, Ryan pulled, Jo pushed, and she was free. Their small audience applauded. Jo bowed.

THANK YOU. Thank you.

"WELL, that was entertaining," Matthew said as they headed for the car. "And people think small towns are no fun. That would never happen at Logan Airport."

Ryan opened the trunk. "If Jo were there, it might."

It wasn't until later that night, when her father was asleep on the hideaway bed in the living room and Ryan looked in on her before turning in, that Jo noticed his hand.

He was about to close her door with it when she noticed the rough, bloodred scrapes on his first three fingers from knuckle to knuckle. She remembered his hand slipping between her and the chair arm at the airport terminal.

"Your hand . . ." she said, coming to him to examine it. She wore a tentlike bright blue cotton gown, and her hair was piled on top of her head after her shower.

He enjoyed her solicitousness, but dismissed the problem with a wave of his free hand. "It's fine."

She ignored his denial and, maintaining her grip on him, drew him into her bathroom. She reached into the medicine cabinet, remembering that she'd seen a tube of Neosporin and a box of Band-Aids. He leaned a hip on the counter and let her work on him.

She was barefoot, and they were eye-to-eye, though she seemed studiously to be avoiding his gaze. He found himself wanting to look into her eyes, wanting to see that warmth and excitement there, that fascination with and enthusiasm for everything, which was so uniquely her.

Cassie had loved life and everything in it—and had always been determined to scoop it all into her experience and coax it into providing her what she wanted.

Jo seemed to enjoy it without needing to control it, and he found himself admiring the way she moved from day to day, thrilled by the unexpected, relishing the surprises.

He was beginning to think that after a month in her company he was learning something.

DADDY, Mama Cass says we're all entitled to a different approach.

JO WAS FIDGETING. She'd bandaged all three fingers, and there was nothing left to do but put the Band-Aids away, but she hated to spoil this moment of domestic intimacy. She liked being closed with him in the bathroom. She could pretend she was brushing her hair and he was shaving as they prepared for an evening on the town, a baby-sitter in the next room with Chelsea. That was fantasy, of course, but it didn't seem to matter. Her whole life this past year had been one enlightening or shattering event after another. She was anxious to deal in a little dreamy escape.

So when Ryan took the box of Band-Aids from her hands, put it aside, then wrapped his arms around her and pulled her close, she thought for a moment that she was simply getting really good at this—that her imagination had virtual-reality capability.

Then she felt the warmth of his hands roving her back, the strength of his shoulder against her cheek, his lips in her hair. It was really happening.

But she'd learned a little since the other night, in the fog on the pier. She simply held him and said nothing, letting all she felt build up inside, letting all she longed for remain unspoken.

It was best that way. She didn't know what to ask of him, anyway. As much as she loved him, she had a better understanding of his love for Cassie. She knew it lived in him still, deep and strong, and she wouldn't have taken a moment of it away from him, even if it meant she could take its place.

The baby squirmed, and she swore she felt its head move, pressing against her pelvic floor. She stiffened in discomfort and uttered a little cry.

Ryan took her weight and put a hand on the baby. "What?" he demanded.

YOU'RE SQUISHING ME. My big toe is in my ear!

SHE SHOOK HER HEAD and laughed softly, drawing a breath. "Nothing, really. Just movement. But the way she's placed now, I can feel every turn of her head."

He relaxed somewhat, sharply reminded of what lay ahead of them. He lifted her into his arms, carried her to her bedroom and placed her in the middle of her blankets. "You're sure you're all right?"

"Positive," she assured him. "Don't worry. It was just a twinge."

"Okay. Good night."

"Good night."

He stood in her doorway a moment, looking at her lying on her side in the virginal single bed, and thought how lonely she looked there, and how unfair it was that she wasn't in some wide four-poster with the man of her dreams and a baby that would be all hers.

But, this baby was all *his*. And that was what decided him.

He went back to her bed, tossed the blankets aside as she gasped in surprise and confusion, picked her up again and carried her to his king-size bed.

"Don't panic," he said, settling her in on the inside and pulling the covers up over her. "I have no designs on your virtue, just your comfort and your safety. I don't want you in there alone if you need something in the middle of the night."

"But…" She pointed toward the living room, where her father slept.

"I know," he said, going to the light switch to turn it off, and closing the door. "If we find ourselves having to explain it to him, I'll worry about it then. Right now, I need you near me."

Jo snuggled into the pillow where he'd placed her, thinking that if he expected an argument from her on that score, he'd be waiting a long time.

"Good night, Ryan," she said.

There was an instant's surprised silence, and then she heard him move to his side of the bed and sit on it to pull off his shoes. "Good night, Jo," he replied.

IF DADDY WANTS US near him, why is he all the way over there?

Chapter Nine

Matthew did laundry, prepared and froze several casseroles for use after they brought the baby home, and accompanied Jo on her walks, though Ryan left them the Volvo and rode in to work with his assistant manager.

Matthew met Buttercup, Bill and Camouflage, and then he and Jo stopped in at Coffee Country, where Devon had everything under complete control.

Jo seated her father at the counter with a mochaccino and went into the back room to put together what she knew would be the last deposit before the baby came. She had to keep busy. Even her father's conversation couldn't distract her from memories of waking up in the dark hours of early morning, curled against Ryan's chest, his arms loosely wrapped around her as he slept.

The first night she spent in his bed, she'd managed to stay on her side, but last night she'd had the Cassie dream again. She had a vague recollection of having recoiled from it—and of reaching for the warm harbor of Ryan's arms. She remembered his body curved around hers, his strong voice in the darkness telling her quietly that she'd been dreaming and to go back to sleep.

When she'd awakened again, he was gone. He'd told her father he had an early meeting with the district manager, who was visiting from Seattle.

The coffee bar had made a lot of money in the few days she'd been home, she noticed, feeling a curious sensation of dispensability. Devon, experienced and charming, had done a fine job of keeping everything tidy and efficient.

If she did decide to walk away from all this when Chelsea was born, it seemed she wouldn't even be missed.

For the past two days, she'd worried over bouts of false labor and considered her options. Spending the nights in Ryan's bed, though all they'd done was sleep, had given her a glimpse of all she could have—if she could just help Ryan see it. Maybe it would be worth the painful distance of being simply his sister-in-law for a while, simply Chelsea's aunt—if it meant that in the end she could have both of them.

But she vacillated, one moment joyfully hopeful that it could happen, and the next cynically certain that it was all in her imagination, that Ryan's concern was just for Chelsea, and that once the baby was born, she, Jo, would be out of the picture. Maybe she should call Lisa, her college roommate who now lived in Port Townsend, on Puget Sound, and see how she would feel about company for a few weeks. If Ryan decided he didn't need her, she didn't think she could stay in Heron Point.

She was a bundle of nerves. Even her father had commented on the walk downtown that she was like grease on a griddle. She would kill, she thought, for a cup of espresso. It was one of the first things she intended to have the moment Chelsea was delivered.

When Jo emerged from the back room, it was to find her father and Diantha in urgent conversation, the woman holding Matthew's hand palm up as she ran her index finger along one of its lines.

"Oh, a very long lifeline," Jo heard Diantha say as she approached the table. "Late eighties would be my guess. And when a robust man like yourself takes care of himself—" Jo noted in amazement that Diantha's cheeks were pink, and her voice was low and husky "—he can enjoy *all* life has to offer well into his early nineties."

Matthew, chin leaning on his free hand, said feelingly, "Now there's a dream come true."

Since neither person had yet noticed her presence, Jo went to Devon, asked him to make Matthew and Diantha another round, and walked the half block to the bank to see if Ryan wanted to join them for lunch.

It would steady her to see him, she thought. She'd come to rely on him a great deal in the past month. And she felt slightly neglected because he'd gone off to work that morning without saying goodbye.

Roberta Dawson smiled her apologies. "I'm afraid he's already left for lunch about an hour ago with the western-district CEO and his entourage."

"Oh." Jo tried to hide her disappointment. "Don't bother to tell him I stopped in. I imagine it's pretty tense for all of you to have management checking on you."

Roberta shook her head. "They're not after us, this time. They're just interested in Mr. Jeffries."

"Oh?"

She lowered her voice. "It's that Los Angeles thing. You know."

Jo sat in the chair beside Roberta's desk, her senses on the alert. She lowered her own voice. "No, I don't. What Los Angeles thing?"

Jo saw the sudden concern in Roberta's eyes. "He didn't tell you?" she asked, sitting back in her chair, as though to put a distance between them. "Maybe I shouldn't have..."

Jo smiled widely and pooh-poohed that notion with a casual wave of her hand. "Don't be silly. My father's just arrived from Connecticut for the birth of the baby, and we've hardly had time to talk." She made her tone friendly, but injected it with a touch of an imperious right to know. "Now, what about Los Angeles?"

"Well..." Roberta appeared reluctant to reveal the news. "It's about the ... promotion."

"Oh, that." Jo had no idea what promotion, but was simply trying to generate confidence. For the moment, she wasn't thinking about what it could mean to her, hoping only to decipher what it meant, period. "They're...they're serious about it, are they?"

Roberta relaxed. "Apparently. It sounds as though they're going to really make it worth your while to move there."

The words struck Jo like a blow, but her only outward reaction was an instinctive covering of her baby with a protective arm.

"That's what you get," Roberta said, "for being with the most imaginative and practical banker in the entire West Coast division." She grinned proudly. "Those were the words of the CEO himself. I heard that when I took coffee into their meeting this morning. From Coffee Country," she added. "Which they enjoyed enormously, by the way."

Jo drew a breath and asked calmly, "Did they say when this will come about?"

"Not until after Christmas."

"Oh, good. Well..." She felt very much as though she'd been nailed to the chair, but she pushed herself to her feet, with more determination than grace, Roberta steadying her arm those last few inches when she had to let go of the desk. "Thank you, Roberta. You've been very enlightening."

Roberta looked worried again as she walked Jo to the door. "You *are* going with him, aren't you?" she asked. "I mean, we all thought, with your sis—" she stopped abruptly, then began again "—with Mrs. Jeffries gone, that you and he would... I mean, there's the baby..."

Jo nodded and smiled sadly, feeling everything that had been positive inside her during the past two complicated days being choked off from its sustenance and dying. "Sort of defies a solution, doesn't it? 'Bye, Roberta. And please don't tell him I was here. I'm sure... he'll want to tell me himself."

She could imagine what he would say as she walked back to the coffee bar to pick up her father. "See you, Jo. Chelsea and I are off to L.A. You don't want to come, do you?" Or maybe "Moving to Los Angeles, Jo. Thank you for giving birth to Cassie's and my child and stepping graciously out of the way. I'll keep in touch."

"Joey," Matthew pleaded as she pulled him from the shop and toward the taxi stand in front of the supermarket. "What's the matter? Are you all right? Is it labor?"

"No," she said, with an edge to her voice that made him give her a second look as he helped her in beside the driver. "It's a lust for blood. Get in, Daddy, so we can get home."

Matthew climbed into the back of the cab and studied the back of his daughter's head with concern. The last time he'd seen that look in her eye, she'd been thirteen and Cassie had "borrowed" her baby-sitting money to bankroll a pie-baking business of her own. Cassie had sported a shiner for a week.

It wasn't the money, Jo had confided to him then, it was the deceit in someone she'd trusted.

"He's moving to Los Angeles!" Jo stormed across the living room, through the dining room and into the kitchen. She filled the teakettle and banged it down on the stove. "Just like that! After Christmas."

Matthew followed her into the kitchen, his arms folded, his brow furrowed. "What?" he asked. "Who told you?"

"Roberta Dawson, at the bank. He was having lunch with the bigwigs from the district. They're promoting him because he's imaginative and efficient. He's sneaky, too, but they probably don't know that." She yanked a tin from the countertop and struggled with the hinged lid. Matthew moved forward to take it from her. He flipped the lid with his thumbs, then offered it to her. She pulled a tea bag out and slammed the tin on the counter. It vibrated like a cymbal. "I suppose he'd have told me before he started packing. Or maybe not. Maybe he'd have left me a note: 'Bye, Aunt Jo. Thanks for everything, but we'll be fine without you now.'"

"Jo." Matthew wandered after her as she marched into Ryan's bedroom and yanked her crocheting bag off the chair. "Honey, don't jump to conclusions until you hear his side."

She gave him a pitying look and marched past him, back toward the door. "He apparently has no intention of telling me. And *I* have no intention of asking."

MAMA JO? Does that make sense? I'm standing on my head, so things aren't always very clear to me, but shouldn't you ask? I mean—isn't it important?

AT THE DOOR, she caught a whiff of Ryan's herbal scent clinging to the robe he'd left over a chair. Tears rose in her throat and collected there, hot and pointed and painful.

She had a mental flash of waking in the night and finding herself surrounded by his arms and his scent. She'd built an imaginary future for herself based on those few moments that reality had just ground to powder.

Well. She'd been prepared to lose so that he could have everything Cassie had wanted him to have, because she'd promised Cassie. But it was standard practice, even in banking, that dishonesty negated any signature or any pledge.

"You have to listen to his side," Matthew insisted. "It's only fair."

Jo went back into the kitchen in answer to the kettle's shrill call. "Fair, shmair. He lied."

"He didn't lie, he just didn't say anything. Maybe he was picking his moment. Can I have second dunk on that tea bag?"

Jo took down another cup and poured water over the bag for a second cup. "Really? And what could he possibly be waiting for? For a moment when I'm more pregnant, more stressed, more hormonally hysterical?"

Matthew waited for her to put the kettle down, then took her arm and pulled her toward the recliner. "Sit down, and *calm* down. If you go into labor while I'm alone with you, you're grounded! Now, here—wrap up in this." He brought her the cotton throw, then went into the kitchen for her cup. He sat in the chair opposite her with his own cup.

"Now think about it," he said. "He's been taking good care of you, hasn't he?"

"He's been taking good care of Chelsea."

He considered that a moment, then conceded the point. "But he brought you into his bed, didn't he?" he asked with a candor that surprised her.

"Because he wanted to make sure the baby was safe."

"Maybe he just wanted to hold you."

"I don't think so."

"Because you've never been able to give anyone the benefit of the doubt." He looked into her face without flinching at her wounded expression. "I'm sorry, but it's true. You're brutally demanding of the people in your life. Cassie was demanding of the *things,* but you're demanding of the people. Not only do they have to do all the things you think they should do, but their motives have to be noble, as well. So, let him explain. Maybe he didn't want to startle or upset you at this stage of the pregnancy. Maybe," he suggested, narrowing his gaze on her, "he was going to ask you to go with him."

She knew that wasn't true. Ryan knew how she felt. He would have told her if he intended to take her along.

She sat quietly, wanting her father to stop talking so she could analyze the plan forming in her mind. It was radical and selfish, but the situation was radical, and she was sick to death of being generous. And she had not made a fine art of pregnancy so that this child could be raised in congested, smog-and-crime-ridden Los Angeles.

She crocheted while Matthew read, a plot brewing under her studiously calm surface.

It was early evening when her father stood and stretched and went for his jacket. "I promised to pick up Ryan tonight. That woman he's been riding with had to leave early for her son's football game. I'll leave a little early and pick up some of those brioches for breakfast tomorrow."

He leaned down to kiss her forehead, and she hugged him tightly.

"Think about what you want to ask him," he advised gently, "without name-calling or accusations, and I'll make myself scarce in the shower."

The moment he was out the door, Jo packed a small bag and called the cab company. This was a rotten thing to do to her father, who'd traveled all this way to be with her at the baby's birth, but it was the only solution she could think of for the baby.

No, Mama Jo. I don't want to leave Daddy. Mama Cass says it isn't a good idea. And I'm going to want out of here pretty soon.

THE CABDRIVER was the young woman with the Elvis button on her cap. She smiled at Jo a little nervously, her eyes focusing on the enormous jut of her stomach. "How's it going? You aren't going to have that in my cab, are you?"

Jo shook her head. "No. If all goes well, I'm having it in Port Townsend."

The cabbie frowned. "I don't have to drive you there, do I? That's two hundred miles away."

"No," Jo replied, watching the road in concern for the Volvo's headlights. But all the traffic was passing right by the condo's turnoff. "Just to the car rental agency."

"SO, you two had a good day?" Ryan asked. He'd driven back, and Matthew studied his profile for signs of guilt as he pulled into the condo's covered parking area.

Matthew slipped off his seat belt and unlocked the doors. "Yes. Jo tried to get you to join us for lunch, but you were already gone."

Ryan nodded as he pushed his door open. "Yeah. District brass was here. They insisted on the steak house outside of town, because someone at their hotel had recommended it. It was good, but I kept dozing off at my desk this afternoon."

"Heavy food?" Matthew asked casually as Ryan set the car alarm and started toward the door to the condo. "Or are you having trouble sleeping?"

Ryan wasn't certain whether the question was genuine solicitousness, or a subtle way to make him comment on the sleeping arrangements.

"Every time Jo moves during the night," he said, prepared to defend the situation if necessary, "I wake up, wondering if it's time."

To his surprise, Matthew smiled reminiscently. "I remember what that was like. Especially the first time. I was a basket case. Cassie was a week overdue."

Ryan unlocked the door, let Matthew inside, then pulled it to again. They walked to the elevators. "If Jo's a week late," Ryan said, "I think I'll need counseling, possibly even incarceration."

They rode up to the quiet floor and stepped off. "What's for dinner?" Ryan asked Matthew.

"Baked chicken," Matthew replied, thinking if the man was guilty of something, he must also be amoral. He seemed completely unaffected by it. "Rice. Carrots."

"Hmmm..." Ryan made an appreciative sound as he turned his key in the lock of their apartment door. "You wouldn't want to stay forever, would you?"

Ryan knew something was wrong the moment he stepped inside. It was too quiet. Her old tape player was usually playing the Mamas and the Papas when he arrived home. He knew the sequence by heart. "Dedicated to the One I Love," "My Girl," "Creeque Alley." And Jo was sitting in the recliner, working on the baby blanket, or setting the table, and playfully harassing her father about getting dinner ready because she was starving.

But there was no one in the kitchen, or in the recliner, and there wasn't a sound.

Of course, Matthew had come to pick him up. That was it. Maybe she'd decided to lie down, or take a shower.

"Jo?" he called. He started toward the bedroom at a walk, telling himself she would be there, supine on the bed, her stomach bulging like a little mountain, her hair fanned out on the pillow like sunlight.

When she wasn't there, he took two hasty steps to the bathroom, then strode anxiously across the hall to the guest room. Not there.

"Jo!" he shouted. He shoved open the door to the nursery, and found everything just as it had been since he'd completed the room three months ago—bright, pristine, waiting.

He turned, panic bubbling up inside him, and saw Matthew standing in the nursery doorway.

Ryan pushed past him and checked the coat closet. The blue coat and her beret were gone, as well as the tote bag that went everywhere with her.

"Her coat's gone!" Ryan shouted, meeting Matthew in the hallway. He didn't want to consider what that could mean.

"Simba's gone, too," Matthew said, a hand on his forehead. "And that package of things for bringing the baby home from the hospital."

Ryan felt a fury so terrible, he was afraid to speak for a moment. She'd done it. She'd run off with his baby, after all those promises that she wouldn't, after luring him into a sense of complacency with her smile and her natural ways. And all the time she'd been perpetrating a deceit.

"You should have told her," Matthew said quietly.

"Told her what?" Ryan was hardly aware of having asked the question, and was paying little attention to the answer. He was calculating times. If she'd been here when Matthew left, and he'd been gone only forty-five minutes, she couldn't have gotten far. Then he heard Matthew say, "Los Angeles."

He refocused his attention on his father-in-law. "What?" he demanded.

"She knows about you moving to Los Angeles," Matthew said. "Someone at the bank told her about your lunch with the district managers today."

"What do you mean? When?"

"When she went to ask you to join us for lunch today."

Ryan closed his eyes and groaned. "Oh, no. No."

"You should have told her."

Ryan didn't bother to argue. He headed for the door at a run, pulling his keys out of his pocket. Matthew followed.

He went to Coffee Country. Devon was closing up, and he looked concerned when he asked if he'd seen Jo.

"No, I haven't," he replied. "Haven't you?"

Ryan was in no mood. "If I had, would I be here?" he asked crossly, going into the back room to look. It was empty.

"I don't know," Devon answered, in the same tone. "Would you? You'd think a man would know how to keep track of the woman who's carrying his baby."

Ryan had Devon's shirt collar in his fist in an instant, but Matthew interceded. "Is there any way this is going to find Jo?" he asked reasonably.

"Jo," Ryan said to Devon in a deadly tone, "is my business, not yours."

Devon pulled Ryan's hand away from his throat. "Then why don't you know where she is?"

Ryan gave him a lethal look, then went to the other entrance and loped up the steps to her old apartment. It was dark, everything in it just as he'd left it the day he moved her into his place. A hole burned in his gut. Where was she?

He looked up Diantha's number in the book and called her from the apartment. She hadn't seen Jo or heard from her, and she was full of worried questions. Ryan promised to get back to her when he found Jo.

"She wouldn't have left town, would she?" Ryan asked Matthew. "Tomorrow's her due date, for God's sake. She wouldn't leave her doctor the day before she was to deliver, would she?"

Matthew would have preferred to believe she had more sense, but he knew her better than that. And he'd seen how angry and hurt she was.

"Is there a car rental agency in this town?" Matthew asked. "A bus station? She can't fly in her condition, can she?"

"Ah, yeah..." The tall, thin man locking up the car rental agency office remembered her. He held both hands way out in front of him. "Pregnant out to here?"

"That's her," Ryan said. "What did you rent her?"

He shook his head. "Nothing. She had no major credit card. You've got to have a—"

Ryan cut him off. "Right. Did she tell you where she was going?"

He started to shake his head, then remembered. "She said something about not needing a major credit card to take a bus."

Ryan repeated his story to the man behind the counter at the Greyhound office, behind the library.

"Yeah, I remember her," he said. He held both hands out in front of him. "Ten months pregnant?"

Ryan nodded wearily. "That's her. Where did she go?"

He shrugged. "Nowhere. We don't have a run north until tomorrow afternoon."

"Did she happen to say where she was going next?" Matthew asked.

He smiled wryly. "She said it was no wonder the diesel-guzzling airlines ruled the travel industry. They, at least, kept a daily schedule. I told her she'd missed our daily Seattle run, but she didn't seem to want to listen."

Ryan thanked him and raced for the airport. As he floored the accelerator, he concentrated on her being there. He didn't want to think about how far away from him she could get by air. Of course, this airline went only to Portland or Seattle, but from there—she could get anywhere.

The ticket clerk, a middle-aged woman with platinum hair and a wide smile said, "Oh, yes, I remember her. Very, very pregnant, and very, very angry when I told her a woman as far along as she was couldn't fly without written approval from her doctor."

Ryan felt relief—but just for an instant. "Did she say where she was going?"

The woman shook her head. "By that point," she said, "she was no longer speaking to me."

Ryan and Matthew sat in the car in the parking lot and stared out the windshield.

"I can't think of anything else to do," Ryan said, "but drive up and down the streets, check the hotels, maybe even the hospital."

Matthew nodded. "Take me back to the condo, and I'll make the calls while you drive around. I'll call you on that cellular thing if I learn anything, and you can call me if you find her."

Ryan turned the key in the ignition, thinking it was a weak and flimsy plan at best, but he could think of nothing better. He felt as though all light had deserted him.

He drove Matthew back to the condominium, turned the car off so that he could take the condo's outer door key off his ring to give it to his father-in-law. And that was when he saw her in the path of his headlights, sitting on the bench in the small landscaped area between the parking lot and the condominium. Simba sat beside her, taller than she was. She was crying.

Chapter Ten

Ryan was almost afraid to move, afraid she would take fright and run away. Then he was distracted from her woeful face by her considerable dimensions, and realized with gallows humor that she couldn't run anywhere. But he still employed caution.

"I'll go make coffee or something," Matthew said. He picked his way through the shrubbery, leaned over Jo and kissed her cheek. She kissed him back, they shared a brief murmured exchange, then Matthew disappeared into the building.

Ryan went to sit beside her. She was no longer sobbing, but tears continued to flow freely. He offered her his handkerchief. The air smelled of wood smoke and river water.

She gave him a suspicious look from under spiked lashes, then took it from him and dabbed at her eyes.

"Do you know," she asked, her tone tearful but quarrelsome, "that a pregnant woman can't leave this town? I think that's a form of discrimination the ACLU should look into."

He leaned an elbow on the back of the bench. She still looked as though she might bolt at any moment. In the glow from the floodlights behind the condo, he could see that her cheeks and nose were red, while every other inch of her that was visible seemed particularly pale. He wanted to touch her, but didn't dare.

"I know," he said calmly. "We traced your path from Ace Auto Rentals to Greyhound to the airport. How'd you get back home?"

She gave him a look that was less angry than frank. "This is your home, Ryan, not mine. My home is an apartment over the coffee bar."

He acknowledged the distinction with a nod, thinking privately that they'd fight that out later. "Then why are you here, and not at the apartment?"

"Because...all my stuff is here." She looked away from him when she replied. "And I left my keys when I thought I wasn't coming back. I came here in a cab."

"So, you came back because you want me to let you in so you can collect your things?"

She looked back at him then, her tear-filled eyes somehow managing to blaze. "I came back to tell you that even though I can't get away with Chelsea—" her voice was strained, but she forced the words out "—you're not going to raise her in Los Angeles."

He studied her quivering bottom lip for a moment, then replied quietly, "No, I'm not."

She swallowed and frowned. "What do you mean? You're moving."

"No," he repeated. "I'm not."

She pointed in the general direction of the bank. "But Roberta said..."

"That I'd been offered a promotion that involved moving to Los Angeles."

She spread both hands, frustrated and perplexed. "Well, that means... "

"That I was offered a promotion," he said patiently, "which I accepted, but only after we cut a deal. I'll have to travel to Los Angeles once a month, but I...am... not...moving there."

She stared at him for several seconds. She fell back heavily against the slats of the bench. "Oh," she said.

When he was searching for her, Ryan had been alternately furious that she would take off on him without one word of warning and terrified that she would succeed in getting away. Now that he knew she was safe, all the things that *could* have happened to a woman in her condition still left him with conflicting emotions.

"Is that all you have to say?" he asked coolly, "after scaring me to death, and walking out on your father when he came over three thousand miles to be with you? Where in the hell were you going, when your due date's tomorrow?"

Her eyes were still wide and pained. The knowledge that he wasn't leaving had provided some relief, but apparently not all she needed. Somehow, that annoyed him further.

"I was going to visit my friend Lisa, in Port Townsend," she replied. Then she asked, her voice raspy, "Why did you decide to stay in Heron Point?"

"Because I want to raise Chelsea here," he replied, his tone aggressive, "among nice people who have time for each other and for things that count. What? You didn't think I had a grip on what's important for a baby?"

Jo, an arm hooked around Simba, burst into noisy sobs. Ryan watched her in mystified fascination. Hormonal hysteria, Matthew had called it. That must be what this was. She didn't seem able to find comfort in anything he said. And he was trying. Considering that a part of him wanted to scream at her and shake her, he was really trying.

Jo was horrified to hear herself choking and gasping. She'd always hated women who cried when they should be making sense, but she seemed powerless over her own emotions.

Tonight had begun as an escape from what she'd thought was Ryan's decision to raise the baby in a giant, bad-smelling, crime-infested city. But as the evening wore on and she grew more and more desperate, she'd realized what was really at the heart of her attempt to escape. And she had to explain it to him. She wasn't sure she was up to it.

"Jo," he said gently. She felt his arm come around her shoulders. That only served to make her cry harder. But she still had to tell him.

"Ryan." She sat up and pulled herself together. She sniffed and wiped her nose and sniffed again. "I . . . have to tell you something."

"Fine. But why don't we go inside, where it's warm?" he suggested.

She shook her head. "No. I have to do it now. While I have the courage."

He leaned back again, an arm along the bench behind her. She could see in his eyes that he suspected. But, curiously, she saw no anger there. That confused her.

"All right," he said. "Tell me."

She raised her eyes to a dark, starry heaven—it was free of fog for the first time in weeks—and silently asked Cassie's forgiveness.

MAMA CASS says forget that and do it! Do it!

SHE HAD TO DRAW A BREATH to swallow her cowardice. "I've told myself . . ." she began in a raspy voice ". . . over and over during the last few months, that . . . that Chelsea isn't mine . . .'' She paused to draw another breath, and a sob rose in her throat. She willed herself not to succumb to tears again. ''But my heart doesn't believe it. Ryan, I love her so much. I've lived for her. I'm . . . I'm her mother.''

She held the handkerchief to her mouth, as though it could hold back the roiling emotions inside her, the groveling pleas on the tip of her tongue.

Ryan's eyes remained dark and quiet. Now that the words were spoken, she expected temper to flare there, accusations to remind her brutally that she'd known and accepted the conditions from the beginning.

But there was still no anger. Just a quiet acceptance that stunned and baffled her.

Ryan had somehow known all along, he thought, that it would come to this. It was contrary to nature to expect a woman to carry a baby for nine months, then willingly turn it over to someone else to raise.

And he'd lived with Jo for a month. He knew just how much love and attention and cherishing she'd invested in this baby. He knew how she talked to Chelsea, and read to her and sang to her—how she'd walk into the nursery when she thought he wasn't watching, and go to the crib and run her hands over the colorful bedding, or turn the musical mobile attached to it, imagining the baby there.

He'd watched her work on the crocheted blanket night after night, smiling unconsciously, humming a lullaby.

He knew Chelsea wasn't his alone.

''All right,'' he said.

Jo heard the words, but for a moment she could not imbue them with meaning. Then she was sure she'd misunderstood them.

"What?" she breathed.

He wrapped his arms around her and pulled her close. "I said, all right. You *are* Chelsea's mother."

Jo heard *those* words and knew she'd gone insane. She felt his arms tenderly, comfortingly enfolding her, and looked up into his eyes to see understanding there.

This was less than she'd dreamed, but far more than she'd ever truly hoped for.

"But...what'll we do?"

"The world is full of unorthodox families today," he said, holding her closer as a sharp night wind wove around them, then moved on to make the evergreens whisper. "We'll just stay together and raise her as the two parents who love her. For now, I think that's all the plan we need."

She looked up at him again in disbelief. "Can you do that?" she asked. "I mean, that's pretty...progressive for a conservative like you."

He smiled. To Jo, who only moments ago had felt like a drowning sailor, that smile was the beacon that would guide her home. "Yes," he said, with a philosophical tilt of his head. "I can. Love eventually makes liberals of us all, don't you think? And I love this baby. Come on. Let's go in."

ALL RIGHT! We're going to stay *together. Mama Cass says...well, she can't say anything. She's crying.*

Ah...Mama Jo. About the space in here...

AS RYAN LED HER INSIDE, Jo felt showered with blessings, bathed in the kindness of a generous God, though she was very aware that Ryan had said he loved the baby, not her. But the same love that had turned conservative Ryan Jeffries into a liberal had turned peace-loving Jo Arceneau into a warrior. All I need is time, Lord, she prayed, and I'll turn him into a screaming radical!

"How does everyone feel about omelets?" Matthew asked when they'd shed hats and coats and stood in the condo's living room. "It's a little late for a big meal."

Ryan glanced at the clock. It was 8:45. It occurred to him that the past two and a half hours had been among the longest of his life. Now a curious peace had settled over him.

That was due, he guessed, to the strange serenity that had overtaken Jo. She was looking at him as though he were somehow divine. He rather liked it, though he knew it was generated entirely, or at least mostly, by her desire to stay with the baby.

But one seldom had the upper hand with her. He intended to make the most of it.

She smiled at Matthew, wrapped her arms around him and told her she loved him.

"I love you, too, you incorrigible brat," he said. "See if I ever come and visit you again."

She kissed his cheek. "You didn't come to see me, you came to be one of the first to see Chelsea Annabel, and you know it. No omelet for me, please. Thanks, though."

"Tea?" he called after her as she waddled toward the bedroom.

"No, thank you," she called back sweetly.

Ryan followed her into the room. She had shaken out the baby afghan, and was inspecting it.

"When did you eat last?" he asked, determined that she wasn't going to let her health slide in the final stretch. He'd been more than lucky to get her back tonight safe and sound. He wasn't going to let anything happen to her now.

She held the blanket to her and gave him that adoring look over the top of it. "I bought some cheese crackers from a vending machine at the airport."

He closed his eyes and shook his head. "And Chelsea's supposed to do her windup on cheese crackers?"

She smiled widely, shook the blanket out again and let it float down on the bed. The delicate colors were soft against the dark blue of his quilt. She had done a beautiful job.

"Actually, I think she's beyond her windup, and stealing third." Then she turned to him with a husky laugh. "Or am I mixing metaphors? I mean, I know they're both baseball, but windup indicates pitching, and stealing third suggests..."

He suddenly realized what she was saying. He caught her arm. "Are you telling me you're in labor?" he demanded.

She nodded. "Pretty sure. At first I thought it was just false labor again, but I had a pretty good one on the bench, waiting for you to come home."

He felt suddenly frantic, and pushed her toward the chair. "Well, why didn't you say something? We have to get you—"

She shook her head, smiling that serene smile. "I think we have plenty of time. They're pretty far apart."

"How far?"

"What time is it?" she asked.

He knelt in front of her. "You mean, you're having one *now?*"

IT'S GETTING DARK and weird in here. Things are moving. Is this it? Is it my birthday?

"Uh-huh. What time is it?"

"Oh, God." He couldn't think. It was only when she

repeated the question that intelligence overrode emotion. He pulled off his watch. "It's 8:51."

She patted his shoulder and breathed out. "Good," she said after a moment. "Twenty minutes since the last one. This is just latent labor. I'm already packed for the hospital, so I'll probably have a couple of hours to make fringe."

Ryan blinked at her. She'd taken charge of her body, as Serena had directed, but she seemed also to have completely lost her *mind*.

"Fringe?" he asked.

She dipped her knees to reach into the crochet bag on the bed and pulled out a skein of yarn. She dipped her knees again and groped inside for something she couldn't seem to find. "Fringe," she replied. "For Chelsea's blanket. Shouldn't you be writing down the time of that contraction, so we sound like we know what we're doing when we call Dr. Mac?"

"Ah...right." Ryan opened the bedside-table drawer, where there was always a yellow pad for working into the night, and logged the time. "We won't tell him you're making fringe. He might decide childbirth has sent you over the edge. What in the hell are you looking for?"

"My fringe measure," she replied. "I cut it out just the other day."

Ryan took the bag away from her, and rummaged through it for her. "What does it look like? God, I can't believe I'm about to become a father and I'm groping in a bag for a fringe measurer."

Jo pushed him into the chair. "Daddy!" she shouted. "Would you bring Ryan a cup of coffee?" To Ryan she said, "Get it together, Jeffries. I'm going to need you."

"Right," he said. He drew a steadying breath. Then he caught her eye and gave her a wry grin. "I think I'd have been all right if you hadn't started talking about fringe."

She pointed to the bag in his lap. "It's just a square of cardboard. You wind yarn around it to measure the length of the fringe."

He frowned as he dug in the bag. "I thought fringe was loose?"

"It is. You wind the yarn over and over the cardboard. Then, when it's taken all it can hold, you cut one end, then you have a lap full of long strands of yarn doubled over to make fringe."

He tried to picture it and couldn't. But he did find the piece of cardboard. You'd have thought by Jo's reaction that he'd found a precious stone. He studied her wide smile and thought the blanket had become a symbol for her—a taking over of something Cassie had started. And her job was almost finished. Or just begun, depending on how you looked at it.

So they were in this together now, he realized with a gripping fist of fear in the pit of his stomach. So far, except for his initial contribution of sperm in a laboratory, Jo had done all the work concerning Chelsea. Now he had to see her through labor and birth. He felt both valuable and desperate to escape.

Matthew appeared with a steaming mug of coffee. His eyes went to Ryan, in the chair with Jo's needlework bag, and Jo, walking around the room and humming while winding yarn around a square of cardboard.

He smiled warily at Ryan. "Are we on 'America's Funniest Home Videos?' "

Ryan stood, put the bag on the bed and accepted the coffee gratefully. "We're having a baby," he said, toasting his father-in-law with his cup. "But we're making fringe first."

"What?"

"Never mind." Ryan turned him back toward the kitchen. "You'd better eat something. It's going to be a long night."

ALL RIGHT. He was getting the hang of this. Of course, it was about time he did. It had been almost eight hours, and they were now in transitional labor.

"Coming again," he warned Jo as he watched the fetal heart monitor register the beginning of another contraction. He firmed his grip on her hand and started breathing with her as she stiffened, grimaced, and finally emitted a primitive, eerie sound of pain.

Her nails dug into his knuckles, but he was more aware of her pain than of his, of keeping her breathing through the contraction to gain her at least the small measure of relief that provided.

"Going, going..." he said, watching the monitor. "Better?"

She sighed, her face flushed and wet with perspiration. He dabbed a wet towel on her cheeks and kissed her hand. "You are doing so great," he told her, amazed at what she'd endured during the long night.

Matthew, unable to bear the sight of his daughter in pain, was wandering the halls and bringing back gossip and reports. He'd come back shortly after midnight to tell them Jave and Nancy Nicholas had had their girl. Six pounds, eleven ounces. "Malia Rose," he'd said. Then he'd frowned. "Are there no Margarets or Elizabeths anymore?"

Jo had laughed. "This is a new generation of women, Dad. They're going to bring prosperity and peace and make men happier than they've ever been."

Matthew had exchanged a smile with him. "Tall order for anyone to fill."

Jo held on to his hand and breathed shallowly, obviously exhausted. He reminded her to take deep breaths, to try to relax.

MAMA JO, I'm coming, I promise. I'm just having trouble with the door!

"MY FEET ARE COLD," she complained.

"Okay. We'll take care of that." Pleased to be handed a problem he could do something about, Ryan went to her overnight bag for the knee socks they'd packed. He freed the blankets, found her feet and tugged the socks on. Just in time for another contraction.

He hurried back to her side to catch her hand and breathe with her through it. She finally fell back against the pillow with a dispirited groan.

"I think its time to choke me with my fringe, Ryan," she murmured.

He smoothed her hair back. "Actually, your dad took the blanket with him to the cafeteria. He's supposed to be working on it."

She smiled weakly. "I'll bet he's watching the sports channel and charming the nurses, and our baby's blanket will be bald."

Our baby. Even as Ryan smiled over her whimsical remark, those two words struck at the very heart of him. He'd accepted from a personal perspective that the baby wasn't his alone, but he hadn't considered what it would mean to share responsibility for a life with another person. With a woman. With Jo.

It was drawing them into an intimacy even deeper than what they'd shared when she was simply carrying Chelsea. They'd be cohabiting, planning together, reaching mutual decisions—pouring their love into the same child.

Was he ready for that?

As he contemplated the thought, Jo went into another contraction. He squeezed her hand, breathing with her, reminding her not to push, and decided that it didn't matter if he was ready or not. It was about to happen.

"Well, the baby will probably be bald, too," he said lightly as she came out of the contraction. "They'll match."

CHELSEA ANNABEL began to appear just before 10:00 a.m. on September 23.

"Bald as a billiard ball," Dr. McNamara said teasingly from his position at the foot of the bed. The blanket and its lack of fringe on two sides had been the joke that eased pain and tension for the last hour as Jo proceeded from labor to delivery. "You'll need fringe on the other side of that blanket. But we need the rest of her, Jo. Push her out."

Ryan supported Jo's back as she held her knees and pushed. Her hair now hung in damp spirals, and he couldn't imagine where she would be able to find another particle of strength with which to expel the baby.

HURRY, Mama Jo! It's so tight in here my head is pointed!

SHE LEANED BACK against Ryan's arm, panting.

Jo felt as though her entire world was ruled by grave exhaustion and excruciating pain. It was a revelation to learn that this kind of misery existed.

There would be a baby at the end of this ordeal, but at this moment, her pain seemed eternal, and it was impossible to consider a result, because a result suggested an end, and this had been going on forever.

She'd been such an innocent, she thought, when she agreed to do this for Cassie.

She realized in a state of near delirium that she hadn't thought about her sister since she'd gone into labor. This had all been so personal—so *hers*.

And Ryan had been a rock. Ryan was going to let her be Chelsea's mother. His hand felt so solid in hers. She clutched it, trying to absorb strength.

"Come on, Jo," he said gently in her ear. "One more push and we'll have her. One more."

She grasped her knees, trying to force the thought from her brain to the baby. Out. Out. Out.

She pushed long and hard. Words of encouragement came from Dr. Mac, and from Ryan, who supported her back and alternately praised and cajoled and bullied.

"I love you."

In the midst of all the excitement and activity around her, though she felt the mind-bending relief of the baby leaving her body, though for an instant everything swam and whirled around her with the cessation of strain, she heard every single one of the three words as clearly as though the room had been otherwise silent.

"What?" she whispered, not even sure who'd spoken. "What did you say?"

Then Dr. McNamara handed her a squalling mass with a bald head and a pruny little face, and her mind was swept clean by adoration of her daughter.

YOU DIDN'T TELL ME it would be this cold! Where's the
warm water? Where's the food? Where's my thumb?

"My... God," Ryan whispered in wonder, leaning over
her. "Chelsea."

His voice held the same note of reverence she felt. His
large hand cupped the tiny head, and the baby moved
against it, still screaming.

Then his index finger went to the barest suggestion of a
cleft in the tiny chin. Jo noticed it, and tears sprang to her
eyes. "Cassie's chin," she whispered.

She heard Ryan swallow, and then he stroked her arm
and kissed her temple. "Your voice," he told her. *His* voice
was choked and tight.

She turned to him, feeling Cassie's absence, but too
filled with joy that Chelsea was here and safe for grief to
even hurt. "She's beautiful," she whispered. "We did a
good job."

He leaned his head against hers. "Yes, we did."

Then the nurse reclaimed the baby to take her footprint
and weigh her.

"Eight pounds," she called from across the room, then
added with emphasis, "and *eleven* ounces!"

Jo groaned and laughed. "Is that all?"

The nurse looked over her shoulder to smile at Ryan.
"We have to tidy Jo up now, take a few stitches. Why
don't you take a break for about an hour?"

Ryan stood, easing Jo back against the pillows, his expression wry. "Sounds like you're in for even more fun. I
owe you big. I'll be back in an hour."

Jo caught his hand. Her eyes brimmed with tears.
"Cassie was here, Ryan," she whispered. "She didn't miss
it."

He leaned down to put his cheek to hers, and she felt the tension in him, one single quake of emotion. She wrapped her arm around his neck and held on.

"It's going to be all right," she promised. "We can do this."

He kissed her cheek and straightened, his eyes turbulent, but his face calm. "Right. See you in an hour."

Ryan felt as though his body and his mind might fly apart. It didn't seem possible that anyone could host the conflicting emotions he felt and survive.

Chelsea was here. Beautiful. Perfect. He felt a happiness and a relief so profound it was startling.

But Cassie wasn't here. Cassie, who had wanted Chelsea so badly, who'd come up with male and female names the night they learned Jo was indeed pregnant, who'd made elaborate nursery plans, elaborate life plans, she'd never been able to carry out.

His pain was as deep as his joy was high.

But he wasn't what mattered here. He had to get it together.

He met Jave Nicholas at the coffeemaker in the waiting room. He offered his hand and a congratulatory smile. "Jo's father was cruising the hall for news and told us about your baby. Good work."

Jave shook his hand. "Thank you. I heard Jo had been admitted. You taking a break?"

Ryan nodded. "A well-deserved one. Chelsea was just born about five minutes ago."

"All right!" Jave poured him a cup of coffee. "Congratulations to *you!* What'd she weigh?"

"Eight pounds, eleven ounces."

"Bigger than ours," Jave said, then added competitively, "But ours has hair."

Ryan grinned. "Got me there. Bald. Very bald."

"How's Jo?"

"Exhausted, but fine, all in all." He took a sip of coffee and closed his eyes as the near-boiling caffeine hit the vicinity of his chest and went down in a hot, restorative stream. "God, that's good. Nancy okay?"

Jave nodded. "Hard to imagine what a woman can go through and come out smiling. I'd have been demanding drugs during latent labor."

Ryan nodded. "And insisting on adoption as a means of acquiring future children."

"Amen." Jave downed the last of his coffee, crumpled the cup and tossed it in the plastic container under the table. He studied Ryan a moment, as though considering whether or not to ask the question on his mind.

Ryan saved him the trouble. "We're going to stay together and raise the baby."

Jave still looked as though he had a question.

"To share parenting duties," Ryan added, thinking that sometimes it was difficult to have friends who cared about you. It made them nosy.

"And that's all?"

"Yeah."

Jave shook his head at him. "I'm glad you take care of my money, and not my personal life. That'll never work, buddy. Nothing generates as much emotion, as much need to communicate, as much temper between parents, as children. You generate all that between a man and a woman who are just sharing space, and you know what results, don't you?"

"I'm sure you're going to tell me."

"Sex."

Ryan rolled his eyes. "Cassie's only been gone—"

"You're a single man with a woman and a child needing you, depending upon you." Jave clapped him on the shoulder. "You'll have to go into hiding if you want to keep your heart out of it."

"Did I hear someone mention sex?" A tall, fair-haired man, white lab coat unbuttoned at the throat, peered into the waiting room. "Nicholas!" he exclaimed, laughing. "I should have known it was you. You passing out cigars? We got word in ER about an hour ago."

Jave waved him into the room. "Hey, Nate. Congratulate another new father. Nate Foster, Ryan Jeffries, father of a bald little girl."

Nate came to shake Ryan's hand. "Sounds like my type. I drive a Jag convertible, and they're not always asking you to put the top up so they don't mess their hair. I suppose you already have rules about her dating older men."

"I'm sure he has some about her dating doctors," Jave said. "Aren't you supposed to be going away or something?"

Nate nodded, glancing up at the clock. "Another couple of hours, then I'm off for four weeks in western Canada." He rolled his eyes. "And God, do I need it. Almost thirty days of communing with nature, listening to the birds, eating fish I've caught myself in some sylvan stream." He smiled wickedly from one man to the other. "Sleeping under the stars. Or at least with a tent flap open to the stars. You two, on the other hand, will probably get very little sleep for the next month. Or the next several years. But I wouldn't be the one to make a point of my own good fortune."

"Someday," Jave warned, "you'll be walking the floor with a colicky baby."

Nate shook his head determinedly. "Not me. You stay away from women with marriage on their minds and you don't get into that kind of trouble."

Ryan turned to Jave. "What do you think? Headfirst in the coffeepot, or a wild ride down the stairs in a house-keeping bucket?"

Jave regarded Nate with a wry twist of his lips. "First one, then the other. I hope you get a tick in your sleeping bag."

"A pregnant tick," Ryan added.

Nate pretended indignation. "Well, it was nice to meet you, too. Geez. Stop by to offer a friendly hello, a little good cheer, and who appreciates you? No one." He looked at the clock again and groaned. "Gotta go." He backed toward the door, suddenly serious. "It really was nice to meet you," he said to Ryan. To Jave he added, "And give Nancy my best."

Ryan frowned wryly at the now empty doorway. "I think I was probably that smug once."

Jave shook his head. "Best emergency room doctor I've ever seen, but he always passes the kids in ER on to someone else. He doesn't like to work on them. Has an aversion to kids in all forms."

Ryan found that surprising in a man who'd seemed so good-natured. "Why?"

Jave shrugged a shoulder. "No idea. He's also very private. Well . . ." He offered his hand again. "This is my third, so I can tell you, your life will never be the same after this moment. So, take care. In a couple of weeks, when our lives settle down again, we'll cruise on the *Mud Hen.*"

Ryan nodded. "I'll look forward to it." Then he went to find his father-in-law.

Chapter Eleven

Jo went two weeks without sleep—or at least that was how it felt. Her eyes burned, everything in her and on her ached, but she couldn't ever remember being as happy as when she held Chelsea to her breast and watched her suckle. The depth of her emotion was as exhausting as the endless cycle of feeding, changing and walking the floor.

Even Ryan didn't seem to exist for her. She knew he was around mornings and evenings, somewhere on the nebulous fringes of her life, but there was never time to find him.

She remembered hearing the words "I love you" at the moment she delivered, knew they had to be Ryan's words. But he hadn't said them again.

She concluded the words had been spoken in the drama of the moment and had since been regretted.

She'd moved out of his room and back into her own, and she felt a little as though she were living alone.

"She cries an awful lot," Jo said worriedly to her father as she paced across the kitchen, bouncing the screaming baby at her shoulder.

WELL, my tummy hurts, and it's not as warm out here as it was in there, and it's all so... big!

MATTHEW, putting lunch dishes in the dishwasher, looked up to say cheerfully, "She's probably tired of looking at you. The doctor said she's fine, she's not allergic to anything. But you never let anyone else hold her. She's probably thinking, "Oh, no! Is that broad with the bloodshot eyes the only person in my life?"

Jo gave her father a scolding frown. "I'm just trying to do everything right."

"Doing everything right," he said, "would include letting her know she has a father and a grandfather. But you barely let us near her. I hear Ryan try to help you with her during the night, but you won't let him."

She stiffened at the unfair accusation. "He has to get up in the morning and go to work. I'm trying to help him get some sleep."

"You're trying," Matthew said, "to keep her to yourself."

"That's not fair."

"It's still true."

She sighed dispiritedly. "Cassie would have done this perfectly."

Matthew closed the door on the dishwasher and considered her. "I think we need to have a father-daughter talk. Bundle up the baby. I'll get our coats."

"But...it's cold," she protested.

"You need fresh air. Come on." He shooed her toward the nursery. "Get cracking. Wrap that bald blanket around her."

The still fringeless side of Chelsea's blanket remained their family joke. But her father didn't look as though he were kidding.

He was carrying the baby in a bright red belly pack Diantha had brought over when Jo came home from the hospital. He wore it unself-consciously, even strutted a little in it, as they walked along the road toward the marina.

Chelsea slept, her still bright pink face at peace, little bow mouth open and almost all that was visible under the pink-and-white knitted hat that matched the quilted snowsuit she wore. Matthew's hands clasped around the baby, held the crocheted blanket to her.

The day was crisp and cold, and an early frost had many of the trees of the hill already turning gold and copper.

"I think," Matthew said as they strolled along at a relaxed pace, "that you have to get some perspective here."

Jo, hands in the pockets of her blue coat, looked up at the tufty white clouds against the bright blue sky. "I have perspective. I'm a mother now. I have a lot to do. I'll get the hang of it."

"Jo, you already have the hang of it. But no one expects you to be Wonder Woman—even Cassie. Raising a child should be a shared experience from the very beginning. You're pushing Ryan away."

She stopped in indignation. "I'm not."

He, too, stopped, unconsciously patting the sleeping baby. "You are. And I know why."

She eyed him warily. "Really?"

"Not because you don't need him. You do. I see it in your eyes every time you look at him."

She folded her arms and demanded in a bored tone, "Then why?"

He looked her in the eye. "Because you don't want him to see you being less than perfect—less than you think Cassie would be in the same situation."

Jo decided that denial would be futile. For a man raising two teenage daughters, he'd understood them uncannily well. He apparently hadn't lost the knack.

She walked on. He followed.

"She was always prettier and smarter," Jo said matter-of-factly. "All I could do to be noticed was be braver, more heroic. That's why I agreed to have her baby. On one level, of course, it was because I loved her. But on another it was because I thought it was heroic. And I thought heroism was a step up from pretty and smart. Now, I'm not so sure. I feel inadequate and terrified."

"Don't you think all new mothers feel that way?"

"Cassie wouldn't have," she said with a sigh. "Cassie always had everything under control."

"Yeah, well . . . life isn't about taking control," Matthew said. "It's about working with what you're given, about making harmony—not necessarily order—out of all of our misfortunes and successes. You used to know how to do that."

"Daddy." They'd reached the marina, and Jo stopped to looked down at the irregular line of boats, their glass and chrome winking in the sunlight. She turned to her father. "I have a brand-new baby, whose father has agreed to let me be her mother, though in truth, she's no biological part of me. We've agreed to spend the next twenty or so years of our lives raising her together while sharing space in a home, but not a bed. And over both of us is the memory of the wife and sister we both adored. Finding harmony there would be a trick for Houdini."

He put an arm around her shoulders and smiled. "Well, if it was easy, it would be fiction. It isn't. It's life." He squeezed. "So just be you and go after what you want."

She looked up at him, not certain what he meant, surprised by what he *might* mean.

He nodded. "That's right. We all loved Cassie. But for the sake of this baby, the two of you have to move on without her. She's gone."

Jo put an index finger to the tiny cleft in the baby's chin. Her voice was heavy. "She's not, though, Daddy. She's in this baby. Every time Ryan looks at her, he sees Cassie."

"And that's just fine, honey, as long as when he looks at you," he said significantly, "he sees you."

RYAN CAME AWAKE at the sound of Chelsea's screech. He got out of bed, as he always did, and went to the nursery door. But this time there was no Jo bustling across the hall, looking urgent and desperate, telling him to go back to bed, that she'd take care of it.

He'd always willingly obliged her, because he knew every time she looked at him she was remembering that he'd told her he loved her. And he wasn't anxious to confront or try to explain what he felt. He was in love with two women, one who'd passed away, and one who was very much alive, and he had no idea what to do about it.

He peered into Jo's room and saw her lying on her stomach, clearly in a deep, exhausted sleep. He pulled her door closed.

In the glow of a Lion King night-light, he went to the crib and leaned over the little bundle of arms and legs, uncovered and moving with robotic stiffness. He replaced the soft quilt Chelsea had kicked off and lifted her into his arms.

The feeling of the warm, wiggling body against him was still new enough to make everything else recede for a moment while he experienced the wonder of it. And—giving him an everlasting sense of accomplishment and near divinity—the baby stopped crying.

He tilted her back in his hand to look into her face, and found her looking right back at him. Jo's book, which he'd been reading whenever he found it out of her hands, said babies saw only in black and white. Since he was dark-featured, he decided his daughter was probably getting a fairly accurate picture of him. He smiled.

Hi, Daddy! I was wondering where you were.

"Hi, Snooks," he said. "What's the problem? Hungry?"

What have we got?

"Wet?"

Yes, I am.

"Yeah? Well, we know what to do about that." He went to the changing table and put her down. She reached up for him with arms and legs, as though she were a little monkey and he the mother monkey—or the tree. The Moro reflex. He'd read about that, too. The primal urge to remain connected.

"I haven't actually *done* this before, you understand," he said, reaching under the table for a cotton diaper. They'd been given several packages of disposables, but Jo had hidden those at the back of the closet for emergencies that somehow superseded environmental awareness. "But I've seen it done several times, and Jo has these all folded and specially prepped with liners."

Chelsea watched him with grave, bug-eyed interest.

Don't forget the wiper thing, and the powder.

"Okay. Off with the old." He tossed the liner away and put the diaper into a covered bucket filled with sudsy water that Jo had against the wall. He wiped and powdered her. "On with the new." He struggled a little with the pins as the baby squirmed.

WATCH IT WITH THOSE, Daddy!

THE DIAPER finally in place, Ryan admired the perfect, doll-like little legs protruding from the bulky mass of cotton fabric. He caught one gently in each hand, his fingers covering it from toe to torso, and marveled at them—knobby little knees, tiny little toes, minuscule toenails.

But Chelsea apparently resented the restriction, and began to bellow.

I WANT OUT OF THIS ROOM. I want to be carried around, sung to, rocked. And what did you say we had to eat?

"ALL RIGHT, all right," he said, lifting her up again and putting her against his chest. She rooted at this throat. "Your mother doesn't like to be held down, either. Well, actually, neither did your other mother. You probably don't even know you've already had two, do you?"

YES, I do. Mama Cass told me all about it. She says to touch you and tell you that she loves you.

RYAN FELT the tiny flailing hand hit his cheek. He caught it and kissed it. "I love you, too, Snooks. Come on. We'll talk about it over a midnight snack."

Ryan held the baby to him in one large hand, and took the bottle of expressed breast milk from the refrigerator. He ran it under warm water, then cradled Chelsea in his arm and teased her lips with the nipple. She complained about the change in position, until she realized it meant milk. Then she sucked happily, grunting and gurgling.

He stroked her cheek with his index knuckle and watched her tiny fist flail the air.

"So—you had a mother whose name was Cassie. Cassandra, really, but she never let anybody call her that. She said it was pretentious. Anyway...she worked very hard to bring you here." The little fist flailed. He considered it her way of encouraging him to go on with his story.

YES, I know her. She says I'm the best thing she's ever done—next to marrying you.

"SHE COULDN'T CARRY YOU, so she gave you to your aunt Jo to take care of until you could be born." He carried the baby to the sofa, put his feet on the coffee table and stretched out. Chelsea lay contentedly on his chest, still guzzling milk. "Then, almost right after that... there was an accident..."

DADDY, I know all this. You don't have to...

HIS THROAT TIGHTENED and he kissed the top of the baby's head. Grief welled up in him, but for the first time in months, he found something easing it; the warm bundle lying atop him.

"This is the hard part," he explained. He heard the tight sound of his own voice in the living room, which was lit only by the light over the stove in the kitchen. He swallowed and went on. "There was an accident," he said again, "and your mother Cassie died. But you were lucky, because you were growing inside Jo, who was taking really good care of you. And somewhere along the way, Jo changed from your aunt to your mother."

The baby drew away from the bottle finally, squirming and fussing. Ryan set the bottle aside, put the baby to his shoulder and patted her back. "I know this is all very complicated, but I think you should know how much... how much love went into bringing you into this world. And how much love greeted you when you arrived. Your grandfather—that white-haired man with the beard who leaned over your crib and made ridiculous noises..."

YEAH. I love that!

"HE CAME all the way across the country just to see you. He's gone home now, but he stopped by the bank before he left and put money into a special account so that when it's time for you to go to college, there'll be enough to send you to Harvard. There'll be time to talk about that later, but that's what you're faced with everywhere you turn, Snookie. Love. Lots of it. It'll be good for you. A little complicated for me, but good for you."

Chelsea burped.

"Good," Ryan said, continuing to pat. "I'm glad you appreciate it. I don't have to tell you, I suppose, how much your mother Jo loves you. Every time you peep, she comes running. I have to get up in the middle of the night to spend time with you. I think she's even forgotten *I'm* here. Not that I want to steal your thunder or anything, but I was kind of getting to like those adoring looks across the room after I told her we could share you. Once, I think I even caught a lustful glance in the bedroom mirror when she thought I was asleep. Or maybe I imagined it. My life seems so damned complicated these days. Whoa. Forget you heard that. *Damn* isn't for ladies. I know it's a sexist attitude, but I don't like it when ladies swear.

"Would you like a puppy?"

YEAH. A big one, with lots of babies!

"YOUR CONDO AGREEMENT doesn't allow pets, does it?" Jo, in her purple velour robe, put a knee on the sofa and curled up beside him. She put a hand to the baby's head, as though she couldn't be that close and not touch her. "And anyway, you might want to approach her about it when she's *awake.*"

"Hmmm..." he said, wondering how much Jo had heard. "And I thought I had her complete attention."

"When I came in, you were telling her ladies shouldn't swear." She gave him a smile that was sweetly indulgent. It relieved him. It seemed the love dilemma could just slide for a while. "She probably figured she didn't have to pay attention to that for at least a year and a half. She won't be talking until then." Then she frowned apologetically. "I'm sorry I didn't hear her. Why don't you go back to bed? I'll put her down."

He shook his head. "This is my responsibility, as well as yours. You have to let me help you."

Jo smiled around a yawn. "I know. My father chewed me out about that. I'm sorry. I was just... You know. Trying to be perfect."

"I'm sure no one's requiring that of you," he said quietly. "Even Chelsea."

Seated beside him on the comfy sofa in the nearly dark living room with their baby on his chest, understanding that perfection was *not* required of her, Jo felt both mellow and deliriously happy. "Were you serious about the puppy?" she asked.

He looked around the beautifully appointed but small living room. "Yes. It's time to start thinking about a yard with a sandbox, a dog to protect Chelsea, room to run." He smiled at her companionably. "And you need more room to spread out than that bedroom gives you."

He caught her eye as he said that. She wondered if there was a message there for her, then decided it was simply wishful thinking. She didn't need space. All she wanted was to be invited into his. But until he understood that, all she could do was agree. "That would be nice."

"I'll keep my eyes open," he said. "River view, or something on the edge of the woods?"

"I love the river view." She yawned again. He hooked an arm around her and pulled her head down to his shoulder.

She tried to take the gesture calmly, not to betray delight. But she couldn't resist snuggling in. "But the nursery's so perfect here."

"True," he said. "But we'll just put all her great stuff in the new one. We can even paint it the same way, reinstall the carpet."

A house, she thought greedily. Ryan and the baby and me in a *house*. Like a kaleidoscopic glimpse into the future, she foresaw birthday parties, Christmas trees, badminton games, tree houses, barbecues, snowmen. She shuddered with excitement.

Ryan, misinterpreting the gesture, pulled the afghan off the back of the sofa and draped it over her one-handed. "Better?"

She took advantage of his misunderstanding to snuggle farther into him. "Mmm..." she said. And as his arm closed firmly around her shoulder, it was her last coherent thought.

"I CAN'T BELIEVE," Diantha said, cooing into the baby carrier that held Chelsea in a quilted pink blanket, "that she's almost six weeks old. It seems like you just had her. I'm glad you decided against hiring Mrs. Bennett, dear soul that she is, and are looking after the baby yourself. Watch Chelsea's eyes follow my bracelets."

Jo, between customers, leaned on the counter beside her daughter and marveled at how she'd grown. She'd gained more than two pounds, was awake and watching her more often, and responded to the sound of her voice. But she seemed to save her smiles for Ryan, who liked to lie in the middle of the floor on his back and use her like a free weight. At those times, she would open her mouth wide, and gurgles of delight would fill the room.

Tom Nicholas, in coveralls and a baseball cap, burst into the bar.

"The usual," he said, reaching to the counter for the paper, then spotting the baby. Smiling, he came to stand beside Diantha and made funny faces at Chelsea.

Chelsea flailed her arms. She definitely had a thing for men, Jo accepted.

Then the counter filled with newcomers, and Jo left Chelsea to the attentions of her admirers.

Ryan came in several moments later, and went straight to the spot where the carrier usually stood, at the end of the counter. Jo watched him raise an eyebrow when he saw that the carrier was there but the baby wasn't. He looked up at her with a frown.

She pointed to the corner of the shop, where Jave and Nancy Nicholas sat, *each* holding a baby. They were standing the babies face-to-face, obviously introducing them. The two of them studied each other curiously— Malia looking horrified, Chelsea grinning broadly, pink gums exposed. Tom sat on the other side of the table, laughing at their expressions.

"Hi, Baldy!"
"Hi, yourself! Where'd you get that wig?"

JAVE AND NANCY WAVED, and Ryan waved back. "Another month of all this attention," he said to Jo as he straddled a stool, "and we won't be able to do anything with her."

Jo began to prepare his latte.

"I need it to go," he said quickly, when she poured a shot of espresso into a tall glass. "Busy afternoon."

"Okay." *Another* busy afternoon? She was aware that her tone was mildly testy as she poured the espresso from the glass into a paper cup. But this was the way they'd been dealing with each other for the past week. Not only had he not repeated his love words, but after several weeks of their coexisting in relative peace, their relationship had taken an unpleasant turn.

Ryan had been tense and she'd been edgy, and they'd engaged in some artful needling. She suspected their house-hunting had precipitated it, though she wasn't certain. But something was keeping Ryan away from her for longer periods. Chelsea managed to snag his attention during the night with a cry from the nursery that invariably brought him to her, his deep voice rumbling quietly in the darkness.

Jo contributed to the tension between them by pretending nothing was wrong. It annoyed him, and she knew it. She found that satisfying.

"It's supposed to be impossible to spoil babies at this stage," she said over her shoulder. "More attention is just more sensory impressions for her to absorb and store. Jave and Nancy have invited us for Thanksgiving."

"That's nice," he said. But his tone didn't match the words. He annoyed *her* by saying one thing when he clearly meant another. "But I was thinking we'd go away for that weekend."

She raised an eyebrow as she turned back to the counter and dolloped foamed milk onto the top of the concoction. "Really. Where?"

"I don't know. Down the coast. East to Bend."

She dropped a stirring straw into the drink. "Who gets to keep the baby?"

He frowned. "What do you mean? We'll bring her with us."

"But whose room does she stay in? Your room or mine? Will we have a connecting door, so whoever doesn't have her will have easy access to her? Or will one of us have to leave his or her room in the dark to visit the baby in the middle of the night?" She fired the questions at him with a sudden vitriol that surprised her, as well as him.

He studied her, eyes narrowed. She turned quickly away, afraid the cause of that little outburst would be as obvious to him as it suddenly was to her.

Ryan stood and took the paper cup in one tense but steady hand. A foul mood had been ripening in him all day, and he was in no position to deal with hers. He decided to ignore it.

"Did you remember the Heron Point Has It meeting tonight?" he asked briskly.

"Merchants have been calling us day and night," she replied evenly, wiping off the espresso machine. "How could I forget?"

He let that, too, pass. "What do you want to do about dinner?" he asked.

She turned to him, an eyebrow raised, the cleaning rag crumpled in her hand. "Eat it, perhaps?"

He grasped his temper with both hands. "Before or after the meeting?"

"*You're* the cook."

"*That's* why I'm asking."

Her expression seemed to crumple for a moment. Then she stiffened and slapped the rag on the counter. "Your call," she said. "I'll do whatever."

"Thank you," he said, his tone suggesting she'd done nothing to earn gratitude.

He stopped at the Nicholases's table on the way out, put his cup down and took his daughter from Jave. He dipped his index finger into the foamed milk and put it to her mouth. She sucked it greedily.

Hi, Daddy! Yum. I'm cuter than her, don't you think? She has all that ugly hair.

"MALIA AND CHELSEA have agreed to have a slumber party in July 2009," Nancy said. "Chelsea has to bring the potato chips."

Ryan had to rouse himself out of his dark mood to deal with her cheerful silliness. "Who's chaperoning this gig?"

"Jave and I will be there, of course. Because now there are boys on the horizon. You know, potential slumber-party crashers."

When he looked surprised, she explained with a broad smile, "Remember Karma Endicott, from our Lamaze class?"

"Oh, right." He began to put it together. "She had a boy a month early, on the same day our two were born.

And Roberta Dawson was out of town. The only one of us coaches who truly did get to escape.''

Nancy nuzzled Malia, who flailed her arms and legs in appreciation. "You have to admit it was all worth it.''

Ryan looked down into his daughter's interested gaze and had to admit that it was. But that didn't stop him from thinking he wasn't sure the same was true of her mother.

He kissed Chelsea's cheek and handed her back to Jave. "When they start talking elopements, put her back in the carrier, would you?'' He chucked Malia under the chin and went back to the bank.

Chapter Twelve

"You're speeding." Jo delivered the accusation calmly, then glanced over her shoulder at the infant seat in the back of the car, in which Chelsea snored happily, unaware of the ripe hostility in the front.

"I'm not speeding," Ryan replied, a ragged edge to his quiet voice. "I have the car under complete control." He wished he could say the same for himself.

Jo tossed her head. He saw the gesture out of the corner of his eyes. She'd worn her hair loose to the Heron Point Has It meeting, and it billowed around her like a spiraled halo.

"That's your answer for everything, isn't it?" she asked.

"What?"

"Control. *Complete* control. Even at meetings."

He made a scornful sound. "So that's it. You were out of order, Josanne. Marsh was still talking."

"Out of order!" she shouted. "It wasn't Parliament, Jeffries! It was a simple downtown association meeting!"

"In which you were out of order."

He slowed to turn onto the road that led to the condos. If Chelsea hadn't been in the car, he thought, he'd have loved to take that corner at full speed and see how Jo liked that.

"You!" Jo said, jabbing him in the shoulder, "are the one who's out of order. Your head is out of order. Your heart is out of order! Your whole damn body..." she suggested hotly in the darkness as they pulled into the covered parking area, "...is probably out of order!"

Silence dropped over them like a blanket. The tension that had governed their lives for the past six or seven days was now a living thing between them—palpable, audible, almost visible.

She reached into the back for the baby, but he brushed her aside, untying the straps and holding Chelsea to him as he stepped backward out of the car. He left Jo to carry the diaper bag and blankets. He marched ahead, unlocked the door and held it silently while she marched through, chin at a defiant angle.

As they waited for the elevator, he kept his eyes determinedly from the short, formfitting blue-and-gold sweater she wore over her favorite long denim skirt. Combined with the graceful lace-up granny boots she wore, it made for a stylish version of the thrown-together look she usually preferred. Everyone had told her tonight how wonderful she looked.

He'd noticed, too. But, though she'd had smiles and glowing baby reports for everyone else, she'd had only sniping and sarcasm for him. When she disrupted the meeting by insisting that none of the booths use foam cups and containers because of their nonbiodegradability, he'd taken a certain satisfaction as chairman of the meeting in insisting that she be quiet until the floor was opened for discussion.

Then, when she'd finally had her say, he'd been more than happy to tell her that the chair had already foreseen that issue and obtained paper receptacles for all involved.

She'd thanked him politely, if stiffly, and folded grace-
fully into her chair. But there'd been murder in her eye.

He'd been more than happy to confront it.

And if she was going to impugn the competence of his
brain, his heart *and* his body, he would happily settle the
question for her. On all counts.

In the apartment, he put the baby in her crib, and
breathed a sigh of relief when she wriggled and grunted,
but never opened her eyes.

*I'M NOT SPEAKING to either of you until you stop shouting.
Good night.*

HE PULLED the nursery door partially closed, and went in
search of Jo. She was not in the kitchen or the living room,
and he was damn sure she wasn't in his bedroom. And her
bedroom door was closed. He pushed it open, and found
her sitting on the side of the bed, pulling off her boots.

"Come out here," he ordered, and went into the living
room to wait for her to comply.

She did. She walked in in her stockinged feet, arms
folded, expression superior, almost pitying. She stopped
within a yard of him.

"What?" she asked.

He had pulled off his suit coat and tie. He now stood in
the middle of the living room, unbuttoning the French
cuffs of his white shirt. "There seems to be a question,"
he said, "about my ability to function on several levels."

Jo looked heavenward. "This is so sophomoric of you,
Ryan."

"I don't think so," he said, folding back the cuff on his
left sleeve. "When I suggested you were out of order at the
meeting, you called me on it. You weren't happy until

Diantha read from *Robert's Rules of Order*." He rolled up the other sleeve. "And you just called me 'out of order.'"

Despite her outward appearance of boredom, Jo watched the tensile grace of his movements in bemused fascination. She had no idea what he was up to. She could only judge by the vague combination of unease and excitement brewing inside her that it was going to be trouble. And that was something she already had in abundance.

She pretended disinterest. "But there are no *Robert's Rules* for the kind of order you're out of."

Sleeves rolled up, he rested his hands on his hips. "Then we'll just have to work it out ourselves—won't we?"

She was tempted to run for it, but she'd endured childbirth not too long ago. She felt cocky. "And how do you suggest we do that?" She knew it was a loaded question, but she asked it anyway.

He took two steps toward her and closed the distance between them. They would touch now, if either one of them reached out.

"Well, we'll take the accusations one at a time," he said quietly. "You suggested my brain isn't functioning." He shrugged a shoulder with almost good-natured amusement. "While I prefer to behave modestly, I'm forced to point out that I'm the manager of a bank, and that I've just been given a prestigious promotion."

"True," she conceded, her arms folded so tightly she wondered if they might break off. They seemed to be all that stood between her and Ryan. When she breathed out, she could feel the cotton of his shirtsleeve against her elbow. She found it difficult to pretend disdain when tension and lust were about to strangle her. "But...a high I.Q. doesn't necessarily... indicate intelligence and common sense."

To her surprise, he agreed. "You're a prime example of that. You're concerned about all the world's causes, but you don't know what's going on under your very own nose."

Her hands were suddenly fisted on her hips. "What do you—?"

He cut her off. "But we're talking about me, aren't we?"

He moved, and she resisted the instinct to shrink away. But instead of touching her, he simply walked slowly around her, like some predator toying with his prey. Again his shirtsleeve brushed the tip of her elbow. She stood her ground, her heartbeat tripping out of control. She felt his breath against her ear as he spoke.

"You said my heart was out of order." He bumped her other elbow, then came around to stand directly in front of her. A breeze could not have fit between them. "I remind you that I have many friends, and a baby daughter who now recognizes me and shrieks with delight every time I touch her." He paused. She prayed for her next breath. "Would someone without a heart," he asked, "elicit that kind of reaction?"

She opened her mouth to reply, but could make no sound. His eyes locked on hers. There seemed to be no breath in her lungs.

He shifted his weight. His cotton brushed against her wool.

"And then you said," he reminded with feigned confusion, "that my body was out of order. What did you mean by that, specifically?"

The words crowded to the tip of her tongue. *I meant that I adore you, that all I can remember when I go to bed is what it was like for those few days to sleep in your arms, and all my dreams are full of images of the two of us making love. I meant that I know your body reacts to mine, but it doesn't seem to reduce you to the same frustration I feel. You're so controlled. You can feel need and desire, but it doesn't force you to reach for me the way I want to reach for you.*

But she couldn't speak.

Then he raised a long-fingered hand in front of her face. "Do you think there's something wrong with my hands?" he asked softly, at the same moment he touched the side of her face. She closed her eyes and swallowed as he ran his fingertips along her jaw to her chin, then gently down her throat until he reached the neckline of her sweater.

Then he finally took that fractional step that brought them body to body, and she found herself in his embrace. Her eyes flew open.

"Perhaps you think my arms don't function," he said, tightening them around her so that there was little doubt. Her breasts flattened against the solid wall of him, and she shuddered with the relief of it, and the subtle agony. Corded muscle held her in place.

"Or my legs?" At that he braced a foot on the ottoman and dipped her backward over his bent knee, as though they were in the middle of some sophisticated tango. She uttered a strangled little cry and gripped his upper arms. The thigh against her back was like oak.

And then she finally saw it in his eyes—passion that ran as deep as hers, desire billowing out of control. Naked need. Maybe he couldn't repeat the words she wanted to hear, but he felt them.

And that was all it took to ignite those smoking emotions in her. She loosened her grip on his arms and slid her hands up to his shoulders and around his neck. She locked her fingers together and pulled his face down to hers.

"Well, if your legs work," she said softly, "you'd better run while you can."

Ryan had watched the expression on her face change from anger, to wariness, to languid desire—and he finally understood what had raged between them this past week. Words of love, once spoken, could not be allowed to slide. They demanded recognition. And action.

He'd thought he couldn't or shouldn't love a woman so soon after Cassie's death, but the new life they shared in his daughter had turned his focus, out of necessity, from what he'd lost to what he held. Chelsea. Josanne.

And this was more than frustration. It was newfound passion. Desire finally free of confusion. This was right. This was what he wanted.

"Watch," he whispered against her mouth, "how well they work." He straightened, lifting her into his arms, and carried her into his bedroom.

Jo tightened her grip on him, unable to believe this was happening. She looked into his eyes when he stopped at the edge of the bed. "Ryan," she whispered, hating herself for needing to give him a way out. "Are you sure?"

He rubbed his chin against her cheekbone. "Are you?" he asked in sudden concern. "It's just been six weeks since you had Chelsea."

She kissed his jaw, touched by his concern, fueled by his willingness to think twice. "Dr. Mac said it was all right." She tightened her grip further and nipped his ear. "I think he knows...I love you."

He set her on her feet, his smile white in the darkness. "I love you," he said, then opened his mouth over hers as his hands reached up under the hem of her sweater to lift it up.

He paused as his fingertips touched a warm, firm breast encased in silky fabric. He felt a strangely primal reaction, a need to feel in his palm the instrument of his child's nourishment and his woman's beauty.

She helped him pull the sweater off, and he reached around her to unhook the nursing bra. He took the full globes carefully in his hands, the strong nipple against his palm. They were warm and heavy, and he heard a small, shuddering sigh escape her.

"Tender?" he asked, stroking a thumb gently across the tip.

She put her hands to his waist and leaned into him for balance, his touch weakening her spine, almost buckling her knees. "No," she said on a little laugh. "Wonderful. I warn you, though. When I'm not pregnant or nursing, I have a very unimpressive chest. You, on the other hand..." She reached up to pull at the buttons of his shirt. Under it was a crisp white T-shirt that she pulled out of his pants.

He dropped his hands from her to shrug out of the shirt and pull off the T-shirt. She ran exploratory fingertips up his muscled torso, through the wiry dark hair covering his pecs, to the impressively wide line of his shoulders.

"...are magnificent," she said.

He kissed her. "That might be mildly overstated," he said, slipping his fingers into the elastic waistband of her skirt. "But thank you."

His fingertip met silk, and he reached into another elastic band and found yet more silk. His hands explored inside the last elastic band and found silk again—but this time it was the silk of flesh.

Jo felt his warm, strong hands touch her hipbone, then move around to her bottom and cup her possessively. She kissed his collarbone and whispered his name.

He drew the layers of clothing over her hips and down her thighs until she could step out of them. Then he tossed skirt, slip and panties aside.

She unbuckled his belt and unbuttoned and unzipped his pants. Ryan closed his eyes as her hands explored as his had done. The tips of her fingernails traced a line over his buttocks, and down the backs of his legs, as she pulled down on his slacks and briefs.

He sat on the edge of the bed to kick them off, then wrapped an arm around her waist and pulled her to the mattress with him.

"The least discomfort," he said, holding her to him as he pushed them to the middle of the bed, "and I want you to stop me."

"I'll be fine," she assured him, fascinated at the realization that she now sat astride him, when there'd been such antagonism between them for so long. Somehow, by some miracle, that had all disappeared, and here was this wildly beating passion that had their fingers linked—as though they had been linked through time and eternity.

She leaned down to kiss his chest, and he held her shoulders away from him so that he could look into her eyes.

"I mean it, Jo," he said. "You have no idea how you'll feel. The book says it could be..."

She melted with tenderness. Every step along the way in this pregnancy, he'd known almost as much about it as she did, because he'd read her book. Before she moved in with him, he'd borrowed it, and since they'd been living together, she would come upon him reading it when she'd thought him busy with something else.

"Do you have to do everything," she asked teasingly, nipping his chin, "by the book?"

"Jo..."

"I will be fine." She kissed a line across his collarbone, then from shoulder to shoulder. "But if you don't stop worrying," she warned, "*I* might hurt *you*—on purpose."

"Joey, I want..." he began, intending to be stern with her.

But she was moving back down his body, stringing kisses along the center of him, and he couldn't remember what he'd wanted an instant ago. He felt her fingertips over his hipbones, in the concavity of his stomach, along the length of his maleness. And when he was sure that would kill him, he felt the ends of her hair like strands of silk following her touch—over his hipbones, in the concavity of his stomach, along the length of his maleness. All he wanted now was to be inside her.

She rose over him and guided him, her artful fingers negating all his efforts to move slowly. She swayed atop him like a flower in the breeze. He braced her hands with his, moving his hips with hers as they traced the circle that defined so much of life—man, woman, eternity.

Jo felt no pain, only ecstasy. She, too, had read that chapter of the book and had been sure the pleasure would far outweigh the possible pain. But even she had had no idea.

She felt as though heaven had opened to her and showered her with its secrets. This was love—not simply love-making, but love-giving, a sharing beyond anything she'd ever known or understood. And sharing it with Ryan gave her life meaning—even apart from her identity as Chelsea's mother, and her own personal pride in herself as a woman.

Then all lofty thought about what love meant was absorbed in the onslaught of physical sensation. The artful circling of him beneath her; the tantalizing beginning, the swelling approach of fulfillment that taunted nearer and nearer. And finally the explosion, the delicious gift of climax that tumbled over and over her, making her body quake with its power.

Ryan felt her fingernails in his knuckles and remembered another moment, on the brink of Chelsea's birth, when she'd dug her nails into him and cried out. Now, as she clung to him with that same desperate need for him, he erupted inside her, all pleasure and revelation, and thought that at this moment she'd given birth again—this time to him.

THEY LAY wrapped in each other's arms, one side of the blankets they'd never turned down pulled over them. Jo had never known such happiness.

"I take it back." She burrowed her nose sleepily into his throat.

"What's that?" he asked lazily, twining one of her spiraled curls around his fingertip. He felt a deep-down joy that radiated to every hidden corner of his being.

She sighed and kissed the underside of his chin. "You're definitely *not* out of order."

His soft laugh was rich and self-satisfied. *"Robert's Rules* was wrong about you, too. Geez."

She leaned her head back to look into his eyes. "I love you. Did I ever get to say that?"

He kissed the tip of her nose. "You can say it again. Repeat it often."

She nibbled at his lips, murmuring, "I love you. I love you."

They were settling down again, arms and legs entangled, when a demanding cry came from the nursery. They groaned together. Then Ryan laughed. "I'll get her."

Jo caught his arm. "Bring her back to bed. I'll feed her here."

Ryan, propped up against the pillows, held Jo and Chelsea in his arms while the baby ate, noisily, greedily.

Jo was delirious with the pleasure of Ryan's arms around her and the healthy, pink-cheeked baby they'd worked so hard to bring to life.

MAMA CASS?

"*It's all right, darling. I'm supposed to be forgotten. Keep eating.*"

RYAN TIED the strings at the throat of his Dracula cape and studied his reflection in the bathroom mirror with a disgruntled frown. In front of him, Jo, in a ruffly pink silk organza top, applied a beauty mark just below her bottom lip with an eyebrow pencil.

"Dracula is so trite," Ryan said, putting a hand to the hair she'd slicked back for him and making a face.

Jo, who'd been listening to his grumblings since she'd brought the costumes home the day before, straightened to study her makeup. "It was all the costume shop had left," she said absently. "And since Chelsea and I went all the way to Longview for them, I should think you'd be grateful." She pressed her lips together and patted down the pile of gold curls atop her head. She tugged her sleeves off her shoulders and studied her reflection critically. "And since Anne Rice brought the vampire Lestat on the scene," she went on, glancing up at Ryan's reflection, "vampires are anything but trite. Show me some teeth."

He frowned doubtfully at her assurances and said, with stubborn insistence, "I am *not* putting on false fangs."

She turned to him, the bottom half of her clad only in ruffly pantalets. She'd left off the hoop and skirts that would have taken up the entire space in the bathroom.

"You've got to get into the spirit of this," she said, looping her arms around his neck. It had only been three days, and she still couldn't believe she had the right to touch him. A sensation like an electric current ran from him to her. "It's going to be fun. Jave and Nancy are going to be there. And I think Tom's bringing Amy."

"Are they on again?" Ryan asked absently, leaning down to nibble on Jo's neck. She smelled like flowers and felt like love, and he was suddenly very aware of all the things they could be doing at home tonight instead of going to Diantha's.

"He...ah...is trying to remain friends with her. But she..." Jo hunched her shoulder as Ryan kissed one of the cords of her neck and pleasure raced along her nerve endings. "Ryan," she protested breathlessly. "Don't start..."

"I'm just trying to get into character," he argued softly, raising his head to give her a swift kiss before moving to the other side of her neck. "You don't want me to arrive at the party in costume, but inexperienced in my seductive vampire wiles, do you? What were you going to say about Amy?"

"She...um...she wants a more...more serious relationship. Ryan..."

"Hmm?" His lips had moved to the swell of her breast above the deep neckline of her ruffly top. And his hand cupped her cotton-clad bottom. She leaned weakly against him, forgetting they were already late for the party.

"We're supposed to be getting ready..."

"I am," he said. It was clear he didn't mean for the party.

Jo heard a baby sound from the front room.

MOM! Daddy! Where are you? Who's the old lady with the peppermint breath?

JO PUSHED on Ryan's shoulders with sudden determination. She had to draw a breath before she could speak. "Mrs. Bennett is in the front room with Chelsea," she whispered.

He groaned against her throat, then reluctantly lifted his head. His eyes were dark with banked passion. "Okay," he said, a grin forming on his lips. "But when we get back from the party, I'm going to make you a vampire, too."

Joy billowed in her at the possessive look in his eyes. She kissed him soundly. "Don't worry," she said. "I'm already yours."

"AH..." Jo and Ryan stopped halfway up the walk to Diantha's home on the hill overlooking Heron Point, and watched a figure burst from the front door and run down the steps. It was completely dressed in a pale color that shone eerily in the moonlight—pants, long top, a hat that covered the head completely, and a mask pulled off and hanging down. "Do you see a white ninja?" Ryan asked Jo quietly, "Or am I finally going under from sleep deprivation?"

Jo peered through the darkness at the figure, now only several yards from them. "I think...that's the hospital's surgery garb," she said, pulling Ryan back with her as the figure continued to approach, moving quickly.

"Amy, wait!" The door burst open again, and a man in a bearskin and a Viking helmet erupted from the pandemonium of laughter and loud conversation inside the house.

When the other figure kept moving, the Viking shouted in a roar, "Amaryllis Brown! Stop this minute!"

"It's Amy," Jo whispered. "And Tom."

Ryan covered her mouth as Amy stopped just a yard away from them, the shadows and her own obvious preoccupation making her unaware of their presence in the shelter of the rhododendron.

"YOU'RE BEING CHILDISH!" Tom shouted as he loped down the walk, stopping a foot from Amy. He pulled off his helmet. Under it was a scraggly blond wig, and he pulled that off, too. "I can't come to the hospital dinner, because I'm in the middle of putting a new roof on Nancy's beach house. I explained that."

"Oh, right," Amy said, her usual sunny disposition replaced by angry cynicism. "And you're going to be doing that at night."

There was an instant's silence. "Yes," he said defensively. "I am. The winter rains are about to—"

"Oh, save it!" she shouted at him. "You aren't coming because you're afraid it might mean we're becoming important to one another, and you're not about to let that happen!"

"Amy..."

"I know you have emotional scars from the fire that killed your friend and ended your career," she said, lowering her voice but not the level of her anger, "and if you want to hold on to them until you're an old man, that's fine. But I have my own problems. And among them is the need to be loved by someone, even though I'm tall and awkward and plain."

Ryan saw Tom straighten, with an expression that seemed to indicate genuine puzzlement. "You're not—" he began.

But Amy wasn't finished. "You're entitled to wallow in your feelings of guilt, and to be shy about your burned leg, and your wounded psyche. But those feelings put me on the outside of our relationship, and that's not where I want to be. Goodbye, Tom.''

He grabbed for her arm, but she yanked it away and ran toward the long row of cars parked along the sidewalk.

Tom said a four-letter word, tossed the helmet and wig, and took off in the other direction.

Jo put a hand to her lips. ''Poor Amy,'' she murmured sympathetically.

Ryan drew her up the walk toward the house. ''Poor Amy?'' he repeated in surprise. He'd helped Tom sell the *River Lady,* consolidate his bills, get a loan to begin his life over again. He knew what he'd been through. ''Poor Tom. He's been to hell and back—almost literally. She's not going to get anywhere by hammering at him.''

Jo let the matter drop, unwilling to point out that that was what had finally placed them in the position of lovers. She'd simply refused to give up on him, to let him belong only to Cassie, even though she was gone.

Jave Nicholas stood in the doorway when they reached it. He was dressed as a pirate, complete with phony beard and mustache, a cutlass dangling at his hip. He was frowning in the direction Tom had gone.

Nancy appeared at his shoulder in a red silk skirt slit up to the thigh, fishnet stockings, a cameo on a strip of black velvet around her neck and a gaudy plume in her hair.

''Maybe you should go after him,'' she said worriedly to Jave.

He shook his head. ''He'd only bite my head off, too.''

''Want me to go?'' Ryan asked, half-seriously. ''I'm qualified to bite back.''

Jave turned to him and laughed, pulling him inside the house. ''Get in here. He'll be fine. He's got to work it out himself.'' He bowed to Jo as he offered her a hand over the threshold. ''Good evening, Miss Scarlett. Just think of me

as a blockade-runner from an earlier time." He drew her
into the party.

Nancy hooked an arm through Ryan's. "So, Count,"
she said, "buy you a drink? We have B negative on tap."

Chapter Thirteen

"It's a shame women aren't wearing those anymore," Ryan said as Jo carefully folded the organza skirt back into a box nested with tissue paper on the foot of the bed. He lay across the coverlet in a brown terry robe, his head propped on his hand as he watched her.

She glanced up from folding the top of the dress into the tissue. "You mean hoops and big skirts?"

He reached out to catch her wrist and pull her down on top of him. His hands ran over the ruffles covering her bottom. "No, I mean these drawers. The ruffles move in a very enticing manner when you move."

Lust flared in her instantly. She could feel his sturdy chest beneath her, his strong arms around her, his thigh raised between hers where his foot was braced on the bed. There was nowhere she would rather be. This morning they'd put down earnest money on a three-story Victorian on a knoll overlooking the river. She was so happy it hurt.

She laughed as she nuzzled his throat. "So, you mean you'd like me to keep them on?"

He nipped her ear punitively. "No, I don't mean that at all. But I think I'd like a picture of you in them that I could pull out of my desk on tedious afternoons at the bank."

He tried to slip his hand inside the waistband and discovered he couldn't. "No elastic in those days?" he asked.

"I think they had it, but it wasn't in common use," she replied, moving his hand to the bow she'd tied at the side. "They used strings instead."

He turned to lay her down on the coverlet. One deft yank unfastened the bow.

"It seems if a gentleman wanted to seduce a lady," he observed, tugging the ruffly pantalets down, "he had to tug on more than her *heart*strings."

She sat up to push his robe off and pull him back to her. "All you'd have to do," she said, stroking a fingertip over his lips, "is flash your pearly teeth. So, if I understand the lore, by morning I'll be a vampire, too?"

He nodded gravely. "And we'll live for all eternity."

"Do we have to bite the baby?"

He gave that a moment's thought. "I don't think so. She probably inherits immortality from me."

Jo leaned up on an elbow. "Are you sure? Now that I think about it, I've never read about vampire babies. Do they even—?"

Ryan rolled his eyes and kissed her into silence. "You used to be the one," he said finally, divesting her of the camisole and nonauthentic bra she'd worn under it, "who was fanciful and didn't care about detail, and I was the pragmatist."

Thought slipped away as his hand closed over her breast. "Love," she whispered, "blurs the lines that divide."

She was right, he thought, as he felt the sole of her foot slip up and down his leg, her hands explore his back, her fingernails leave a tantalizing trail of sensation.

Each of them had changed, and what separated them in action and philosophy seemed so much less important than what connected them.

He held her against him, lips to lips, breasts to chest, eager maleness to waiting femininity.

Jo opened for him like a flower, and enclosed him with all the love and hope she felt in their closeness, in their daughter, in their future.

Feeling spiraled out of control inside her. Ryan thrust deeper, and they climaxed together, lives and destinies entangled.

"Ryan!" she cried in a whisper.

"Cassie!" he breathed against her shoulder. "Oh, Cassie."

Complete stillness fell upon the bedroom.

In the silence, Jo heard the name like a shout in her brain—and felt her life shudder to a stop.

Ryan heard the echo of his own voice and closed his eyes in disbelief. No. He hadn't said that.

Jo stiffened in his arms, and he tightened his embrace instinctively, turning so that she lay in his arms. "Don't," he said urgently. "I'm sorry. It was a slip of the tongue. I was...it was all so perfect that for a minute I was..." He backed away from the words he'd been about to speak, afraid she'd misunderstand. "Jo, I'm sorry. I didn't mistake you for her. I swear I didn't."

Jo felt as though a train had run over her, as though everything inside her was crushed and broken.

But she loved him enough, she wanted a life with him enough, to listen to her brain telling her over and over that it had simply been a slip of the tongue. It hadn't meant that when he made love to her he thought of Cassie. It hadn't.

She wrapped her arms around his neck. "Of course not," she said, with a conviction she thought sounded genuine. She kissed his throat and snuggled closer. "It's all right. Don't think about it anymore."

"Jo..." he began. But the baby cried, and she wriggled out of his arms to go to her.

He caught her wrist and tried to pull her back. "Jo, listen to me."

She smiled but pulled her hand firmly away. "Go to sleep. I'll feed Chelsea and be right back."

She walked out of the room and closed the door. Ryan fell back against the pillow with a groan, his arm tracing the empty expanse of bed beside him, He had a feeling that, however innocently, he'd made a fatal mistake.

IT WAS A PERFECT DAY for boating. The *Mud Hen,* newly refurbished, sailed amid the soft swells of the Columbia River, with far more dignity then her namesake.

"I wanted to change the name," Jave said to Ryan as he guided the small craft up the channel. They passed two braying, glossy harbor seals lying on a buoy, a lone heron majestically perched on a piling, and a host of cormorants ranged on a long-abandoned dock, several of them with wings outstretched. He pointed a finger at Tom, who lounged against the boat's cabin with a can of cola in his hand. "But Little Brother thought it gave her character. Character. Do you believe it?"

"No, I don't," Ryan replied, more to elicit a response from Tom than because he agreed—the same reason, he was sure, Jave had raised the subject. Tom had been morose and withdrawn all morning—and the reason was below decks with Jo and Nancy, making sandwiches. "I wouldn't try to raid the coast in it, or anything. Somehow, I don't think the *Mud Hen*—" he repeated the name loudly, teasingly, in Tom's direction "—would raise terror in the hearts of the common folk."

When Tom didn't even turn in his direction, he frowned at Jave.

Ryan had been surprised to see that Amy had been invited to join their company, considering how her evening with Tom had ended just a week ago. But he understood that women were inveterate cupids, and Nancy, apparently, was one of the most optimistic. But Tom and Amy hadn't spoken to each other since each's initial shock at finding the other in the boating party.

That had resulted in an old-fashioned gender separation that had kept the women in the galley and the men at the wheel.

Ryan was frankly relieved. Jo had been terminally sweet and cheerful since the night he'd called her Cassie, and he was beginning to feel as though he were living with a doll rather than a woman.

It was all his fault. He understood that. But in an effort to pretend her feelings *weren't* hurt, Jo was behaving with all the sincerity of a Stepford wife. She conversed charmingly, she made love eagerly, she sat close to him and touched him. But there was an air of staginess about it that was getting on his nerves.

All his attempts to talk about it were smilingly rebuffed, because the baby needed something, or because she had to carry out some chore relating to the Heron Point Has It event the following week. He didn't know what to do about it.

Ryan turned to lean against the rail and watch the bright green coastline of Washington go by. He was surprised when Tom suddenly came to lean beside him.

"There's no point," Tom said with a sigh, "inviting a woman into your life, when you don't even have your life together yet." Then he turned to Ryan with a level gaze. "Is there?" he asked. "We all know your situation. Your lady's smiling, but she looks a little too desperate for me to believe that all's well with the two of you."

"Jeez, Tom," Jave said, turning the small boat into a wooded harbor. "Why don't you hit him with a sledgehammer?"

Tom clapped Ryan's shoulder in a sort of philosophical apology. "I was just making a point. I don't think he's the one to get on my case about Amy."

Ryan raised an eyebrow. "I don't recall saying a word."

"You don't have to." He inclined his head in Jave's direction. "You pontifical types who know what's best for everyone don't even have to open your mouths. Your manner radiates disapproval."

"No one disapproves of *you*," Jave said, pulling down the bill of his cap as bright sunlight embroidered the water of the bay. "We disapprove of your self-protective cowardice."

Ryan turned to Jave. "Jeez, Jave," he said, echoing his friend's own words. "Why don't you just hit him with a sledgehammer?"

NANCY OFFERED Amy a tissue. Jo sat beside her, an arm around her shoulders in the galley's tiny nook. Malia and Chelsea sat in their carriers, both lulled to sleep by the movement of the boat.

"I'm sorry," Nancy said. "In retrospect, I can see it was stupid, but when I called you yesterday and failed to mention that Tom was coming along, I thought I was just helping you two communicate." Her voice lowered regretfully. "I guess I didn't realize it was so... over."

Amy's face crumpled again, for the fifth time in the past half hour, and Jo tightened her grip on her.

"The worst part is—" she was weeping now "—he's a great guy. Except for that unwillingness to share what hurts."

Nancy arranged sandwiches on a plate. "I reacted that way after my first marriage," she said. "I gave Jave a terrible time. Remember?"

Amy nodded.

"But he didn't give up on me."

Amy sniffed and drew a deep breath. "Well, he probably had more self-confidence than I do. As the ugly duckling in a beautiful, intelligent bevy of Brown women, I'm just barely holding my head above water. I don't think I'm strong enough to keep us both afloat. It has to be over, or we'll both drown."

Nancy smiled. "Lots of seagoing metaphors, there. Maybe it's time to take this picnic ashore and get some fresh air. Jo and I will stay between you and Tom. Don't worry."

As the three couples ate with artificially boisterous good cheer, Jo considered her situation with Ryan in a new and unsettling light.

She had forced Ryan into this relationship. There had been clear signs of interest in her on his part, but he'd obviously needed more time, more distance from everything he'd shared with Cassie. But she'd seen a glimmer of opportunity, and she'd pushed.

But she remembered their lovemaking, their quiet moments with Chelsea, the insignificant, unremarkable everydayness of the past few weeks of their lives and found it hard to believe that it wasn't what God intended. She was so happy with him. He'd seemed so happy with her. Until he'd called her by her sister's name.

A simple mistake? She tried to think so. She wanted him to believe she thought so. But the more time wore on, the more deeply it hurt to remember that, during one of the most personal moments of a woman's life, she'd been mistaken for another. For Cassie, who'd always had everything she, Jo, wanted. And apparently still did.

CASSIE WAS BACK. Jo bumped into her on the street in downtown Portland, while she was pushing Chelsea in a stroller. They were all moving in slow motion through a glittering fog. Jo ran to her, her mouth open in silent shock, her arms open to welcome her back to life.

"Cassie!" she heard herself exclaim. Then she crushed her in her arms. "God, Cassie, I've missed you!"

"Jo!" Cassie greeted her with the warmth and affection they'd always shared. She hooked her free arm in hers and laughing, led the way down the street.

Jo was aware of overwhelming joy, tempered only slightly with a vague sense of disbelief. Cassie was back. It couldn't be, but it was. They were arm in arm, pushing the baby together, the way they'd dreamed it would be, in the beginning, over that Thanksgiving weekend.

They walked together in happy conversation, the baby gurgling and flailing her arms. Then the fog dissipated and the scene became sharply, terrifyingly familiar.

"I know all of this won't be easy for you," Cassie said.

Jo saw herself laugh. "I'm doing it as a labor of love," she replied. "And when I'm *in* labor, remind me that I said that."

Then they stopped at the street corner to cross. Jo watched in horror as she saw herself turn to look at a marigold-colored sweater in a shop window. She willed herself to turn, to reach for Cassie to stop her from crossing. She heard herself groan, knowing she would experience that agonizing paralysis, that sense of impending horror swelling even as she was frozen in that moment in time.

But this time was different. She watched herself turn away, saw herself cover the distance that separated them in several long steps taken in slow motion. Then she saw herself snatch the baby from Cassie and watch without uttering a word of warning as she stepped into the street.

The sound of brakes screeching mingled with her scream. The high-pitched sound filled her ears, dominated her reality, went on and on and on.

RYAN SHOOK HER and shouted her name. The quality of her scream filled the room with her anguish, and deepened his desperation to wake her.

"Josanne!" he shouted as he pulled her up into a sitting position. He accompanied her name with one solid single shake. "Wake *up!*"

She came to with a start, the scream waning to an ever smaller sound that, conversely, conveyed an ever deeper pain.

He still held her arms and looked into her eyes, trying to help her come out of the nightmare. "It's over," he said. "You're awake. It's me, Jo. You're okay."

She finally focused on him, and he saw recognition there, awareness of where she was. Her hair tumbled past her shoulders in wild and curly disarray, and her blue eyes looked into his with an expression he couldn't read—except to know that it didn't look at all like relief.

Then her mouth contorted, and she fell against him with a sob.

"Jo..." he murmured softly, leaning against the pillows and pulling her into his arms. She wrapped hers around his bare middle and held on with a desperation that concerned him.

He glanced at the clock. Almost five. They'd made love just hours ago, and she'd been eager and responsive, if still a little remote, as though only part of her were engaged in the act. Afterward, he'd tried to coax her into conversation, to talk about the boating trip and the situation with Tom and Amy. When she simply shrugged over their relationship, he'd brought up the house they were buying, but her answers had been monosyllabic, and she'd finally fallen asleep against him.

He pulled the blankets over her bare shoulders and wrapped his arms around her to hold them in place. Apparently whatever was bothering her, whatever was creat-

ing a gulf between them, had worked on her subconscious
while she slept.

He tightened his grip on her, hating to see her in pain,
but privately grateful that now he had something he could
deal with. He waited for her sobs to quiet.

Jo held Ryan tightly and forced herself to confront the
truth. She could not have Ryan and Chelsea. The dream
had just told her that she'd stolen them from Cassie. She
hadn't been responsible for Cassie's death, of course, but
she'd stepped in eagerly to benefit from it. And it wasn't
that simple.

She felt Ryan's lips against her temple. "Tell me about
it," he said gently.

She remained still, her cheek against the solid warmth
of his shoulder, her arms wrapped around him. She closed
her eyes to commit the moment to memory. It would have
to last her a long time. She knew what she had to do.

"I dreamed about Cassie," she said, her voice heavy
with tears. "We were walking down the street in Portland, and she had Chelsea."

Ryan felt his own emotions roil at the memories of that
day. He hadn't been with them. They'd parted company to
shop separately, and made plans to meet for lunch. He'd
waited for them for more than an hour before a police-
man sent by Jo finally came searching for him and explained about the accident.

He remembered the overpowering rage, the need to destroy things, to scream his horrible grief. Then, finally,
he'd understood the overwhelming enormity of his loss,
and everything inside him had died.

Pain scraped at him now, but it was for the woman in his
arms and not for himself. In the intervening time, she'd
eased his loss and given him his daughter—something new
and wonderful.

"Go on," he said encouragingly.

She shook her head against him. "No. It'll hurt you."

He rubbed her shoulder. "I can take it."

"It's about . . . the accident."

"I'm listening."

Jo told him everything. She told him about the paralysis that always overtook her during the dream, and how this time it had been different. Her voice a strained whisper, she told him about snatching the baby from Cassie and watching her cross the street.

Then she pulled out of his arms and sat alone on her side of the bed, the blankets clutched to her. "Do you see what it means?" she asked, staring into the darkness.

"Yes," he said, putting a hand to her back. It felt fragile to his touch. "You saved Cassie's baby."

She turned to him, her eyes glistening sadness in the shadows. "I *took* Cassie's baby," she said. "I tried to take you."

He understood with sudden insight what was troubling her. "No," he said, leaning forward to look into her eyes. "We *gave* you the baby to carry for us." He put a hand to her face. "And I give you my love willingly. You haven't *taken* anything from me."

She held his hand to her, turned her face to kiss its palm, then put it away from her. "I rushed you, Ryan. I have you all confused. You just think you need me because of the baby, and because you miss Cassie."

He stood angrily, snatching his robe off the foot of the bed and putting it on. She was upset, he told himself. Distraught, even. He had to remain calm. But he didn't feel calm.

"You know me better than that," he said from the foot of the bed. "I don't use anyone for my purposes. I was going to hire Mrs. Bennett to take care of Chelsea, remember? And I do miss Cassie. I will probably always miss her. But I *love* you!"

She listened, but she remained stiffly unyielding, knees pulled up under her chin, her arms wrapped around them.

"It won't work between us," she said.

He didn't want to hear that. "Not if you don't think it will."

She uttered a protracted sigh. "I wanted to slip into Cassie's place."

"You made your own place."

Jo wanted to believe that—but he'd made love to her and called her Cassie. And she couldn't blame him, because she'd pushed him into a relationship before he was ready.

"I think the trouble is," she said with sudden acceptance, "that Cassie and I are occupying the same place. And that isn't healthy for you or me. I think I have to go."

She pushed the blankets aside and got to her feet. Ryan couldn't move. "What do you mean?" he demanded.

She gave him that distant Stepford-wife smile and went to the closet. He'd moved her clothes from the guest room just a week or so ago. "Why don't we talk about it later? You have to be at the fairgrounds in an hour, and I have to load Devon's truck with my supplies for the fair."

"Oh, no." He caught her arm as she tried to walk past him toward the bathroom, a skirt and sweater over her arm. "You're not going to bring up separation, then tell me we'll talk about it later. We'll talk about it now. You're not going anywhere."

She shook her head and raised one hand to smooth her hair. It defied the action, springing up in wild abandon, like the personification of the woman herself.

"First of all," she said, with a sudden control he found frightening, "it isn't separation. We're not married. We're just living together to share the duties of raising a baby."

"Bull."

"Okay, it got physical, and that confused us. But it wasn't love."

"It *is* love," he insisted.

She sighed patiently. "Ryan, we could argue yes-it-is-no-it-isn't all day long, but what would it prove?"

"That one of us has to win the other over," he said.

"All right," she granted. "Then let's talk about this later, when we have time."

As though on cue, Chelsea announced with a screech that she was awake. Jo pushed her clothes into Ryan's arms and smiled faintly. "I guess you get first go at the shower. Would you lay those on the bed for me?"

Jo rocked as she fed Chelsea, and listened to the sound of the shower. Tears streamed down her face, and she let them, telling herself there would be plenty of time later to be strong.

MAMA CASS says she doesn't like what you're thinking. And you're getting tears on me.

RYAN PULLED UP in front of Coffee Country and saw that Devon was already there, loading boxes into a black Chevy pickup. Chelsea, in her infant seat, dozed in the back of the Volvo.

"When I drop her at Mrs. Bennett's," he said as Jo opened the passenger side door, "I'm going to ask her if she'll keep her until later tonight. I'm making reservations at Chez Pasta, and we're going to talk."

She smiled. There was no point in arguing. "All right," she said. Then, because she knew she would need to remember it later, she leaned across the seat and kissed him quickly. At least that was her intention.

But he cupped the back of her head in his hand and held her there while he prolonged the kiss, deepened it artfully with the tip of his tongue, then released her.

"Think about that today," he said, "and tell me that anything about the last few months we've shared suggests that we don't belong together for the rest of our lives."

Jo looked into his eyes and memorized everything about him that she loved. Then she opened the car door and stepped out.

"Bye," she said, then reached into the back to touch the baby's foot. Pain radiated everywhere inside her. "Bye, baby," she whispered, and closed the car door.

Ryan drove away with a tap on the horn, and Jo quite literally felt her heart sink.

Devon opened the coffee bar's door. "Hey, Jose," he said. "you want the coffee candies, too, or just—?" He stopped in surprise as she raced past him into the bar, her eyes glazed with pain and spilling tears.

FOR THE FIRST TWO HOURS of the commercial fair, Ryan didn't have a moment to think. He had to deal with a pop machine that poured carbonated water and no syrup; the vintage clothing exhibitor who wanted to be moved from beside the Rotary Club's sausage-and-onions booth, pleading that everything lace had probably already been ruined by the smell; and an electrical outlet at the back of the building that was smoking.

By the time he'd called an electrician and the pop vendor who'd supplied the machine, and moved Frothy Fashions next to an herbalist, he was desperate for a cup of coffee.

He was about to head for Jo's booth when Tom Nicholas brought him a double espresso.

"Here you go, big guy," he said. "You look stressed."

Ryan smiled thinly. "Generally, banks are a lot quieter than this, and money problems are easier to solve."

Tom nodded. "I suppose so. Either you have it or you don't. Simple."

"Something like that."

"Ah..." Tom pointed to a booth in the far corner. "Riverview Hospital's in a dark spot," he said, with studied nonchalance, as he indicated the absence of an overhead fluorescent there. "You think you could find a trouble light or something she could just hook on the top of the booth?"

"I'll see what I can do." Ryan studied him suspiciously. "Did Amy ask you to ask me?"

He shook his head. "We're not speaking. I overheard her talking about it when I walked by." Tom raised his cup to him. "Thanks. Better get back to my booth."

Were relationships in general impossible, Ryan wondered, or just those among himself and his friends?

He headed toward the front door to check the morning receipts.

By noon, the Heron Point Has It commercial fair had admitted four times the visitors they'd expected, and many exhibitors had approached Ryan about signing up to participate the following year.

Only Diantha glared at him, over the crowds of people studying her natural, organically grown products. He was used to that from her and almost didn't give it a second thought.

It was early afternoon before he had a moment to himself. He headed for the Coffee Country booth to see if Jo had managed to have anything for lunch besides her own fare. He found Devon behind the counter.

"Where's Jo?" he asked.

Devon glanced up at him while restocking a pedestal plate with scones. "Taking a break. Booth-hopping, I think."

Ryan might have accepted that and walked away, had he not caught the hatred in Devon's eyes. He knew the young man had always disliked him, but he'd never seen quite that degree of condemnation in him before. It reminded him with sudden sharpness of the look he'd gotten from Diantha.

Connected with the conversation he and Jo had had early that morning, those looks brought to mind a thought too ugly to consider. No. She wouldn't have.

"She say what booth?" he asked, his calm tone edged with grim suspicion.

Devon glared up at him again. "Why don't you just look around?"

Ryan's calm evaporated. He grabbed Devon by his shirt collar and pulled him toward him so that their noses almost met over the counter.

"I've *been* around all morning. I haven't seen her. I thought she was here. Where is she?"

Devon hesitated for an instant, but it was long enough for Ryan to know that something was wrong, and that Devon had been sworn to silence.

He tightened his grip. "Where," he demanded, his voice deadly quiet, "did she go?"

"I don't know," Devon replied. The anger in his eyes subsided slightly. It wasn't fear, Ryan saw, but general concern for Jo. "I told her it was stupid."

Ryan freed him out of self-protection. He was sure fury had made lethal weapons of his hands.

Ryan ran across the building and sideways down a narrow aisle until he reached Diantha's booth. He cut into her conversation with a customer.

"Where's Jo?" he demanded. "And don't bother telling me you don't know."

She raised a judgmental eyebrow. She excused herself to the customer, then said to Ryan, "She was perfect for you, you know."

"I know!" he shouted at her. The customer whose conversation he'd interrupted backed out of the booth. He lowered his voice. "Diantha, I know. I told her that. But she didn't believe me. Where is she? Please."

She considered him a moment, then sighed and folded her arms. "She went to Connecticut."

He stared at her in disbelief. "Connecticut," he repeated flatly.

Her manner softened, her voice quieted. "To her father."

"For how long?"

She looked apologetic. "She asked me if I wanted to buy Coffee Country."

Ryan forgot that he had a reputation for control. He ran to find Tom Nicholas, grabbed his arm, and brought him with him to the parking lot.

"I have to leave," he said. "I think all the major crises are handled. The high school drama club has agreed to clean up as a fund-raiser. So all you have to do is lock up after everybody's gone." He handed him a key as they reached his car. "I know it'll cost you a few hours and I'm sorry to take advantage, but I've got to—"

Tom cut him off. "Of course I'll do it. Just tell me nothing's wrong with Jo or the baby."

The baby.

Ryan forced himself to refocus his attention one more moment. "Jo's left," he said. "I've got to get her back."

"All right." Tom backed away. "Go. But drive carefully."

The baby!

Ryan tried to dial Mrs. Bennett on his cellular phone as he raced the Volvo toward her little duplex behind the Methodist church. But her line was busy. He closed the phone in frustration and tossed it aside.

Had Jo taken the baby? No wonder she'd given him so little argument about talking the problem out tonight.

She'd had an escape plan. And she'd probably taken his daughter.

By the time he reached Mrs. Bennett's, anger and desperation were so entangled inside him that he could barely see. He took the porch steps two at a time and banged loudly on her door. And he didn't stop until the old woman pulled it open.

"Mr. Jeffries," she said in concerned surprise. "Is something wrong?" She held Chelsea in her arms, wrapped in the blanket with the fringe on only three sides.

Ryan heard a strangled sound come from his throat, and then he reached for his daughter. She stared at him, big-eyed, and it was all he could do not to burst into tears.

DADDY! I'm so glad you're back. Mama Cass says Mama Jo left for...

HE HELD HER AGAINST HIM and buried his nose in her blanket. He had to pull himself together.

"I'm sorry, Mrs. Bennett," he said after a moment. Holding the baby with one arm, he reached into his breast pocket with the other and handed the sitter twice her usual rate. "Everything's... Plans have changed," he said. "I'll take Chelsea with me now."

She looked surprised, then reached behind the door and handed him the diaper bag. "Well, of course that's fine, but I thought you and Jo had a hot date tonight."

He'd thought so, too. He smiled his thanks and held Chelsea tightly to him as he walked back to the car.

He drove home, glancing often in the rearview mirror at the baby, who made loud, high-pitched, happy noises from her infant seat.

DADDY! You're gonna go get Mama Jo, right? Daddy?

CHELSEA WAS ASLEEP when he reached the condo, but he couldn't make himself put her down. The fear that she'd been taken was still too new, too complete. He balanced her against his shoulder as he went to the kitchen and dialed Matthew's number. His answering machine picked up. He left a message.

Then he sat down in the recliner, the baby a comforting weight in his arms, and accepted the feeling of devastation. Jo had left him. But she hadn't taken the baby. Knowing how much she loved Chelsea, he saw it as a gesture of how much she loved *him*.

Of course, she'd made that clear over and over during the past few months. What she hadn't understood was how much he loved her. This morning, all his efforts had fallen on stubborn ears.

He didn't know what else to say.

Chapter Fourteen

Matthew Arceneau held his weeping daughter in his arms. He had no idea how to help her. Deep sobs had racked her since he'd picked her up at the airport an hour ago and brought her home to his farmhouse at the edge of a wood.

She'd told him about Ryan thinking he'd fallen in love with her, then calling her Cassie while they made love. Then she told him about the dream in which she'd snatched the baby from her sister, then done nothing to stop her from walking out in front of the car.

"It's foolish," he said, "to change the entire direction of your life because of a dream."

She finally pushed out of his arms, ran a hand over the hair she'd tied back in a braid and sniffed. "It explained everything to me, Dad," she said, sitting up and dabbing at her red nose with a crumpled tissue. "I thought I could just step into the situation as Chelsea's mother and Ryan's love, because I'd always loved him, and deep down I guess I thought it was my right. But you can't force love on someone. They'll love whomever they want to love."

Matthew watched her ball the tissue into an impossibly small piece, then reach behind him for the box and place it on the sofa cushion between them.

"You said he explained to you why he called you Cassie. That sounds logical to me. That...," he said, smiling fondly at her, "and the fact that it isn't impossible for a man to love the woman he's lost and still love the woman who's vital and beside him and helping him find his way again. It isn't that he loves her memory more than he loves you, it's that he loves you both. Is that so awful?"

"I don't know." She snatched up a new tissue, her brow furrowed, her eyes focused on her memories of the dream. "Why did I take the baby from her, but not stop her from crossing the street?" she asked. "All the other times I was paralyzed, but this time I wasn't. This time I could have stopped her." She looked into Matthew's eyes, fresh tears brimming. "I wonder if it means—?"

He'd read her mind since she was a child. He read it now. "That you wanted her out of the picture so you could have Ryan and Chelsea?" He blurted out the words so that she could hear them for the nonsense they were. "No. Absolutely not. When Cassie was here, you never betrayed your feelings about Ryan. Neither of them ever suspected. But with her gone, you did what a heart filled with love is supposed to do—you tried to give it. You haven't stolen anything from Cassie, Jo. Cassie's gone."

Jo took one more tissue, blew her nose, then drew a deep breath and sat forward.

"It's better this way," she said, trying to think of something other than the ache in her arms to hold Chelsea, the ache in her breasts to feed her, the ache in her heart where her love for Ryan would always be. "It just wasn't meant to be, from the beginning. He's always belonged to her. Now he has his baby, and he can find someone to love on his own, without encouragement from a prejudiced party."

She smiled affectionately at her father. "Thanks for letting me stay for a few days. I'll start job-hunting first thing in the morning, then I'll get an apartment and be out of your hair." .

"Stay as long as you like," he said. He let the subject of Ryan drop. She'd made up her mind, and arguing with her would be futile until she was ready to listen. "It's not like I have a parade of women through here and need my privacy."

"I'm sure the fault's not on your side." Jo stood and gathered up their pottery mugs on the coffee table. "Diantha was pretty taken with you."

He smiled. "I liked her, too. She might visit me next summer."

Jo raised an eyebrow. "She didn't tell me."

He took the cups from her and gave her a look of paternal superiority. "You don't know everything, you know. Why don't you go put your things away, and I'll call for a pizza? Oh, wait." He sobered suddenly. "Ryan's left four messages," he said. "I have to return his call. What do you want me to tell him?"

That I love him, she thought. *That I will always love him.* But she drew a breath and said, "That I arrived safely and am fine, and that I send my best." She had to swallow before she added the next. And even then her voice came out thin and hollow. "And ask him how Chelsea is."

"What if he wants to talk to you?"

"Tell him I'm asleep."

"That won't solve the problem. He'll just call again tomorrow."

"It solves the problem for today. And right now I can only handle a day at a time."

"I'M SORRY, Ryan." Matthew's reasonable, professorial voice came quietly across the phone line. "But she won't talk to you. She's . . . convinced it's over."

Ryan closed his eyes against the words, then opened them again, telling himself that he didn't have to lend the words any credence.

"I'm booked on a flight out in the morning," he said. "And tell her not to try to hide. That I'll just keep looking until I find her."

"Give her a little time," Matthew cautioned.

Ryan swore. "Time isn't going to change anything, Matt. She thinks I'm confusing love for Cassie with love for her."

"She told me. Look. You've both had such a difficult year. Why don't you just let her be for a few weeks? Let her think things through."

Ryan uttered a scornful sound. "You know her," he said. "She thinks that she's right about everything. Do you really think time will change her mind?"

Matthew hesitated.

Ryan hadn't expected him to lie, but seeing that possibility now as his last hope, he wished he would.

"No," Matthew said finally. "But there's probably a way to bring that about, if we could just come up with it."

"Like what?"

"I don't know. Think. Meanwhile, I'll pray. I'm supposed to ask how Chelsea is."

"How does she think she is?" Ryan demanded angrily. He held the phone away from his ear so that Matthew could hear the squalling from the nursery. "She's fussy. She knows something's wrong. She's gotten nothing but bottled milk all day. Tell her Chelsea's very, very unhappy, because she misses her mother."

"I'll tell her."

"Thanks, Matt."

Ryan hung up the telephone and hurried to the nursery to pick up the baby. She continued to cry for a moment, then quieted as he walked with her into the kitchen to run a bottle of store-bought formula under the hot water.

THAT stuff again? You mean she isn't back yet? I want you to know I'm very upset. I want my mother!

"IT'S GOING to be all right," he assured Chelsea as he settled her in the crook of his arm and gave her the bottle. He paced the room with her, too restless himself to sit.

"Your mama Jo's just confused," he said, stroking a thumb over the warm and very bald little head.

The small pink scalp reminded him of their jokes about the bald blanket, and that reminded him of all the hours Jo had put into finishing it—and how it remained unfinished yet, like the resolution of their relationship.

Well, there had to be a solution. Cassie had believed there was a solution to everything.

And there in the middle of his dark apartment, with the baby dozing off in his arms and the lights on the guiding buoys visible from his window, it came to him.

He stopped pacing and stood still—the power and the possibilities of it playing out in his mind.

It could work. Or he could lose everything.

But he didn't have to think twice. Jo's love was all-or-nothing stakes.

JO HAD SPENT THE DAY on the sofa with an ice pack on her head. Her brave resolution to go job hunting in the morning hadn't taken into account the physical results of a broken heart.

She'd awakened with a pounding headache from a night of crying, acute nausea from six pieces of green pepper-and-pepperoni pizza in a stomach that hadn't seen food in sixteen hours, and a general misery that made stepping out of the house impossible.

Her father had walked her to the sofa, covered her with a blanket, brought her a pot of tea and the TV remote and gone off to school.

She pushed the blanket aside and sat up gingerly. She gave her head a few minutes to stop thumping and spinning, then stood, holding on to the back of the sofa, and made her way carefully to the kitchen.

Her father would be home soon. She should have something ready for dinner.

She opened a cupboard, and found nothing that reminded her of home, but suddenly she saw in her mind's eye the day several months ago when Ryan had moved her into his condo and she'd browsed through the cupboards. She put a hand to her heart, where pain throbbed.

She leaned against the countertop, weak from the emptiness of a future without Ryan and Chelsea. All the hope she'd once had in every moment of every day had been ground to dust by loneliness. And she'd been gone less than twenty-four hours. She couldn't imagine how this would hurt a month from now. Or a year.

The thought was too horrible to contemplate. She found canned soup and sandwich makings, and was about to tackle the task of preparing them when the doorbell rang.

She turned slowly to look at the door, dread in her heart. Oh, no! Her father told her Ryan had planned to fly out to Connecticut, but that he had talked him out of it. What if he'd changed his mind? What if he'd come anyway, determined to bully her into coming back to Heron Point?

She felt a moment's sunburst of excitement at the thought. God, how she missed him! How wonderful it would be to wrap her arms around him, to feel him holding her!

Excitement dissipated as she accepted that she would only have to send him back alone. He didn't belong to her.

The doorbell sounded again, and she braced herself to walk across the room and answer it. If she ignored it, and it was Ryan, he would only wait until her father came home, and she would be forced to confront him anyway.

As the doorbell rang a third time, she put her hand on the knob and pulled the door open.

It was dark outside, but her visitors were brightly lit by the old coach lantern on the porch.

She stared in openmouthed shock at the baby. "Chelsea!" she gasped, grabbing the baby to her. She was dressed completely in white wool, a ruffly cap framing her pudgy pink face. She gave Jo an openmouthed smile, little hands flailing the air. The infamous blanket was wrapped around her.

"Oh, baby!"

MAMA JO! Thank goodness! But this still isn't right. Daddy's still at the other place.

JO CRUSHED Chelsea against her, feeling the little mouth already rooting at her neck. The baby's warmth and freshly powdered smell brightened the deep-down darkness that filled her being.

Then she noticed the woman who'd been carrying Chelsea.

"Diantha!" she said, in complete amazement. "What are you doing here?"

Diantha, in a natural suede jacket with fringed collar and cuffs, smiled wryly. "Well, it's a cinch the baby wasn't going to get here on her own. So, here I am. I always wanted to belong to an escort service, but this isn't precisely how I imagined it." She turned to wave off the cab idling at the curb. "Thank you!"

"But..." Jo continued to stare at her in perplexity.

Diantha pointed beyond Jo, to the cozy-looking living room. "Could we talk about this inside?"

"Oh! Of course." She stepped aside, pausing to nuzzle Chelsea while Diantha picked up an overnight bag and went past her into the house.

Jo closed the door, her mind darting in a hundred different directions as she tried to make sense of Diantha's turning up on her doorstep with Chelsea. How had Diantha gotten the baby away from Ryan? Why had she wanted to?

Diantha stopped in the middle of the living room and looked around with a smile. "Traditional, but very nice." Then her expression altered subtly, and her color rose. "Where's your father?"

"Still at school. He's due home soon. Diantha, I don't understand."

Diantha nodded and reached down to push aside the blanket on the sofa, then sat down. "Been a couch potato today, have we?" she asked. Then she took a good look at Jo as she sat beside her with the baby, and smiled sympathetically. "Ryan sent me." she added.

Jo placed Chelsea on the sofa cushion between them and began to remove her hat and snowsuit. "What?" she asked in surprise. "Why? Why would he do that?"

Diantha shook her head as she reached into her coat pocket for a rattle that she shook over the baby's head to distract her while Jo fussed with her clothes.

MAMA CASS says it's because he... Oooh! I like that. Can I have it?

"I'M JUST HERE to escort the baby," Diantha said. "I'm going back tomorrow."

Jo wrapped the blanket around Chelsea and cradled her in her arms. She felt such happiness at the sight of her, but concern, too, over what her presence meant.

"Why," Jo asked patiently, "did Ryan ask you to bring her here?" She tensed suddenly as a possible answer occurred to her. "Is something wrong? Is he all right?"

Diantha unfastened the buttons of her coat. "No," she said, "I wouldn't say he's all right." She angled Jo a bland, wide-eyed glance as she shrugged out of her coat. "Maybe you haven't heard, but the woman he loves walked out on him without warning and moved across the country."

"Diantha."

"I know. You mean physically. Yes, he's fine. There is nothing wrong." She delved into her purse and produced a small, square envelope. The name Jo was printed on it in neat block letters. "He asked me to give this to you, and to tell you to read it when you have a quiet, private moment."

Jo accepted the envelope. It was thick and cream-colored, and was engraved with Ryan's return address. Once *her* address. Heron Point Condominiums, number 27.

Emotion frothed inside her. What had he done? She looked up at Diantha, what should have been a joyful turn of events somehow making her terribly sad. "But he wanted her so badly," she said, mystified. "He loves her so much."

Diantha patted her shoulder, her manner distinctly maternal. "And what does that tell you, my little thick-headed double Aquarius?"

Jo frowned at her friend. She knew being a double Aquarius meant that Aquarius was not only her astrological sign, but her rising sign as well—the sign that had passed over the eastern horizon when she was born and consequently exercised great influence. But how that related now, Jo had no idea.

Apparently reading her mind, Diantha explained simply, "You're eccentric, and you think deeply, and because of that you think you know everything. But you don't. So think again. Think hard."

Matthew walked in while Jo was still staring at Diantha. He was almost as shocked as Jo had been to see his two new guests. He tossed coat and briefcase aside and came to scoop his granddaughter from Jo's lap.

"And how is my precious Pumpkin?" he asked, dangling her over his head. She shrieked at him. "And what are you doing here?"

PUMPKIN? Those fat orange things? Malia Rose's grandfather calls her Angel.

HE PULLED HER into his arms, took the bottle Diantha handed him and sat opposite them in a platform recliner.

"Diantha, it's wonderful to see you, but what on earth is going on?"

Diantha explained while Jo took down another can of soup and made sandwiches. Her friend and her father talked through dinner, and afterward, while Jo tidied up and played with the baby. Her father was animated and witty. Diantha's eyes sparkled.

"How's Coffee Country?" Jo asked. Diantha answered succinctly that Devon, bored with school, was happy to work it full-time until she could hire someone to share the hours. Then she turned to Matthew and resumed their conversation.

Jo carried the baby to the spare bedroom she'd used the night before, mentally calculating all the things she would need to make the baby comfortable. First priority was a crib.

Having the baby would affect all her plans about working, and probably about renting an apartment. She would have to find a rental house, somewhere that accepted children. And she would have to look into child care.

She told herself she was excited. But she wasn't. She was thrilled to have the baby—it felt as though some vital part of her that had been severed the morning before had been painlessly replaced. Well—not precisely painlessly. Because she did feel pain. It just wasn't her own. It was Ryan's.

She couldn't imagine why he'd sent Chelsea to her. She knew how much he loved his daughter, how he played with her with genuine delight, how he gave her her bottle with the utmost tenderness and fascination, how he watched her sleep, a proud smile on his lips.

She remembered how empty she, Jo, had felt last night, when an entire continent separated her from Ryan and the baby. She could imagine how he felt at this moment. She glanced at the clock. Almost 8:00 p.m.

It would be almost five in Heron Point. Ryan would just be leaving the bank, in the darkness of the late-fall evening. He would smell the river and wood smoke as he walked to his car, and he would hear the lonely bellow of the sea lions. And he would know that when he got to the condominium, there would be no one there.

Her eyes brimmed and her throat burned with unshed tears.

Jo put on the light on the bedside table, placed the now sleeping baby beside her on the coverlet, propped a pillow up against the headboard and leaned back to read Ryan's note. It was block-printed, like her name on the envelope.

Hi, Jo,
Spoke to your father last night, and he told me you arrived safely in Connecticut. I wanted to come out and talk to you, but he said you would prefer I didn't, so I've sent you all my love instead. The thought of you alone without your baby hurt me even more than my own pain. So I've asked Diantha to take Chelsea to you. I've sent on Simba and the rest of her things express mail, so they should be arriving within forty-

eight hours. Take care of both of you. The work is not very skilled, but Bert showed me how to finish the fringe on Chelsea's blanket, so rest easy. Your circle's complete.
Ryan

Jo sat absolutely still, as pain and joy and a dozen other emotions she couldn't quite isolate or identify swelled inside her.

She reached down to inspect the fringe on the blanket Cassie had begun, that she'd almost finished, that her father had taken to the cafeteria to work on while she was in labor—and saw that the fringe had been finished on the bald end of it. It was pulled through evenly and with care—but a sob of happiness escaped her when she saw that it was on backward. She ran to the living room for the cordless phone.

RYAN WAS LATE for work. Very late. He took a last sip of tasteless coffee and glanced at the kitchen clock. It was almost eleven. There'd been no word from Jo, though Diantha had called very late last night to tell him that Jo had been ecstatic at the sight of Chelsea. That news had provided all the comfort he knew the situation could provide him. And that was fine. He'd known the chance he was taking when he sent Chelsea to Connecticut.

But it was one thing to do the noble and heroic thing, and quite another to live with it. He hadn't even gone to bed last night, knowing he wouldn't sleep. He'd prowled the dark apartment, the silence ringing loudly in his ears.

He'd gone into the nursery and touched all the things Jo and Chelsea had touched just a few days before, and sworn that he felt their impressions on it, smelled the lingering fragrance of baby powder and Jo's gardenia scent.

He'd known grief before, but that had resulted from a life God had taken from him. But this grief seemed to run even deeper and hurt even more, because Jo and Chelsea were alive and well—he simply couldn't have them. And that was a torture he'd have to live with. He just didn't know how he was going to do it.

He'd showered and shaved hours ago, he just didn't want to leave the condo, where the essence of them still lingered. He didn't even have to concentrate to see Jo sitting in a corner of the sofa, the baby at her breast, a smile on her lips as she hummed a Mamas and the Papas tune.

But he forced himself to put the coffee down, put on his jacket, and go to the door. Jo and Chelsea would be happy together. He had to find comfort in that and get on with his life.

He stepped out into the hall, locked the condo door behind him and pushed the button for the elevator.

He'd tackle some big project today, he decided. He'd review an impossible loan application, or work on that tangled checking account that no one at the branch seemed able to reconcile. That should keep his mind occupied so that he could get through the day. The night was too grim to even consider at this point.

The down bell rang, and the elevator doors parted.

Ryan took a step forward to get on—and everything inside him jolted to a halt. Air clogged in his lungs, blood ebbed in his veins, and his brain refused to function.

I'm seeing Jo in her blue swing coat and her magenta beret, and Chelsea in the white snowsuit and bonnet I put on her to send her to Connecticut.

He blinked. They were still there. And beside them with the diaper bag and a small suitcase was the cabbie with the Elvis button on her hat.

"Ryan! Oh, Ryan!" Jo wept as she flew into his arms, stepping on his foot, cutting off his air, the baby's cries as she was pressed between them threatening to shatter his ear drums.

I'M TIRED OF THE PLANE! I'm tired of us not being to-gether! I want it to be just like this, all three of us—and I'm not going to stop screaming until someone tells me that's the way it's going to be!

THEY WERE very much flesh and blood, he decided in a kind of disbelieving stupor. And they were back.

Jo, her free arm still in a stranglehold around his neck, her left foot still squarely on his right one, the baby still screaming, kissed his cheek, his jaw, his chin, then his lips.

"I love you," she said, her mouth just centimeters from his as her eyes, drunk with love, seemed to devour his face. "And you love *me!*" Her grip tightened on him even further. "You sent me the *baby!*" she whispered, a sob in the sound. "You would have let me have Chelsea!"

Ryan kissed her soundly, feeling as though a star had exploded inside his being. All-or-nothing bets were hard on the nerves, but God, when they paid off...

"She's ours," he said, pulling the beret off her and tak-ing a handful of her hair. "And you're mine. Do you un-derstand that? Do you finally understand that?"

"Yes. Ryan, yes!"

Ryan kissed her again. Then she pulled out of his arms when the baby suddenly stopped crying.

"Are you okay, Chelsea, baby?" Jo asked.

SNIFF. Yes, thank you. That's better. Mama Cass says she has to go now. She's going to trust the two of you to be happy together and to make me happy. Did you hear me? What do you have to say?

RYAN, an arm around Jo, leaned down to kiss the baby's forehead. "Everything's all right now, Chelsea," he said.

Jo leaned into his shoulder. He enclosed both of them in his embrace.

"I'm sure this is the way Cassie would want it," Jo whispered.

"Maybe she knows," Ryan said. "I'm sure if she does, she's happy."

CASSIE, on her way home and no longer needing a spokes-man, touched Ryan's cheek and Jo's hair.

"Who," she asked, "do you think gave you the idea to send Jo the baby?"

RYAN NOTICED the cabdriver still standing there, smiling at them. She'd put the bags down.

"Sorry." He laughed, reaching into his breast pocket for his wallet. "You probably haven't been—"

"No." She held both hands out in front of her in a gesture of refusal, her smile widening. At Ryan's look of surprise, she gestured from him to Jo and the baby. "Hey. Love me tender. This one's on me."

Ryan caught her hand and pressed a bill in it. "Then here's a tip. Thank you."

"You're welcome."

Ryan took the baby from Jo, then put an arm around her and turned her toward the apartment.

BYE, Mama Cass. I'll take it from here. Don't worry. I love you.

THE CABBIE turned at the sound of the elevator's bell. The doors parted.

An elegant older woman with a mesh shopping bag smiled at the cabbie. "Going up?"

CASSIE WATCHED her family walk into their home. "I love you, too, baby," she whispered. "I love you all." Then she heaved a sigh of relief, and swept past the cabbie, calling, "Hold the elevator!"

HARLEQUIN® AMERICAN ♦ ROMANCE®

"Whether you want him for business...or pleasure, for one month or for one night, we have the husband you've been looking for. When circumstances dictate the need for the appearance of a man in your life, call 1-800-HUSBAND for an uncomplicated, uncompromising solution. Call now. Operators are standing by...."

I ♥ 800 HUSBAND

Pick up the phone—along with five desperate singles—and enter the Harrington Agency, where no one lacks a perfect mate. Only thing is, there's no guarantee this will stay a business arrangement....

For five fun-filled frolics with the mate of your dreams, catch all the 1-800-HUSBAND books:

> #596 COUNTERFEIT HUSBAND
> by Linda Randall Wisdom in August
> #597 HER TWO HUSBANDS
> by Mollie Molay in September
> #601 THE LAST BRIDESMAID
> by Leandra Logan in October
> #605 THE COWBOY HIRES A WIFE
> by Jenna McKnight in November
> #609 THE CHRISTMAS HUSBAND
> by Mary Anne Wilson in December

Coming to you only from American Romance!

HFH-1

MILLION DOLLAR SWEEPSTAKES (III)

No purchase necessary. To enter, follow the directions published. Method of entry may vary. For eligibility, entries must be received no later than March 31, 1996. No liability is assumed for printing errors, lost, late or misdirected entries. Odds of winning are determined by the number of eligible entries distributed and received. Prizewinners will be determined no later than June 30, 1996.

Sweepstakes open to residents of the U.S. (except Puerto Rico), Canada, Europe and Taiwan who are 18 years of age or older. All applicable laws and regulations apply. Sweepstakes offer void wherever prohibited by law. Values of all prizes are in U.S. currency. This sweepstakes is presented by Torstar Corp., its subsidiaries and affiliates, in conjunction with book, merchandise and/or product offerings. For a copy of the Official Rules send a self-addressed, stamped envelope (WA residents need not affix return postage) to: MILLION DOLLAR SWEEPSTAKES (III) Rules, P.O. Box 4573, Blair, NE 68009, USA.

EXTRA BONUS PRIZE DRAWING

No purchase necessary. The Extra Bonus Prize will be awarded in a random drawing to be conducted no later than 5/30/96 from among all entries received. To qualify, entries must be received by 3/31/96 and comply with published directions. Drawing open to residents of the U.S. (except Puerto Rico), Canada, Europe and Taiwan who are 18 years of age or older. All applicable laws and regulations apply; offer void wherever prohibited by law. Odds of winning are dependent upon number of eligible entries received. Prize is valued in U.S. currency. The offer is presented by Torstar Corp., its subsidiaries and affiliates in conjunction with book, merchandise and/or product offering. For a copy of the Official Rules governing this sweepstakes, send a self-addressed, stamped envelope (WA residents need not affix return postage) to: Extra Bonus Prize Drawing Rules, P.O. Box 4590, Blair, NE 68009, USA.

SWP-H1095

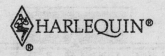

WESTERN *Lovers*

Available in November

Two more
Western Lovers
ready to rope and tie your heart!

DESTINY'S CHILD—Ann Major
Once a Cowboy...
Texas cowboy Jeb Jackson laid claim to the
neighboring MacKay ranch, but feisty redhead
Megan MacKay refused to give up her land without
a fight. Surely Jeb could convince the headstrong
woman to come to an agreement—*and* become his
lovely bride!

YESTERDAY'S LIES—Lisa Jackson
Reunited Hearts
Years ago, Trask McFadden had wooed
Tory Wilson—only to put her father behind bars.
Now Trask was back, and Tory vowed she'd never
let him break her heart again—even if that meant
denying the only love she'd ever known....

WL1195

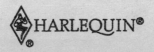